FOUR ON ONE

Well, that done it. All four of them Piggses went for their guns at the same time, and mine was out in a flash too. My first shot hit that big Pigg, the one what had been talking, right in the mouth. A bullet tore right into my left chest and knocked me right over onto my back. I was shocked and stunned, I can tell you. The actual feel of it was more than I ever expected or even imagined. I seed the hole, and I seed all the blood, and it was all mine. By the time I could raise up my shooter again, I seed where bullets was splatting into them other three Piggses from all different kind a directions. Anyhow, that's what it looked like. When all four saddles was fin'ly empty, and all four Piggses was laying dead or dying, I relaxed and laid on back my own self. I figgered I was a dying too. But I didn't keer too much about that, 'cause the bastards what had did it to me was all dead too, and there was four a them and only one a me.

I figgered it was a pretty good score to go out with.

Praise For Robert Conley and
FUGITIVE'S TRAIL

"Cherokee writer Robert Conley is one of the most inventive writers America has ever had. In Kid Parmlee he has created a second-hand Billy the Kid who will charm your damned ears off and send you down a trail of fun, frivolity and adventure. Go buy it right now, read it and enjoy it."

—Max Evans, author of *The Rounders*, *The Hi Lo Country* and *Bluefeather Fellini*

"Robert Conley is possibly one of the most underrated and overlooked writers of our time, as well as the most skilled. Versatile: poetry, humor, historical, Western, mystery, even horror. Now, Kid Parmlee. Neither a traditional general Western character, a super-hero or anti-hero caricature, he is simply Kid Parmlee, a human being. In his pathetic way, Kid Parmlee is not a very good person, but also only as bad as survival requires. Simple yet clever, good and bad, sad and funny, failure and success . . . 'The Kid' holds up a mirror to the human condition."

—Don Coldsmith, author of the Spanish Bit Series and *Bearer of the Pipe*

FUGITIVE'S TRAIL

ROBERT J. CONLEY

St. Martin's Paperbacks

FUGITIVE'S TRAIL

Copyright © 2000 by Robert J. Conley.

ISBN: 0-312-97508-2

Printed in the United States of America

St. Martin's Paperbacks edition / August 2000

St. Martin's Paperbacks are published by St. Martin's Press, 175 Fifth
Avenue, New York, N.Y. 10010.

10   9   8   7   6   5   4   3   2   1

Chapter One

The only thing I ever really keered about in my whole life was my ole dog, Farty, and he really was, too. That's how come him to get that name in the first place. Me and Maw and Paw had us a little ole place out on the dry prairie in West Texas. It weren't nothing to brag about, and, hell, I never did figger out just how it was that ole Paw was trying to make us a living. We had us an ole muley cow and some scrawny ole chickens. Paw had a swaybacked nag he rid into town ever' now and then. But we sure as hell weren't making no money off a the place. From time to time, ole Paw would go off by hisself for a few days or maybe even longer, and then he'd come on back home with some groceries and some money in his pocket and most always those times a jug or two a good whiskey, but I never knowed where the money come from. I don't know if Maw knowed or not neither. If she did, well, she didn't seem to keer none. Reflecting back on it, though, I reckon that he must a been up to no good.

And we wasn't exactly what you'd call a happy family. Things was most pleasant when Paw was off somewheres, 'cause then him and Maw wasn't yelling around at each other. Most often, whenever Maw yelled at Paw and got the best of him, why then he'd turn on me. Neither one a them two seemed to give much of a shit about me, and that's probably why I keered so much for Farty. He keered about me. Me and Farty was like best friends.

Well, it was one a the days Paw was going into town, and I whined around something fierce till he agreed to let me go on along, but I had to walk alongside him riding on that ole swayback. Ole Farty, he just naturally tagged along. When we got into town, Paw headed right straight for the saloon. But he give me a dime first and left me out on the street. Me and Farty. I flipped that dime a time or two feeling right well heeled, and then I walked across the street to the general store what was owned and run by ole Andy McFarland, and I went right inside there and bought myself some hard candy. Then I stepped outside feeling like a real big shot, with a chunk of that candy poking my jaw way out. I was sucking on one, and I had some more down in my pocket. Why, if any a them snotty town boys had come around a-looking for trouble, I was sure in the right mood to whip their ass.

Ole Farty, he was just laying there right smack in the middle a the board sidewalk, and here come a damned ole bastard what looked to me like he was up to no good to begin with. He was a big fella, rough-looking, and he sure needed a shave real bad. I couldn't tell if he was a farmer or a cowboy or what by the way he was dressed, but he was some kind of a working man, I guessed, and he stopped right there by Farty like he didn't want to have to step over no damn dog.

"Get out of my way, you goddamned mutt," he

says, real gruff like, and ole Farty, well, he done what he was best at. He farted. And it was a right smelly one too. Well, that ole boy tuck offense at that gesture of Farty's. I guess he tuck it personal, and he went and kicked poor ole Farty in the side. Kicked him hard, knocking him clean up in the air and off into the street. Farty yelped at the kick, but he soon recovered from it, and he turned on that bastard and bared his teeth and snarled real menacing like. The bastard pulled a little sissy pistol out a his pocket and shot Farty dead. Just like that.

"You old son of a bitch," I shouted. I was genuine horrified and outraged. There was some ax handles in a barrel right there by the door into the general store, and I didn't take no time to think about what I was doing. I just grabbed one a them ax handles, and I swung it as hard as I ever could. I hit that ole boy across the back of the head, and it sounded for all hell like I had hit a watermelon and split it, and he dropped down just like a sack of grain. Then I went and picked Farty up and started walking out of town heading home with him. I was bawling, too, like a damn baby. I told you I keered about Farty.

And, oh, that was a long walk, I can tell you that. My arms was aching from the dead weight of poor old Farty, and I was running tears that was making muddy river streaks down through the dirt that was caked on my face. My legs was okay, 'cause I was used to walking, and even my bare feet wasn't bothering me none. Old Farty's blood was on my shirt belly and on my arms, and I think that it was even on my face where I had hugged him. I wasn't even thinking none about that shit I had hit. I had hit him and forgot him. All I was thinking about was just only Farty and nothing else.

Well, I fin'ly got back out to the house, and Maw come out to see what was the matter with me. First thing she asked me though, she asked me, "Where's your Paw?" I told her that he was still in town, I guessed. "How come you to come back home by your own self?" she asked me then, and I told her that I didn't rightly know. I guess I hadn't even thought about Paw whenever all that had happened. I'd just hit that bastard and then picked up poor dead Farty and headed for home. The last thing I knowed about ole Paw, I told her, he'd gone into the saloon.

At long last, she seemed to notice that I was a-standing there with tears all down my face and my dead dog in my arms, and she come on out to me, and she said, "What happened, Sonny?"

"Farty's dead," I said.

"I can see that," she said, "but how'd it happen?"

"A man shot him," I said. "For no reason. The son of a bitch."

She slapped me hard across my face then, and she said, "Don't never use that kind of talk in front of me. You know better'n that."

I didn't say nothing. I just shut up and stared at her.

"What do you mean for no reason?" she said. I told her what it was that happened, and I didn't leave nothing out, not even old Farty's fart. I told her the whole story. Then she said, "You hit that man with a ax handle?"

"Yes'm," I said.

"You hit him hard?" she asked.

"Hard as I could," I said.

"How bad do you think you hurt him?" she wanted to know.

"I don't know," I said. "I think maybe I kilt him. I don't keer neither."

"Oh, Lordy," she said, and she went to wailing and pulling her hair. "My only boy's done a killing. Lord God A'mighty, what did I ever do to deserve this?"

I turned and walked away from her, still carrying Farty, and I walked away out behind the house till I found a good spot for a burying. I laid him down there real gentle like, and I knelt there beside him for a spell. I could hear Maw still caterwauling from way back there where I was at. It begin to come on me then that what I done was some serious, but I was still a mourning so for Farty that it didn't really bother me none. Not just then. Not yet.

I fin'ly got up and walked to the shed behind the house and got me a old rusty shovel with a broke handle on it, and I walked back to where I had left Farty. I dug him a good deep hole there, and I put him down in it and covered him up. Then I got two sticks and tied them together in the shape of a cross to make a marker for him, and I jobbed that makeshift cross into the soft dirt that I just covered old Farty up with. I didn't take the broke shovel back to the shed. I just tossed it aside. I stood there and mopped the sweat off my brow with my shirtsleeve, and then I fin'ly realized that there weren't nothing more I could do, not for Farty and not for me. I walked back over to the house. Maw was setting at the table just a staring at the tabletop real blank.

"Did you burry your dog?" she said.

"Yes'm," I said.

I heard the plodding of a slow horse, and I went

to the door and looked out. "Paw's coming," I said. Maw just set there. Outside, Paw slipped down offa the back of old Swayback. He turned to face the house, and he seen me a standing there in the doorway. He just stood there for a minute or two just staring at me. Then he said, "You look a mess, boy. Go wash your face." I walked out to the pump while he went on inside. After I'd washed myself up some, I went on back in. Paw was setting beside Maw by this time. He looked up at me. "He's deader'n hell, boy," he said. "You kilt him."

"I don't keer," I said. "He shot Farty." I didn't know if Paw would jump up and beat the shit out of me or what for saying what I done, but I was feeling that it just didn't make no difference to me no more. He didn't even get up though. He just set there.

"They'll be coming out here for you," he said. "Andy locked up his store and rode for the sheriff."

"They going to hang me?" I asked him.

"I don't know, boy," he said. "I don't know if you're old enough yet for hanging, but there's some as would say if you're old enough to kill, you're old enough to hang. I just don't know. But one thing I do know for certain. If they don't hang you, old Pigg's kin'll be after your ass. One way or another, you're done for."

Maw sobbed at that.

"Who's Pigg?" I asked him.

"Who's Pigg?" Paw said, and he shuck his head kind a slow. "You kilt a man dead, and you don't even know his name. The man you kilt was named Joe Pigg, and he comes from a whole family of real bad ones. Brothers and cousins. They won't let it go.

When they hear about it, they'll be a looking for you. You can bet on that."

"Well," I said, "I reckon they'll have to ketch me, before they can do anything to me."

"You'd best run far and fast, boy," he said. "And you'd best get started right now. Don't waste no time." He stood up then, and he shoved a hand down in his pocket, and he come out with ten dollars and give it to me. It damn near astonished me, for Paw had never in my life give me more'n a dime or a nickel at one time. Then, "Take the horse," he said. I stared at him, but all he done was to just set his ass back down. Maw never looked up at me. I turned around and went outside. I looked back once. Then I crawled up onto old Swayback, and I turned her and headed her west. And that's the whole story a me leaving home, and that's also just about everything I know about my own maw and paw, 'cept to say that Paw's last name was Parmlee, and so, a course, that's my name too. I sure don't know much more than that.

Old Paw had said that I'd best move far and fast, but I don't know how in hell he thought I could move fast with just ole Swayback under me. That poor old thing should ought to a been put out to pasture a long time before that. I hoped that no one would come after me too soon, 'cause for sure they'd ketch up with me the way that old horse was a moving. And I never had the heart to whip her up or to even try to get her moving no faster than just her own ordinary plodding along pace. I was thinking about my own self too, for I figgered that if I was to run her, it might kill her, and then I'd be afoot. So I plodded west.

I knowed that we didn't live very far from the New Mexico border, but I didn't know how many miles

that meant, and even if I'd knowed that, I wouldn't a
knowed how many miles I could cover in a hour on
old Swayback, and I didn't have no way a knowing
whenever a hour had passed neither. The only thing
I knowed, or at least I thought I knowed it, was that
the sheriff wouldn't be able to come after me if I was
to get across the border into New Mexico. 'Course
them Piggs wouldn't give a damn about that.

So anyhow I just rid along headed west. I didn't
have no destination in mind. I didn't have no idea
where I was going nor what I was a going to do. All
I knowed was that I had left home, and I wasn't never
going back. I had me a swaybacked horse, ten dollars
and a pair of overhauls, which I was wearing. I had
one tore and bloody shirt. That was all. I didn't have
no boots or shoes. It come to me that I sure wouldn't
be hard to spot riding along like that, and after I had
rid for a while, I commenced to looking back over
my shoulder ever' now and then. After a while, too,
I begin to feel hungry, and I et all them pieces a hard
candy that was in my pocket. Well, that made me
thirsty, and I realized then that I had made a bad
mistake. I had rid away from home without no water.
Nary a drop.

I was sure in sorry shape, and there was a part of
me a saying that I'd ought to turn around and go right
straight back home and get myself better prepared for
this here journey to wherever it was I was going, but
a course, I knowed that I couldn't do that. Likely the
sheriff was already on my trail, and maybe so was
them other Piggs. I hadn't tuck off right, but there
just weren't no way I could go back and start it all
over again. I was stuck on the trail just the way I was.

I kept going, and I felt like I wanted to cry some more, but I never, and what's more, I told myself that I would never cry again. Never. And I ain't neither. Well, hardly ever.

But I fin'ly got to thinking that I was just too damn easy to spot. It wouldn't take much of a description a me to set a posse or the Piggses on my trail. I was moving along slow, and the land all around me was just as flat as a griddle cake. They'd be able to spot me sure from miles away. I got to thinking then that I had ought to do something about it. Several some-things. I had ought to get me a good horse for one thing, one that would look better and move faster. The other thing I had ought to do was to get me some new clothes. Some boots and a shirt and a pair a reg-ular britches. I had to get them things for myself so I wouldn't stand out on the flat prairie like a sore thumb a looking like old Parmlee's runaway kid. I had me ten dollars, but I didn't have no idea a how far it would go. Hell, I'd never seed that much money at one time, much less worried about how much it would buy. I figgered though that I wouldn't be able to buy myself all a them things with it.

I also had to find me and old Swayback some wa-ter, and I figgered I had to do that pretty damn soon. I didn't have no idea where nor how to look for it neither, but I was pretty damn sure that we wouldn't neither one of us get much farther without it. Then, a course, the next thing after that would be food. And even if I was to find myself a place to buy me some clothes with my money, then I wouldn't have none left for food. Hell, it seemed like I was on a dead end trail.

I even thought a little farther on than all that.

'Course, plodding along like we was, I had all kinds a time to think. But I thought that eventually I was going to have to find myself some kind of work, something to do with myself to make me some money, 'cause my ten dollars sure weren't going to last me my whole lifetime. I'd thought that ten dollars was a whole lot of money whenever ole Paw had give it to me, but with all the thinking I was doing, it come to seem like just a little bit after all. Hell, it had my head a swimming with all the thinking.

I wondered how tough it would be to find me a job somewheres—whenever I got to somewheres. Then it come to me that I didn't even know where the next town was at. The closest one could be in any direction. The only reason I was riding west was 'cause I knowed that New Mexico was thataway, and I'd get myself into a different jurisdiction, and then I'd only have the Piggses to worry about and not the law too. I was headed for no town that I knowed of. I was just hoping for one was all.

And so I started in to putting a whole lot a energy into them hopes. I kept hoping that I'd see me a town just any minute, and whenever I rid on into it, I'd find out that I was already in New Mexico, and then someone would see me and say something like, "Oh, you poor boy. Come on and let me get you something to eat." And I'd eat me a good steak dinner, on that person, a course, and then that same kind person would say, "Come on along with me, sonny boy, and we'll get you some nice new clothes." And I'd get myself all outfitted up real smart like, and then that person would offer me a good-paying job that would start that very next morning. I wished for all that as hard as ever I could, but I just kept riding along and seeing nothing but the same old brown flat up ahead and all around me.

But it come to me along about then that likely nothing like that would ever happen to me, and that maybe the only way I'd get me some new clothes would be to buy them, and then I'd be broke, and I'd still be needing me a horse and food, so what all that meant was that the only way I'd ever get ever'thing I needed would be if I was to steal it. It tuck me a little while to even really form them words, even in my mind, but once I had done said it to myself, I thought more and more about it. Then I said to my-self, hell, I'm already wanted for a killing. How much worse could it get if I was to steal something?

Then I thought that if I was to go to stealing, I might ought to get at it right away while I'm still in Texas, 'cause I'm already trying to run for the border to get out of the reach of Texas law. So if I could just get me a good horse and a good suit of clothes, a good meal and a canteen full of water, maybe even a little more money in my pockets, why, I could head for that border in better shape and style. What I didn't know was where I was going to find me anything to steal, and even if I was to find it, how was I going to steal it? I didn't have no gun.

That was the other thing I needed me. I needed me a gun. I thought that I'd sure like to have me a good Colt .45 in a rig where I could have it hanging down on my right hip. That's what I'd like to have. And I'd like to have me a real Texas hat with a star on its crown, a nice red shirt and a good new pair a jeans tucked down into a pair a black, high top leather boots. That was what I had begun to dream about. Then I'd come back out of the dream and get to wondering just how I was going to make any of this come about.

Well, by God, I fin'ly come to a stream a not bad-looking water, and I couldn't hardly believe my own good fortune. I got offa old Swayback and let her drink her fill while I done the same thing. I tried to drink enough water to make my belly forget that it was hungry, but I learned pretty soon that I couldn't do that. I did drink so much that I was sloshing inside. That weren't none too comfortable, but I didn't know how long that drink was going to have to last me, and I didn't have no canteen nor nothing at all to tote water in. Damn, I felt stupid. How could a man take off horseback for New Mexico outa hot and dry West Texas and not even tote along some water?

I seen some game too along about then, and a course I didn't have no way to bring any of it down. I told myself it didn't matter none, 'cause I didn't have the time to stop and build a fire and cook nothing anyhow. I just crawled back on ole Swayback and started in a plodding west again. But the more I rid, the harder I got, and I quit a wishing for that kindly reception I had imagined, and I started in a wishing more harder for a gun so that I could steal me the things I needed. I started in thinking more a myself as what I really and truly was and that was a fugitive. Hell, I was on the run.

I was a wanted killer, and that made me an outlaw, and I forced myself to think hard, and to accept myself for just that. If I was to be an outlaw, I told myself, I'd be a hard one, and I'd be a good one. I'd be the goddamnedest outlaw that ever come down the pike. I had my jaw set hard, and I was riding along trying my best to look tough and mean, and I reckon that the truth was that I looked pretty damn silly, riding old Swayback in my bare feet and my old overhauls, but I was developing the right attitude, I can tell you that. I knowed that much. And just then I seed a house a setting all by its lonesome off to the north a the trail.

Chapter Two

I got all kinds of excited just a looking at that lonesome house off over there. I was thinking about food and water and clothes and guns and money and a fresh, good horse. A course all I had to help me try to get any of them things was just that ten dollars and my own natural meanness. I didn't have no weapons to hold nobody up with nor nothing like that. I wanted to get my young ass on over there, but I had to set and think about it a spell. I thought that I had to have me some kind of a plan if I was to get what I wanted. Then I fin'ly figgered out that I really didn't know what them people might have that I would want, and I couldn't actually make no real plans, not knowing what might be available to me over there. So I fin'ly decided to just plod on over there and act like just only what I for real was, and that was a poor kid out alone and in desperate need. Maybe they'd feel sorry for me and feed me some at least. Maybe not. I guessed I'd just have to take myself on over there and find out.

Well, I had just rode up alongside a clump a scrubby old trees and brush when I seed a man come out a that house. I nudged old Swayback back into the cover of that scrubby stuff and watched from there. The man went on around behind the house and in a few more minutes he come back out all mounted up on a fine looking horse, and he went a riding back off in the same direction from what I had just come from. Only he weren't riding right at me. He was cutting a angle from his house kind a southeast toward the trail. He'd hit it back behind where I was a lurking at. I decided to wait him out. Whenever he had fin'ly plumb disappeared, I moved on out of my cover and headed on over for his little house. I rid slow and easy. 'Course, that was the only way old Swayback ever went.

I thought that man might of left a woman in there or something, but nobody come out a the house whenever I rid up close, and so I just set there on old Swayback and waited for a bit. Fin'ly I hollered out. "Anyone home?" I yelled. Nobody give an answer, so I slid down off my old horse and walked on over to the door and banged on it a bit. I still didn't get no answer, so I looked back down the long road, and that rider was long gone. There weren't no one else in sight neither. That made me kind a bold, and so I just went on inside. I found me some bacon and some beans and some hard biscuits, so I whomped myself up a right good meal and et my fill. I was some nervous, so ever' now and then I got myself up and run to the front door and opened it to look outside, but I never seen no one coming.

When I was about as full as I could get without hurting myself, I found me a sack and commenced to stuffing it with ever'thing I could find to eat that would keep along the trail. I put in some tins of beans and peaches and what was left of them hard biscuits. I even put in a slab a bacon. It was salt cured and had ought to last me a while. I dropped a couple of pans and a knife and fork and spoon down in there too. I rummaged around all through the house, and I found me a suit of clothes that weren't way too big for me, so I put them on. I found a canteen too, and I filled it with water to take along with me. Well, pretty soon I was all dressed and well outfitted for travel. The boots I had found was uncomfortable. They was loose on my feet, and they seemed hard, but I figgered I'd best wear them. At least I weren't barefoot no more. I found me a hat too, but it come down clean over my ears. I put it on anyhow. I rolled up a couple a blankets to take along with me.

Then at last I come to the real treasure. I opened up a chest that was setting at the foot a the bed. I thought at first that it weren't nothing but a bunch of extra bedclothes, but I decided to dig a little in it. I throwed quilts and blankets out till, by God, there was a six-gun burried down there. And it was a Colt, all right, but it sure weren't the model that I had been dreaming about. It was a .41, the 1877 model what they called "Thunderer." It had a four-and-a-half-inch barrel on it, and it was a double-action revolver. There was also a box a .41 shells there, so I figgered it was all right. I dropped that box a shells in my new coat pocket, and I tucked that Colt into the waistband a my new trousers.

I looked around a little more, but I never found no money nor nothing else I felt like I really needed, and I had begun to get more nervous hanging around in that house so long. I gathered up all my ill-got gains and went outside. I was a little disappointed to be so well set up now and still a riding on old Swayback, and then I recalled that the man who had rid off from that place had brung his horse out from behind the house. Just for the hell of it, I walked around there, and damned if I didn't come on a little ole corral with three good looking riding horses in it. There was also a couple a saddles and blankets and all the necessary tack just a hanging there on the fence rails just a waiting for me.

Well, it didn't take me long to pick out a sweet little roan mare and get her all saddled up and ready to go. I was just about to ride off, and I had me a thought. It was likely to be a while before that feller come back home, but whenever he did he for sure would know right away that he had been robbed, and almost for sure he would go to the law and tell about it. I already knowed that I was being hunted, and I sure didn't want to leave no clear trail. I fetched my old overhauls out of the house, and when I rid out, I tuck them with me and led old Swayback away too.

On down the trail I burried them overhauls under some rocks. Riding along on that fine horse, setting in a good saddle, with boots on my feet, a wearing a full suit of clothes and toting a Colt six-gun, I told myself that I was a sure enough outlaw. 'Course, the man I had killed, I had hit from behind with a ax handle, and my first stealing wasn't no bold holdup neither. It was just sneak-thiefing, but, hell, I had me a posse on my trail, and I was headed for New Mexico. I was a sure enough fugitive from justice a living off the land and looking over my shoulder, and I felt pretty damn good about it too.

It was getting to be late in the evening, and I could tell that it would be dark before long, so I needed to locate myself a likely spot for a camp for the night. Well, I seed a thin line a trees off in the distance, and

I figgered that meant water, so I headed d'rectly for them. By the time I got there, it was dark, and so it weren't the easiest thing to do to locate the spot where I wanted to lay myself down on the ground all night long, but I fin'ly did. I had et so much back at that house that I weren't near hungry yet, so all I done was to just take keer of the horses, and then spread out my blankets and lay me down to sleep.

Well, it was a quiet night, and in the morning I gathered up some sticks, built me a fire and had myself a hot breakfast a bacon and beans. I rolled up my blankets, got my new horse ready to go, and then decided to try out my new Colt. I checked her over, then tuck me a few practice shots at some rocks on the other side a the river. I weren't none too good with it, but I figgered I could hit a man if he was close enough to me and I had a need to do it. Fin'ly I mounted up and rid on west. I left old Swayback there. There was plenty a water and grass. I figgered she'd be all right, and she must not a give a damn about it herself, 'cause she never even made out like she even thought about follering me.

I felt pretty good riding out of there. I was thinking about how quick it comes easy to call stole stuff my own and to feel like it really is, but after a few hours of riding along with nothing for company but the horse I was a setting on, I begun to get pretty bored with my new role as a outlaw fugitive. And as the sun rose on up higher in the sky, the heat commenced to come on strong. Real soon I had to pull off my new jacket and lay it across the saddle behind me. I kept a looking around in all directions too. I said I was bored, but I sure weren't relaxed. I looked ahead looking for signs a life or for some boundary marker to tell me whenever I was leaving Texas, and I looked behind me for any sign a the pursuing posse or a the Pigg family. I rid on and on, though, and never seed nothing. It was like as if I was the only human critter on the face of the whole entire earth.

I stopped again 'long about noon and had myself some more beans and bacon and hard bread, and I washed it all down with a little water. Then I figgered I had best give some a my water to my horse, and I done that by pouring some into the crown a my hat and holding it for the horse to drink out of. I wished then that I'd a got something for the horse to eat, 'cause the ground round about there was pretty barren. I mounted up again and headed on west. "First chance we get," I said to that ole horse, "I'll feed you real good. I promise you that. I'll let you eat as long as you can stand it."

Come evening I found us another watering spot, and even though there was still some good riding time left in the day, I decided to stop for the night. I figgered that if I was to go on to take advantage of the daylight hours, I might not be so lucky as to come across another good camping site. I was sure too that the mare could use some good grazing and a good long drink a water, not just a hat crown full. So I made me another camp and fixed me up another meal. Then I just laid back beside my little campfire and rested myself a waiting for the sun to go on down. And I thought back on what had for sure been the longest day of my whole life.

All that long day I hadn't seed another live human being, nor a house nor nothing man-made. I sure was longing for some company, but I knowed too that if I was to see anyone a coming, I wouldn't know if it

was the law or the Piggses after me or what. I had
powerful mixed feelings about the prospect of seeing
people. If them Piggses was to catch me, I knowed
that they'd kill me in a minute. I didn't know what
the law would do to me, if it was to catch me, being
as how I was just a kid. They might lock me away
or they might hang me to death. I just didn't know,
but I didn't want to find out neither. Fin'ly I went on
to sleep, and I guess I slept all right, though I did
have some troubling dreams run through my head
ever 'now and then.

   Whenever I fin'ly woke up, I could tell that it was
early daylight, but my eyes hadn't yet actual focused
on nothing. They was still trying to open up, and they
felt kinda stuck together too. I rolled over on my side
and yawned, and then I rolled back over on my back
and rubbed my eyes a bit. I started to set up and try
to open my eyes at the same time, and then I seed
legs and feet wearing tall boots, and they was standing all around me. I blinked and swiped real hard at
my eyes when I seed that, and then I set up right
straight, and I reached fast for that new Colt revolver
of mine.

   "Whoa, there, boy," one a the men said. "You going to kill all of us with that thing?"

   I thought for a bit about what he said, and I reckoned that I might could kill me one or two of them,
but then the rest of them would kill me for sure. I
hadn't had time to count them yet. "I ain't going to
let you hang me," I said. "I believe I'd ruther get
shot."

   "Now, who's talking about hanging?" the man
said. "Or shooting for that matter?"

"You ain't the posse?" I said.

"We for sure ain't a posse," he said. "You got a posse after you?"

"If you ain't it, then I ain't saying," I said. "Likely I done said too much already. Where are we at?"

"We ain't much of nowhere," he said. "Where you headed?"

"New Mexico," I said.

"Well, you made it that far," he said.

"You mean, I'm in New Mexico?" I said.

"That's right," he said.

"Well, hell," I said. "Then I ain't got to worry none about no posse. Say, you ain't the Pigg family, are you?"

"Boy, you sound like you must be in a hell of a jam," he said. "Put that damn six-shooter down, will you? My name's Rod Chambers. Me and these other boys are cowhands working for the Boxwood outfit. We seen your camp and thought we'd stop in and ask for your hospitality. That's all."

"Oh," I said. I put down the gun, and I stood up kind of slow like. I wiped my hands on my britches, and then I stuck out my right hand to shake with old Chambers.

"I'm—I'm Parmlee," I said. He shuck with me, and then he interduced me to the rest a his gang.

"These boys here is Shorty, Tex, Mac and Bo," he said. I figgered they must all have other names, but then, I had another name too, what I hadn't give out. I wondered if I should ought to have give him a total fake name, but it was too late to worry about that. I had done give it out proper, although not complete. I shuck with each a them other cowhands, and Chambers said, "Mind if I stoke up your fire some?"

"No," I said. "Hell no. Help yourself."

He knelt down and commenced to poking at what was left a my little fire, while ole Tex went after some more sticks for it. "You got any coffee?" Bo asked me.

"No, I ain't," I said.

"Well, we got some," he said. "I'll fetch it."

Well, by God, before long, between their stuff and mine, we had us a hell of a breakfast a cooking. They seemed like pretty good guys, and I was glad to have their company. I was special glad to know that I had made it safe clean out a Texas, and that from there on I'd only have to watch out for them Piggses and not for no posse too. I kind a wished that I knowed what a Pigg looked like though. As far as I knowed, the only Pigg I had ever saw was the very one what I had kilt, and I kept on a trying to recall just what he had looked like, but I couldn't really quite call up his damned ugly features. I knowed for sure I wouldn't be able to spot his kinfolks just by looking at them.

Well, we et up the breakfast and drunk us a couple a pots a coffee, and then we cleaned up the dishes and put out the fire. We all saddled up our horses and mounted up ready to ride on out a there in our own directions. Chambers looked over at me.

"Where you headed, Parmlee?" he asked me.

"I don't rightly know," I said. "I ain't figgered it out yet."

"Well, why don't you just ride along with us?" he said. "If you're needing a job, I reckon I might be able to fix you up. I'm foreman over at the Boxwood."

"I ain't never punched no cows," I said.

"You can learn, can't you?" he asked me, and I opined as how I likely could, so he told me to ride on along with them, and I did. It wasn't like as if I had no other major prospects just then. I thought about how I had felt whenever I first woke up that morning and seed them boots standing all around me, not knowing if they was posse or Piggses, and all of a sudden it felt kinda good to be headed for a regular job with folks what didn't want to kill me or nothing like that. And besides, after the way I had felt looking at them boots that early morning, I begun to consider that maybe I wasn't really cut out to be no bad outlaw after all.

We rid on for two full days before we come up to the main headquarters a the Boxwood. It was a hell of a big spread. Ole Chambers give me a bunk in the bunkhouse and interduced me all around. Since I weren't no real cowhand, he put me to work doing all kinds a chores: fetching firewood, peeling taters, washing dishes, just any old damn thing, but I didn't mind. Hell, whenever he put me to mending fence, I felt like as if I had been promoted way on up there.

The other thing was that I found out that ole Tex was some slick with a handgun, and I begged him into teaching me. I used my stole Colt, and I got to be pretty good with it, but it tuck me a fair amount a time in the doing. I recollect the first time ole Tex tuck me out. He set up some empty tins, mostly beans and peaches tins what we had a plenty of around the ranch; he set them up on a fence rail, and then he said, "Plunk at them, Kid," and so I slapped at my Colt like for a real fast draw, you know, and I bruised the heel a my hand and never even pulled the damn thing out. Ole Tex, he never laughed at me for that, but he just only tole me to slow it down and to be easy and deliberate like. So with my hand a hurting like hell, I tried it like he said. Then I went and wore a blister on my thumb, the one what thumbs back the ole hammer, you know, and Tex, he said that I had ought to lay off for a spell, but I wouldn't have none a that. I taped up my thumb and just kept right on at it. Eventual the bruise went away and the blister healed over, and I become a little better at it each day. Well, my draw got smooth and easy and deliberate like, but my aim weren't worth snake shit.

I blowed the head off a old rooster one time. It would a been a hell of a shot too, if I had been aiming at the damn thing, but I weren't. I was aiming at a damn bean tin on the fence rail. But Tex, he kept a working with me and giving me pointers and all, and after some weeks a doing it ever' day, I begun to knock them tins offa the fence rail. It sure made me feel good to see them fly. And whenever I had got to where I didn't hardly ever miss them at all no more, why, then I begun to work on making my slow and easy and deliberate draw a little more faster and so on. Well, I turned out some slick. I longed for a real Peacemaker though, like the one what was hanging at Tex's side, and I saved my wages up till I could afford one. It tuck me a little to get used to it, but then I got to be pert near as good as ole Tex hisself. 'Course I got myself some new clothes and a pair a boots what fit me, and I begun to feel real cocky, being a real working cowhand and a good hand with a gun to boot. Why, I was a drawing and whirling most ever'where I went, and more than once ole Rod, he had to tell me something like, "Kid, we ain't paying you to show off with that damn gun." Well, I kinda settled down some then, and whenever I was at work, I tried to concentrate on my learning there too.

I strung wire till both my hands was all cut up, and once or twice I had a wire snap off and come back and bite the hell out a me. Fin'ly they graduated me up to riding the herd with them, and the first time I ever roped a calf, the little shit pulled me right outa the saddle. I landed on my face and my belly, and I sure did get laughed at that day, I can tell you. But then I learnt to lap that rope around the saddle horn so that it wouldn't happen no more. The first time I helped to cut the nuts off a calf I like to got sick with the sight and just the thought of it, and they laughed at me real good then, too. In fact, that very evening, ole Cookie, he served them balls up to me on my dinner plate, and I couldn't eat them, and that got me a worse laugh than what the cutting had got.

One morning my ole horse puffed out his belly when I went to cinch him up, and then when I started in to climb aboard, the damn saddle slipped off to one side, and I tuck me a hard fall. They hee-hawed me then too. Another time out on the range, I had roped me down a calf and was feeling some smug about how slick I had did it, but just then its mama cow come a running at me and knocked me over backwards and run right over me. Ole Rod come a running.

"You hurt, Kid?" he said.

"Naw, hell," I told him. "I'm all right."

Soon as I said that then Rod and Tex and all the other boys commenced to laughing at me again. I got a whole hell of a lot a laughing at while I was a learning, but ole Tex, he told me not to take it personal. "It's just all a part of the learning," he said.

"All of us has gone through it." So I tuck it as best I could, and as time rolled on, by the time I was sixteen year old, I become might hear as good as any hand on the ranch. I thought I had my whole life laid out in front a me right there on the ole Boxwood with Rod, and Tex, and all the rest a them ole boys, and the boss and his lady too. Hell, we was like family, and that was a real new feeling to me. I hadn't never had that feeling back home with Maw and Paw.

Then one day a feller come riding into the ranch, and he hauled up there in front a the big house. Chambers seed him a coming and walked over there to meet up with him. I was standing over by the corral, and I could sorta hear what they was saying over there. After the howdying was did, the feller pointed over to the corral, and it didn't take long for me to realize that he was talking about the horse I had stole might near two years earlier. I figgered that maybe he was the man I had seed ride away from that house that day way back then, and I was glad I weren't wearing his clothes or his gun no more.

Chambers walked him over to the corral, and he kind a give me a look out a the corner a his eye. "She just showed up out here one day a while back," he said. "We brought her on in to take care of her. You'll find her in good shape."

"You got no idea how she come to be in these parts?" the feller asked.

"No idea," said ole Chambers. Then he looked over at me. "Parmlee," he said, "fetch that roan mare out for this man." I done it and tuck the line over to the stranger. He tuck it from me and thanked me.

"Likely someone stole her from me," the man said,

"then rode her over this way and abandoned her to pick up a different one to hide his trail. Well, I sure thank you for looking after her."

When that man rid away leading his horse, I stood there a staring at Chambers, waiting for him to ask me for some explanation. He never. He just turned and went on with his business. I can tell you, I was embarrassed, but I sure did appreciate what ole Chambers done for me. He must a knowed that I had stole that horse, but he never said nothing about it—not to the owner and not to me. It was like as if he figgered that nothing I had did before he picked me up along the trail mattered none. The only thing he keered about was what I had did since then a working for him there on the Boxwood.

But that weren't the end of it. No, sir. 'Cause you know, them Piggses had never give up a-hunting for me. And the way I got it figgered after all that happened is this way. The Piggses had follered my trail to the house where I had stole that roan from. Maybe they had talked to the ole boy, and then maybe he had told them that someone had come by when he was out and stole all that stuff from him. Maybe they had even found old Swayback where I had left her. They knowed that I had got my ass on into New Mexico. They also knowed, a course, that they was hunting a kid name a Parmlee. Maybe they had told that man my name.

Well, a couple a years had gone by, you know, but them Piggses was stubborn, and that man whose horse I had stole was still pissed off. I figger that when he fin'ly found his horse, he had hunted up them Piggses again and told them just where he had found it.

Maybe he even told them that he had heared me called by that name. Anyhow, whatever the truth of all that might be, they rid onto the ranch early one summer morning. Piggses. They was four of them.

Chapter Three

Well, hell, I weren't actual standing just right there whenever the bastards come a riding up. I was off to the corral fetching out a fresh horse to ride. I had been sent out on a early morning errand, and when I come back I needed to get me a fresh horse before I could ride on out to where the rest of the boys was busy catching up calves what needed to be branded. But ole Rod Chambers, he was out in front a the big house where the boss lived, and ole Tex was with him, I guess. I guess they had just been in the house a talking to the boss about something or other, and when they come out onto the porch, they met up with them four Piggses what had just rid up. I don't know just exact what had transpired out there, but them Piggses must a asked after me by my own right name, 'cause pretty soon, ole Tex come around to where I was at in the corral. He sidled up kind a close to me, and he had a look on his face, and I knowed right away that something out a the ordinary was up.

"Kid," he said, and there weren't nobody around to listen, but he was still keeping his voice down real low. "Kid," he said, "you'd best mount up and ride on out of here lickety-split and lay low for a spell."

"What's up?" I asked him.

"They's four riders over to the house," he said. "Strangers. They call themselves Pigg. They're looking for you, and they ain't friendly."

Well, my heart kind a fell down into my belly at that unpleasant news, but I gulped hard once and then got myself braced all up. After all, it weren't nothing to get all excited about. It was just something I'd knowed all about for a long while that I was going to have to face up to one fine day, and so here it was. That's all.

"I been expecting them," I said. "Matter a fact, I wonder what tuck them so damn long to find me."

"Me and ole Rod'll stall them off for you while you ride out of here," Tex said. "Now get going. Go out to that north line shack where we was at last week. I'll fetch you up some supplies after a while."

Well, I think I done told you that ole Tex had been training me up with a six-gun for some time by then, and I was already feeling kind a cocky about my own prowess with same, so I just set my jaw and hitched at my britches, and I said real firm like, "I ain't running from them Piggses, Tex."

"Hell, boy," he said, "they's four of them, and they look like toughs to me. You can't fight them all."

"Tex," I said, "whenever you and Rod and them first picked me up out there on the trail, I was a running from the Texas law and from them Piggses. I knowed that the Texas law couldn't follow me out here, but I knowed just as well that them Piggses would, sooner or later. I knowed they'd catch up with me one a these fine days. I ain't running from them no more, and that's all there is to it. You just stay clear when the lead starts in a flying, you and Chambers."

"What the hell do they want you for anyway?" Tex asked me. He had shoved his old beat-up hat way back and was a scratching his head, and his face was all wrinkled up in a kind a puzzlement.

"I kilt one a their kin back in Texas," I said. "Back before you all found me on the trail."

"But you was only 'bout fifteen year old back then," Tex said.

"Fourteen," I said, correcting him.

"How'd you kill him?" he said.

"Hit him in the back a the head with a ax handle," I said. "The son of a bitch shot my dog."

"Well, I'll be damned," said Tex. "You sure you won't take on out of here? I believe that them four mean to kill you."

"I'm sure," I said. I hefted my Colt just a bit to make sure it was sliding easy in its holster. Then I headed on over toward the gate. Ole Tex, he just give a shrug and come on up alongside a me. We walked along together on over to the front a the big house, and sure enough, there was ole Rod standing facing four men who was still just setting horseback. I seed the boss hisself a standing up on the porch and watching. Rod seed us a coming, and he give me a real strange look. I guess he was trying to figger out why the hell I was coming out there 'stead a running away like Tex had told me to do. I figgered that Rod had sent Tex to warn me and to tell me to get the hell out a there. I most always done just whatever the hell Rod told me to do, but this here didn't have nothing to do with the job. It was personal.

I walked right out square in front of them four Piggses, standing with my back to ole Rod, and I said, "Rod, you and Tex step on out of the way." Then I looked right hard at the biggest Pigg of the four of them. "If your names is Pigg," I said, "then it's me you're a looking for. I'm Parmlee. You ain't got no fight with these others here. Let them stand clear, and then make your move."

"We ain't looking for no fight with anyone but you, Parmlee," the big Pigg said. "Nobody kills a Pigg and gets away with it. You killed Joe, and we'uns is been hunting you ever since."

"Tuck you long enough to find me," I said.

"You're a cocky little shit, ain't you?" Pigg said. "Before we kill you, tell me just one thing. How come a little weasley shit like you to kill poor ole Joe the way you done?"

"He shot my dog," I said.

"That it?" Pigg said, like as if he couldn't hardly believe it. "You killed a human person over a dumb animal? Hell, boy, a goddamned dog ain't worth killing a man over. It sure ain't worth dying over."

"Joe Pigg weren't fit to kiss my dog's ass," I said. "And my dog's name was Farty."

Well, that done it. All four of them Piggses went for their guns at the same time, and mine was out in a flash too. My first shot hit that big Pigg, the one what had been talking, right in the mouth, but it was my only shot. A bullet tore right into my left chest and knocked me right over onto my back. I was shocked and stunned, I can tell you. Hell, I'd never been shot before, never really even hurt real bad. 'Course, whenever I went out there, I knowed there was a real good chance a me taking a bullet, maybe even getting my young ass kilt. Even so, the actual feel of it was more than I ever expected or even imagined. I seed the hole, and I seed all the blood, and it was all mine. A couple more bullets hit the ground right close around me too. By the time I could raise up my shooter again, I seed where bullets was splatting into them other three Piggses from all different kind a directions. Anyhow, that's what it looked like. When all four saddles was fin'ly empty, and all four Piggses was laying dead or dying on the ground, I relaxed and laid on back my own self. I figgered I was a dying too. I sure felt weak and kind a fading, but I didn't keer too much about that, 'cause the bastards what had did it to me was all dead too, and there was four a them and only one a me. I figgered it was a pretty good score to go out with.

But I got the surprise a my young life when I didn't die. I just laid there a bleeding, and right soon ole Rod was a hovering over me. Tex come up on the other side, and I could see that he was only just then holstering his Colt. He had jumped in and helped me out. Likely Rod had too. I had told them to stay out a the way, that it was only just my fight, but they had went and jumped in it anyhow. I wondered about that. I wondered why they had did that. "They're all done for," Tex said. "How's the kid?"

"He's hit bad," Rod said. "We got to get him fixed up real quick. You ride for the doc."

"All right," Tex said, and he was gone in a second. Then I heared the boss's voice coming from somewhere off where I couldn't see.

"Get him in the house," he said.

Then old Rod, he just picked me right up the way you might carry a dang little baby, and he toted me right inside the big house what I had never been inside before and then on back to a bedroom somewheres, and he laid me right down in the biggest and

softest bed I had ever even been near in my whole
entire life, and me all dirty and all bloody, and the
next thing I knowed, someone had tore off my shirt,
and then someone was a washing the blood off a me,
and someone had jobbed something into that bullet
hole a trying to stop the bleeding, I guess. It seemed
like I had a whole mess a folks worrying over me,
and it was all kind of fuzzy to me. I could see sort
of, but I wasn't seeing real clear, and I hadn't said
nary word to no one since I had tuck that bullet. I
guess I was just kind a staring at the world around
me and wondering how come I was still in it.

But the funny thing about it all was that it never
hurt me none. I must have fin'ly passed on out
though, 'cause when I next come to and kind a come
back to my senses, I was all cleaned up and bandaged
up all good and proper, and, by God, that hole in my
high chest was a hurting me then. It was a kind of
throbbing with pain, you know. I kind a raised my
head up just a little, and then I moaned out kind a
loud, 'cause it hurt when I moved, and then I seed
Mrs. O, that was the boss's lady, her real name was
Mrs. Oliphant, 'cause the boss was Mr. Oliphant, but
we all just always called them Mr. O and Mrs. O,
well, I seed Mrs. O kind a hovering over me and
looking real concerned, like she keered about me for
real.

"Just take it easy, young man," she said. "Take it
easy. The doc's been here and took out the bullet. He
says you'll mend right enough, but it's going to take
a spell. You feel like sitting up and taking some
broth?"

"Yes'm," I said, "I guess so," and it sounded to
me like my own voice was a way far off somewheres,

and it didn't even sound like me, but I reckon she heard all right, 'cause she went on out of the room, and by and by she come back in with a tray with a bowl a setting on it. Well, she set that tray down on the bedside table, and then she helped me to get all set up, and then she put fluffed up pillas back behind my back for me to lean back and rest myself on. It hurt me some to move around like that, but I managed to get myself all set up with some kind help from Mrs. O. And then, by God, if she didn't set right down beside me on the edge a the bed, and she picked up that tray again, and she went and spoon-fed me from out a that bowl of steaming beef broth.

It was so damn good, and it felt just for all the world like as if it was a putting the strength right back inside a me and a working already to heal up that bullet hole. I really and truly thought I could feel it doing that. But mostly I was a thinking that my own mother wouldn't never a treated me so good as what that fine lady was doing, setting there on the bed beside me like that and spooning that hot broth right into my mouth. And I don't know what it was come over me so powerful strong, but all of a sudden there was tears a pouring down my cheeks, and I couldn't do nothing about it. Not a damn thing.

"There, there," she said, and she tuck up the fine white napkin from off the tray, and real gentle like, she daubed at my cheeks and my eyes with it. "You're going to be just fine. Does it hurt very bad?"

"Oh, it ain't that, ma'am," I said. "The hurting didn't make me do that. I can take it. And I ain't skeered a dying or nothing like that. It ain't that neither. It's just that—well, no one ever treated me this good before in my whole entire life."

Well, I be damned if she didn't set that tray aside right then and just reach her arms around me and hold me real close against her breast, and when she went and done that, I really commenced to bawling. She let me bawl till I was total bawled out, and then she went and mopped up my face again, and then she finished feeding me that bowl of broth. When she was fin'ly all done, she told me to just lay back and close my eyes and try to get me some more sleep. Well, I done what she told me to do, and she pulled the covers up over me real snug, up to my chin, kind a tucking me in, you know, but I didn't sleep. Not right off. I closed my eyes all right, but I just laid there a thinking about that wonderful kind lady and how good and sweet she was a treating me, and I couldn't help it, but I was thinking about my old maw too, and I was thinking how she had slapped me across the face the very last day I ever seen her before I run off from home for good and ever.

Well, it tuck a while, but I sure enough did commence to getting better. I was up and around before long, but my left shoulder and arm was sure enough stiff and useless. I used them a little bit each day just as much as I could till I was feeling most good as new. By God, I had been shit on and shot at and hit, and I was still alive, and I was getting well. I was a for real working cowhand, and I had killed myself two damn Piggses, and at just only sixteen years of age, I had just come to believe that I was one hell of a tough, gunfighting man. Then one morning, I was setting out on the front porch a the big house all by my lonesome a sipping at some nice hot coffee Mrs. O had give me, when Mr. O come out of the house with ole Rod, and then Mrs. O come right out behind them. They all had kind a long faces on them, but Mrs. O's look was the longest.

"Parmlee," said Mr. O, "generally I give unpleasant chores like this to Rod here to take care of, but in your case, I mean to talk to you direct."

I looked up at him feeling right curious, and I said, "Yes sir?"

"I'm letting you go," he said. "I have to. I think you're about healed enough now to travel." He handed me a roll of bills, which I tuck, but I really didn't know why he was giving them to me or why I was a taking them, so I just set there staring at him and holding all that money out there in front of myself. "That's all your back pay plus a little bonus," he said. "Cut yourself out a good horse. Your choice. And take a saddle and tack. That's all I can do for you. Rod tells me that you'll make a good cowhand one of these days. You're a hard worker. I'm sorry to have to do you this way, but I've always made it a policy to keep no wild hands on my place. You drew four gun hands onto my place after you. Then instead of hiding out a spell, you came right out to face them. We had four killings on the place as a result of that, right here in front of my own home. I got to let you go, boy."

I looked over at Mrs. O, and damn me if she didn't have tears running right down her cheeks.

"Can't we make this one exception?" she said. "He's so young, and it really wasn't his fault."

"No, Mother," the old man said. "We can't."

"Hey," I said, standing up and setting my coffee cup aside. "I understand." And I really did too. I thought about what a fine lady that Mrs. O was and

how good she had been to me all the time I was laid
up like that. She sure didn't need no one like me
hanging around her place and bringing my kind of
trouble around. I was right proud of Mr. O for seeing
it that way too. I was glad for her to know that he
was taking good keer of her like that. "I don't want
to be the cause of no kind of trouble around here.
You all have been real good to me. More than I
reckon I deserve. I'll just be pulling right on out, but
first I just want to thank you all for everything you
done for me."

Well, I couldn't say no more, without getting sappy,
so I just tucked all that cash into my shirt pocket and
turned away real quick and stepped down off a the
porch and started in to make my way on over toward
the corral. I was about halfway over there whenever
ole Rod caught up with me and handed me my own
gunbelt and my hat. I was glad he done that, 'cause I
had knowed they was still back there inside the house,
and I just felt real awkward about going back in there
myself after I had just been told to move my young ass
on out a there. I reckoned that either Mr. O, or maybe
his wife, had ducked back inside and got hold of them,
then give them to Rod to take on out to me. Anyhow I
tuck them from ole Rod and thanked him. I stuck the
hat up on top a my head and strapped on my Colt. At
the corral, Rod helped me catch up a good horse and
saddle it up. It was a brown stallion, one I had rode before, and I liked him. We had got along good together.
He didn't have no name that I knowed about. I just
called him "ole horse." I led ole horse on over to the
bunkhouse, tied him there to the hitch rail, and went inside to gather up my gear. I noticed that ole Rod had
went back over to the big house.

Well, I made myself a blanket roll out a all my stuff and went outside to tie it on behind ole horse's saddle. Then Cookie, he had picked up on what was going on with me, and he brung me along some trail food to pack in, and I made sure I had myself a couple of canteens full of water. I wasn't about to get myself out on a long trail unprepared again, like I had did before. I had learned that lesson real good the last time. Fin'ly I mounted up on ole horse to ride on out of there. I was going out past the big house when Rod come a running out and waving to me. He had some kind a paper in his hand. I hauled up short, and he come on over. He held that paper up for me to take.

"It's a bill of sale for the horse," he said. "In case anyone ever challenges you on its ownership. This paper will prove he's yours. Mr. O signed it and told me to give it to you. Kid, I'm sure sorry about this. I tried to talk him out of it."

I tuck the paper and shoved it inside my shirt. "Thanks," I said. "It's all right. And he done the best thing. Tell him, and the Missus, tell them that I said thanks for everything, and say, will you tell ole Tex so long for me?"

"Sure I will," he said.

I felt a kind a choking down in my throat, and I knowed that I was about to bawl again if I weren't careful, so I never said another word. I just turned ole horse right smart and give him a little kick and rode off kind a quick like. I had a real kind a hurting feeling inside a me. It was like I was riding away from something I would never again find in my whole life. I had never felt thataway before. When I had rode off from home on ole Swayback, I had been skeered. Hell, I was a kid and didn't know what in hell it was that might be fixing to become a me. I didn't have no idea where I was a going or nothing, or even if I would ever make it there. I was skeered, but I wasn't sad on account of leaving home or nothing like that.

But this time, riding off from Rod and Tex and all my other buddies at the Boxwood outfit, and especial that sweet Mrs. O, I felt real sad. I felt like, hell, they was my family. I felt like I reckon I should have felt when I had left Maw and Paw and Texas, but I didn't never feel that way about them. I sure enough felt it, though, riding off from the ole Boxwood. I rode hard for a spell, and I was a crying hard at the same time. Looking back on it all, in spite of how much a man I thought I had become, I reckon I was just still a snot-nosed kid after all.

Chapter Four

Like I said before, I didn't know where the hell I was headed. I did know that Texas was east of me, and I was real keerful not to ride east. I didn't have no reason to take my ass back to Texas. So I headed north and maybe a little west. I spent a couple of lonely nights on the trail a thinking about all the boys back at the bunkhouse on the ole Boxwood, and maybe even I cried a little now and then. I thought some about Maw and Paw too, but I never cried when I was thinking about them. About all I could think a thinking about Maw was how she had slapped me hard across the face that last day I ever seed her. And whenever I thought about Paw, I just thought that after he knowed I had killed that man, he give me some money and a swaybacked horse and told me to skeedaddle on out a there, and that was the most generous day a his whole entire life that I knowed about.

Well fin'ly I stumbled onto a little town. It was called Ash Grove, and I found out right soon that most of the locals liked to call it Ass Grove, so I done the same thing. It weren't much of a town. It had a saloon and a general store and a eating place all right under the same roof, and it was also the only place in the town what could sort of serve for a hotel, 'cause they did have rooms upstairs, but they wasn't really meant to be hotel rooms. They was rooms for the gals to take their customers into to give them a quick romp for a few bucks is what they was. Well, I weren't proud and I weren't no prude, so I asked the man if I could rent me one a them rooms for a spell. He asked to see the color a my money, and I showed it to him and paid him in advance. Why, then he give me a room right fast.

I didn't hardly get no sleep that first night for I could hear all the sounds coming from the next room to mine and maybe from other rooms as well. The walls wasn't none too thick, and the sighing and moaning and groaning and giggling, the gasps, the creaking bedsprings and such, just kept my full attention and kept me wide awake and a wondering just what was going on in them rooms with them gals. I sure did long to know, and I didn't just want someone to tell me about it neither. I was longing to know all about it at first hand.

I reckon I did fin'ly get off to sleep, but I was so used to getting up early back at the Boxwood that I done it when I didn't have no need to. So I was up the next morning without having had too much sleep. I went on downstairs and into the eating part a that there establishment, and in there I ordered myself up a good breakfast a chicken eggs, ham, 'taters, biscuit and gravy. I et that all up in a hurry and washed it down with about a pot of coffee, I guess. Then I paid for it all and went on outside.

I couldn't think of a damn thing to do with myself, so I walked back over to the stable where I had boarded ole horse and checked up on him. He was the one and only person I knowed in that town. He was just fine, so I only talked to him for a few minutes, and then I left again. I don't know what's worse: being out on a lonely trail without no particular destination in mind or being in a town with folks all around you and you not knowing none of them. I was really thinking about them gals, too, but none of them was nowhere in sight. I figgered that, having worked all night, you know, they was just natural sleeping the day away.

So I was just kind of lounging around lazy like outside when I seed a cowboy come a riding up. He tied his horse there at the right rail in front of the main establishment, the one where I was a living, and went on inside. Just then this here other cowhand come a sneaking out a somewheres and went right on over to the first ole boy's horse. He looked around hisself kinda skulky like and didn't see no one out loose but me. He give me a grin and a wink, like as if he was letting me in on a little joke a some kind, then he tuck and loosened up the cinch on that other ole boy's horse. Well, he meant for that ole boy to take hisself a hard fall whenever he started to mount up. That's what he meant to cause to happen.

I just acted like as how I never even noticed that grin and wink nor even what he done with the cinch. I was just minding my own business. By and by, the feller come out of the store, and he stood there on the sidewalk and rolled hisself a smoke. I guess that's what he had gone inside there to buy. He poked that fresh rolled cigareet in between his lips and then he brung out a match and scratched it on the ass of his britches. He lit that smoke. Then he stepped on down to his horse and tuck ahold of the horn. His foot went up to the stirrup, and to this day I don't know how come I didn't just keep a minding my own business, but before I knowed what I had did, I said out loud, "I wouldn't step up on that, mister. Someone has done loosened your cinch."

He looked over at me, and then he checked the cinch, and he seed then that I weren't lying to him. Not a bit of it. He tightened her back up again and swung up into the saddle. Then he looked over at me. "Thanks, kid," he said. "Who done it?"

I give a shrug. "I don't know no one in this town," I said.

Just then the actual culprit stepped right on out into the open with a hard scowl on his ugly face, and he give me a sure enough mean ass look, and then he looked on over at the other feller, and he said, "I done it, Sandy. What about it?"

Sandy said, "I got orders not to fight with you Lazy Snakes, Cutter, but don't push your luck."

"Why, hell, Sandy," Cutter said, "I was just playing a little joke. I wouldn't try to start no fight with you. You know that. All us Lazy Snakes hands is peaceable. 'Course, I might just dust the britches of this busybody little brat here for messing up the fun."

I stepped out then and faced that Cutter. "You can try it," I said.

"Well, now," said Cutter. "What do we have here? A new Billy the Kid?"

"Some folks do call me Kid," I said, "but my name ain't Billy."

"Leave him alone, Cutter," said Sandy. "Hell, he's just a kid, like you said."

"Stay out of it, Sandy," I said. I told you I had been lonesome and bored, and so I was actual kind of enjoying this.

Cutter squared off facing me, and he kind a shuck his hands and arms to loosen them up. I seed that his Colt was a hanging low on his thigh. Right hand side. "You think you can take me, do you?" he said. "You know how to handle that iron you're toting, baby face?"

"I aim to take off your left ear before you can clear leather," I said.

Well, he didn't say nothing to that. He just looked madder'n a bitch dog if you had picked up one a her sucking pups, and he went for his Colt real fast, but he weren't fast enough. Ole Tex had taught me good. I jerked my own Colt out and triggered it before his was even clear, and it was either the best shot or the luckiest shot I ever made, 'cause I seed the blood fly when my bullet tore into his left ear, just like I had bragged it would. He shrieked something awful, turned a loose a his Colt and slapped at the side a his head with his left hand.

"Goddamn," he said, "you shot off my fucking ear."

"Told you I would," I said.

Then he turned and run off to somewheres, still holding the side a his head and trailing a stream a blood all down the street. I ejected the spent shell out a the chamber a my Colt and put in a new one. Then I holstered the Colt. I give Sandy a nod and started to go back inside the establishment where I was a bunking. Sandy said, "Hold it a minute there, Kid." I turned back to look at him. "That's all right, ain't it?" he said. "You said that some calls you kid."

"It's all right," I said. "What is it you want?"

"Can I buy you a cup of coffee?" he said.

"Sure," I said. "Why not?"

He clumb back down out a his saddle again, and he walked on over to where I was a standing. "I didn't mean for you to get in no fight over me," he said, "but I do appreciate your warning about the cinch."

"It weren't nothing," I said. "I just didn't think the man's joke was none too funny, that's all."

We went on inside and got ourselves a table and some coffee. Sandy offered me the makings of a cigareet, but I told him no thanks. I never told him that I didn't know how to roll them things. He finished off the one he was smoking on and snubbed it out in a ashtray what was setting there on the table.

"Old Cutter," he said, "works for the Lazy Snakes Ranch just east of here. I work for the Three Forks outfit. Them's the two biggest operations for hundreds of miles around here, and they're pretty much rivals in the business. There's been trouble brewing for years. It's bound to break out into a real fight sooner or later."

"Pretty big outfits, are they?" I asked him. I knowed the answer, but I couldn't think a nothing else to say, so I just went and said that dumb question.

"You could say so," he said. "And I reckon each one thinks the other'n is too big and would like to cut it down to size."

"Couldn't be your Three Forks outfit could use another hand, could it?" I asked him. "I can do any kind of ranch work what needs to be did, and I ain't too proud."

Sandy give me a look and kind a squinted his face up. "Well, I don't know, Kid," he said, "but I'll check on it. I'll ride back in here tomorrow and let you know. Where you staying?"

I thumbed in the direction a the stairway, and

Sandy grinned. "You mean, up with the whores?" he said.

I kind a laughed, and then he did too. "Yeah," I said. "It's pretty lively up there too."

"I bet it is," he said.

Pretty soon after that he excused hisself and said that he had to get on back out to the ranch, but he promised me again that he'd come back into Ass Grove the next day and let me know if they might have a spot for me out at the ole Three Forks. I thanked him kindly for that, and he left. Well, I felt pretty good. I felt like I had just made myself a new friend, and I might even get myself a job out of it. I give him a few minutes to get on out of town, and then I walked into the store part of the establishment and bought myself the makings. I went upstairs to my room and commenced to practicing on rolling them cigareets.

Well, I used up damn near all the tobaccy and all but two a the papers before I got one to hold together, and it weren't none too pretty neither, but I went and smoked it just the same. It made me cough a bit, and the smoke got into my eyes and made them water some, but I had rolled me a smoke and smoked it. I went on ahead then and rolled up the last one and lit it, and then I left the room, smoking my cigareet as I walked down the hallway, down the stairs and back into the store to buy more makings. I got them and put them in my pocket, puffing all the while, just as if I had been a doing it for years, and then I went into the saloon and stepped right up to the bar. The bar-keep come walking over to where I was at, and he give me a look that there weren't no mistake about. I knowed he was fixing to say something about how

young I was and then tell me to get the hell out. But
before he could open his mouth to start in, the feller
setting about two bar stools down from me piped up
with, "Say, that's the kid what shot off old Cutter's
ear. Damn good shooting, Kid."

"Thanks, mister," I said.

"What'll you have?" the barkeep said.

"Give me a rye whiskey," I said, and by God, he
brung it. He poured me a little short glass full and
then left the bottle setting right there in front of me.
Now I was just a snot-nosed kid, like I done told you,
but I weren't too stupid, not even back then. I didn't
want to look like no fool with my first ever drink a
whiskey, so I just picked it up and tuck me a little
sip a the stuff, and, damn, but it burned my throat a
going down. I sipped at it ever now and then, real
keerful, and all the time I watched the crowd behind
me in the big mirror what hung up over the bar back
on the wall behind it, that is. I had always heard tell
that once you start in acting like a gunslinger, folks
will be after your hide, and I had kilt myself two men
now and shot off a left ear, so I weren't taking no
chances. I was just a little bit nervous, but I was trying
hard not to show it.

At first I seen some eyes staring at me, and maybe
some ole boy kind a pointing at me to show his buddies, but pretty soon they all seemed to forget all
about me. I managed to sip down all a that whiskey
and pour myself a second one. My head was feeling
somewhat light, maybe even a bit dizzy. It come on
me just then that it might not be such a good idea,
me having just shot off a ear, to get myself too woozy
in that place. I had poured myself a second drink,
though, and I didn't feel like I could walk off and

leave it just a setting there. That wouldn't look none
too good. I figgered I'd have to sip at it real slow for
some time. Just then I seen someone moving toward
my back. I seen it in the mirror. But it weren't no
man looking to get hisself a gunslinger. No sir. It was
a gal.

She come up and sidled up beside me there at the
bar and kind a snuggled herself right up against me.
I glanced over at her, most embarrassed, and she
looked right at me and smiled. She was most nearly
as big as me, 'cause I never did get much growth on
me. I could smell her sweet perfume, and I could feel
her soft flesh pushing at my side. My God, I felt hot
and flush just then. My legs turned some weak on me
too, but I felt something ferocious stirring down there
between my legs.

"Buy me a drink, Kid?" she said.

"I was just fixing to drink this one and then go on
up to my room," I said.

"How about some company?" she said. "You can
take the bottle and the glass with you. Hey, Jonah,
give me a clean glass, will you?"

The barkeep slid a glass along the bar, and she
caught it. Then she looked into my face again, and
she said, "Well, how about it?" Now, I ask you, what
was I to do? I kinda nodded to her and turned away
from the bar, and she turned with me, a holding onto
my arm real tight, and it was a good thing she did
too. I staggered just a little getting myself out a that
there saloon and then crossing over to the stairway,
but the gal held me up, and we made it up the stairs
and on into my room. I put the bottle down on a small
table in there, and then I set down real heavy on the
side a the bed and tuck me a sip out of my glass. The

room had commenced to swaying around a little. The gal set down beside me. I tried to say something, but I guess I just stammered.

"Hey, Kid," she said. "Is that the right name for me to call you? Kid?"

"It'll do," I said.

"Well, Kid," she said, "I'm guessing that's your first whiskey. Am I right?"

"That's right," I said, and I remember wondering why I had admitted it to that gal. She put her arms around me and pulled my head down to lay it against her right side titty, and she just held on to me like that for a spell. It was real nice, and I was wishing that I hadn't got myself so damn tiddly.

"Am I your first gal too?" she asked.

"Yes," I said, and the only thing I could figger was that it was the whiskey making me so honest with her. I didn't really like folks a knowing that I never had no whiskey nor no woman.

"Well," she said, "don't you worry about a thing. I'll look after you all right. I'll look after you all night if you want me to." I figgered I could afford that all right, 'cause I figgered that I would be getting me a job the next day, and so it wouldn't matter too much if I was to spend even my very last penny.

"Yeah," I said. "Stay all night. Please."

She hugged me tighter against her, and she said, "I ain't going nowhere, Kid. I'm right here, and I'm going to stay right here."

"What's your name?" I asked her.

"I'm Sherry Chute," she said. She tuck the glass out of my hand. "Here," she said, "you're about to spill that good whiskey on the floor." Then she stood up, and I felt like I was weaving all over the place

without her to lean on. She put the glass on the table
beside the bottle, and then she come back on over to
me. She knelt down and pulled the boots off a my
feet. Then she stood up and commenced to pulling
my shirt off a me. Well, I sure didn't resist her none,
and pretty damn soon, she had me all undressed nekkid and stretched out on the bed. "Just relax, Kid,"
she said. "Sherry will take care of everything."

And oh, Lord A'mighty, but she did. She meant
just what she said. First, she finished undressing herself, and I couldn't help myself, I just stared straight
at her. I think that my eyes was wide and my jaw had
dropped down on my chest. I had never before saw
a nekkid woman, much less been in the same room
with one and me nekkid too. Well, I felt something
on me snap right up to attention while I was staring
at all the glories a her wonderful womanness. Then
the next thing I knowed, she was laying right there
on top a me, me just a feeling her flesh all up and
down my body. Somehow the room quit spinning. All
my concentration was on the lovely lady what was
laying on me. I smooched on her for a spell, a running
my hands up and down her back and butt and legs,
and then she got real serious.

What she done—well, what didn't she do? I believe that woman done everything to my young virgin
body that a woman can do to a man. When she fin'ly
stopped, 'cause I couldn't go no more, she went and
got my glass a whiskey what was still mostly full. It
was still that second glass I had poured for myself
back down there at the bar. She brung it over to me
and said, "Now sip a little of this, darlin'." I sipped
it some, and she said, "You want a smoke?"

"Sure," I said.

She found my makings and real quick like rolled two fine looking cigareets. She was good at that too. Then she lit one and tucked it in between my lips. She lit the second one and laid herself back down beside me. "You're just about the most wonderful thing I ever come across," I said.

"Hey," she said, "you weren't so bad yourself. When I first brought you up here, I was afraid you were going to pass out on me, but you never, and what's more, you got a lot of staying power, Kid." I had to admit that I reckoned I did have, after all what I had just did. We finished them smokes, and I finished my second glass of whiskey. Sherry leaned over me and kissed me real sweet on the lips, and then she said: "You all right now?"

"I'm fine," I said. "I ain't never been better. Not in my whole entire life."

"That's great," she said, and she commenced on me all over again. We done it all a second time around, and I think she pulled out one or two new ones on me. Anyhow, I don't know what time it was, but we fin'ly got to sleep way into the night. Hell, it was morning. I know that much, but how far along the morning had got, I don't know. I do know that it was bright sunlight whenever I woke up again, and old Sherry was laying right there beside me a sleeping like a baby. I thought that she was the most beautiful thing I had ever saw.

Well, me getting out of the bed stirred her up. She looked at me real groggy like, but even so, she pulled me back into the bed, and we went at it yet again. When we was done that time, I asked her if she wanted to go get some breakfast with me, but she asked me to just leave her be right there in my bed.

She needed her sleep. She did remember to make me pay up before I left the room. I paid her, and I still had a little money left. I thought about ole Sandy just then, and I sure did hope he'd come around with a job for me. I stepped out in the hall and stood there for a minute while I rolled me a smoke. Then I lit it and headed for the stairway. I found me a table in the eating place and set there a smoking and drinking coffee even after I had finished up my breakfast. I counted my money again, and I figgered that I could spend a while in the place and have me some more romps with Sherry. But sooner or later that and the meals I'd have to have would wipe me on out. I sure was anxious to see old Sandy.

Chapter Five

It was early the next morning, like he'd told me it would be, 'bout the same time I'd first saw him, when ole Sandy come a riding back in to Ass Grove, and there was another feller riding alongside of him. I was just a standing there on the sidewalk smoking me a rolled cigareet, just like an old hand. I had got to be pretty good at it by then. Them two rid up and hauled their ass up right there in front of me. As they was dismounting, Sandy said to the other feller, "This is him right here." They both swung on down, lapped the reins of their horses around the hitching rail and then walked over toward me. I seed the other feller giving me a hard study.

"Morning, Kid," Sandy said, and he stuck his right hand out towards me. I tuck it and shuck it.

"Morning, Sandy," I said.

"Holster," Sandy said, "this here is the Kid I was telling you about. Kid, this here is my boss, Morgan Holster."

Holster stuck out his hand, and we shuck. "Howdy, Mr. Holster," I said.

"Just Holster," he said. "Just call me Holster like everyone else does. Have you had your breakfast yit?"

I had but I lied, 'cause I figgered that was a kind a invite, and I meant to get something out a ole Holster, whether it was a job or just only a free meal. "I reckon I could stand a bite," I said.

"Well, let's go inside then," Holster said, "and have us some eggs and coffee and talk some things over."

He started on in, and behind his back, ole Sandy give me a wink. We follered Holster on in and got us a table. Pretty soon we had us some coffee, and we was waiting for our meals. That waiter was all right. He never let on to Holster and Sandy that he had just served me up one platter of eggs and ham, and it weren't all that long ago neither. He did give me a look though, whenever I ordered up a stack of flapjacks and some more ham to go with them.

"Sandy tells me you're looking for a job," Holster said.

"Yes sir," I admitted. "That's right."

"You done cow work before?" he asked me.

"I worked for the Boxwood outfit down south a here for a spell," I said. "I reckon ole Rod Chambers or even Mr. O hisself would speak a good word for me if they was to be asked."

"I know both of them," he said. "They're good men. How long was you with the Boxwood?"

"Nigh onto two year," I answered him. Then he asked me what I was askeered he was going to ask me, and I weren't quite sure how I would answer it when it come.

"How come you to leave Boxwood?" he said.

I tuck a sip a my coffee and glanced over at ole Sandy, but he just only kinda raised his eyebrows like as if to say that he couldn't be no help to me on that one. I was on my own. I thought it all over real quick in my head, and I told myself just then that the damn world surely wouldn't come to no end if I weren't to get that one job.

"I kilt a man," I said, "and Mr. O cut me a loose."

"You mind telling me the circumstances of the killing?" Holster said.

So I told him all about the Pigg family, and how come me to leave home the way I done, and how I come to meet up with ole Rod Chambers and got signed on at the Boxwood, and how near two year later them Piggses come around to the ranch looking to kill me. I told him the whole truth. I didn't leave nothing out.

"Kid," he said, "you got a name?"

"Parmlee," I said.

"First name?" he asked.

"Kid'll do," I said. I just really didn't want to tell no one my give name was Melvin. It hadn't never seemed like a real proper name to me, and especial it didn't seem so now that I was a real cowhand and maybe even a gunfighter.

"All right," he said. "Kid'll do. Sandy says you'll do any kind of work around a ranch. That so?"

"I done it all," I said, "and I'll do any of it again if it's called for. If I work for a man, I'll do what he pays me to do."

"That's good," Holster said, "but I got to be up front with you, Kid. There's more to it than just that."

"I'm a listening," I said.

"One of the main reasons I'm interested in you," he said, "is what Sandy told me 'bout what you done here yesterday morning."

"You mean whenever I shot that feller's ear off?" I said.

"That's right," he said. "I want cowhands, but I want cowhands who can also handle themselves in a fight if it comes to that. And I want hands who won't mind getting in the middle of a fight if it happens."

"I can take keer a myself," I said, "and I ain't never yet run from no fight."

"But what if it ain't your fight?" he said. "What if it's my fight?"

"I reckon if I was a working for you," I said, "then your fight would be my fight."

Well, we finished up our breakfasts, my second one, and we had us some more coffee and chatted some. Holster told me then about the Lazy Snakes, but he never really told me no more than just the same thing what ole Sandy had done said about them. It was pretty damn clear, though, that they was the ones that Holster was a thinking we might have to shoot it out with one a these days. But the main thing is that I had myself a job when everything was all did and said. Whenever we got up from that table, I run up to my room and grabbed my few things up in there. I seed Sherry and told her a hurry-up good-bye. I told her 'bout my new job, and I promised her that I'd be a coming in to see her ever' chance I got. She was still groggy and never said much. Then I hurried on. Sandy and Holster was waiting for me downstairs.

Once we was outside, they mounted up while I run down the street to the stable to get ole horse, and pretty damn soon the three of us was a riding along together out to the Three Forks Ranch. I felt pretty good, I can tell you. Hell, I had been run off from my own home a snot-nosed kid with hardly nothing to my name, and I had wound up working two years for a big ranch. I had learned the business pretty good and learned how to handle a gun. Then when I had lost my job, I picked up another one easy as falling off a horse. Yes sir, I felt good about my situation, but at the same time, 'cause a my two breakfasts, I felt 'bout as full as a tick dug in between the eyeballs of an ole redbone hound. I was sure hoping I'd be able to make the ride out to the ranch without having to embarrass myself in some way.

Well, luck was with me, 'cause I weren't the first one to have to speak out for a stop along the way. They was some bushes beside the trail, and all three of us went into them bushes to relieve ourself in one way or another. I felt some better after I had stood up and rehitched my britches. We all mounted up again and commenced riding the rest of the way to the ranch house.

I tell you what. The Three Forks was a fine spread. I had thought that the Boxwood was something else when I first seed it, but the Three Forks made the ole Boxwood look like a squatter's nest. I got to thinking there was a whole lot more in this ole world than I ever even dreamed about when I was a growing up in that little shack my ole paw had nested us in back yonder just outside a Sneed, Texas. For just a minute then I wondered about what Maw and Paw might be doing and how they was getting along, but pretty quick I put them on out of my mind. I sure didn't worry about them none.

Anyhow, the first a the ranch I seed was when we come to a fence what run farther than I could see in both directions, and we come up to a wide gate. A big arch was up over the gate. It was made out a wood, and it had letters burned in it what read "Three Forks Ranch." I tell you, it looked real elegant. We rid right under that big arch, and we still had us a long ride to go on down the lane what led on up to the main ranch house. It was a two-story house with a roofed-over porch wrapped all the way around it. I seed three or four chimbleys on the roof a that big house.

When we come up right close to the front porch, ole Holster just stopped his horse and clumb down off its back. He handed the reins over to ole Sandy. "Take care of the kid," he said, and he went right up on that porch and on into the big house. I give Sandy a quizzical look, and Sandy said, "It's his house. He's the boss. I told you that, didn't I?"

"You mean he owns the whole place?" I asked him.

"Yeah," Sandy said.

"Hell," I said, "I thought you meant he was the foreman or something."

"I'm the foreman," Sandy said.

"Well, I be damned," I said.

We rid on over to the corral then and put the horses away. Then Sandy tuck me on into the bunkhouse and interduced me around to the hands that was in there. He give me a bunk and a place to stash my belongings. It was already getting kind a late. The sun was down low, so he said that he'd get me started out proper first thing in the morning. I went on ahead and turned myself in for a good night's sleep. I sure hadn't had one the last two nights back in Ass Grove.

Well, I worked for them people for about a year, and all that time I was seeing Sherry pretty regular.

In fact, I was thinking that whenever I had saved me up enough money, I just might marry up with that little ole gal. I hadn't said nothing like that to her nor to nobody else, but I was sure thinking a lot about it. The other thing that was going on was that we was constantly sparring with them Lazy Snakes boys. Always sizing one another up, you know. Whenever a Three Forks guy and a Snakes guy would meet up with one another in town, there'd be words passed between them. Once there was even a fistfight, but there weren't no shots fired in all that year. I could see that it was a coming though. Sure as hell. Sooner or later. There was a big fight a coming. Maybe a full-out range war.

Well, my ole brain was surely agitated most all the time, what with me having a full-time cowboying job, and being constantly on the guard for a range war what might be springing up on us just anytime, and then too thinking about Sherry and when would be the right time to pop the marrying question on her, and wondering too about what married life with ole Sherry would be like whenever I was to get around to it. I sure didn't have no time to think about nothing else, I can tell you that for sure and certain.

I did manage to keep up my practice with my six-gun, though, and the boys had plenty a opportunities to watch me knock cans off a fenceposts and bounce rocks around and such. One time a rattlesnake skeered a cowboy's horse, and I whipped out my ole shooter and tuck that rattler's head clean off with just one shot. 'Course, they had all heared about the time I had shot the left ear off a old Cutter's head, and they had also heared that I had been forced to leave my previous job 'cause of a killing I had did. So I was knowed all around as a real genu-wine bad-ass gun-fighter, even though I still looked most like a snot-nosed kid, which I guess I really was, even though I could shoot a gun and weren't skeered a no one nor nothing.

It was kind a funny right at the first, 'cause some a the folks in town and some a the Lazy Snakes hands too thought for a spell there that ole Holster had done gone and hired hisself on the real, honest-to-God Billy the Kid. It was all 'cause a what ole Cutter had said to me just before I shot off his ear. Someone had heared him wrong and thought that he had really called me Billy the Kid, meaning that's who I really was. One day in Ass Grove, ole Marty Feldspar, the owner a the Lazy Snakes spread, seed Holster, and he accused him right then and to his face.

"I hear you hired yourself a real famous killer, Holster," he said.

"Who do you mean?" said Holster.

"Heard you hired on Billy the Kid," Feldspar said.

Just about then I stepped out a the store, just in time to hear what the old bastard said, and I said, "I guess you must be talking about me, Mr. Feldspar, but I really ain't no Billy the Kid."

"Who are you?" Feldspar said.

"They do call me Kid," I said, "but my name's Parmlee. Kid Parmlee."

"You the one shot Cutter's ear off?" he asked me.

"I done that," I said. "I didn't feel like killing no one that morning, even though he asked for it, and I would a been justified if I'd a done it."

So folks stopped thinking that I was really Billy the Kid, but then they was saying things like, "Ole Holster has got hisself a regular Billy the Kid a working for him." You know, they kept on a making me out to be just like Billy the Kid, and they kept on accusing poor ole Holster of hiring hisself bad-ass gunfighters and killers 'stead a cowboys. Why, hell's fire, I hadn't done nothing for Holster in a whole entire year but just only work cows. That's all. And I sure hadn't done no more shooting around the town neither, not since I de-eared ole Cutter. But folks do like to talk. If I hadn't knowed it before, I learned it in that first year I worked for the Three Forks Ranch.

Well, one evening the ole cookie cooked us up a great pot of beans, and I et a good share of them. I thought they was pretty good too, but he must a done something wrong along the way, 'cause after a while my guts got to rumbling something fierce. I kept finding ways to get myself off away from the boys so I could fart without it being noticed. But whenever it come time to go to bed, there weren't nothing I could do for it. I was keeping the boys awake with my farts, and I was fouling the air something fierce in the bunkhouse too. I couldn't hardly stand it my own self, but I guess the boys was skeered a my reputation as a regular Billy the Kid, so other than making a few grumbling remarks and groans and other painful noises, they just left me alone.

They left me alone till I was good and sound asleep, and even then I never knowed what they was doing nor who was a doing it till it was too late to fight back, but what they done was they throwed a sheet over me and roped me up in it real good, and then they carried my ass on outside. 'Course I woked up when they was a tying me, and I commenced to hollering and screaming and kicking and thrashing about and threatening to kill ever'one on the whole damn ranch, but it never made no difference. They hauled my farting ass on outside and dumped me on the ground kinda rough like and just left me lay there. Even then my farts never let up, and it was just awful inside that sheet. Hell, it was like being wrapped up in a fart sack all night long and tortured. I like to gagged myself to death, and I never got no good night's sleep neither.

Well, in the morning, someone cut me loose and run, so that whenever I fin'ly got myself out from under that goddamned tangle a sheet I couldn't see no one nowhere near. I never knowed who it was what had tied me up, and I never knowed neither who had fin'ly gone and cut me loose. I got up then, and I went and washed myself up a bit and changed my clothes, and I just couldn't hardly get enough of that good fresh air. I had done farted myself out though overnight, so I was okay in that respect, but I was god-awful embarrassed about the whole thing. In fact, you could say that I was downright humiliated. I couldn't hardly look no one in the face, and a course, I couldn't really just go on ahead and kill them all for what some few had did to me, although I did kind a feel like doing just that.

I was lucky it was my day off, so I just got all my stuff together and packed it all on my ole horse and headed on into town. I had been paid too, and so I didn't have no intention a ever going back to the ole Three Forks Ranch. I didn't tell no one though. I just rode on into town like me or any a the boys would do on his day off. Well, I fooled around some till I was pretty sure that ole Sherry would be up and ready to start her day, and then I went to look her up, but I found her with a big man with a hairy chest and a handlebar mustache. They wasn't doing nothing when I barged in her room, but they was both just laying there nekkid like as if they had just finished, and it surely did piss them off whenever I walked in there. Hell, I guess if I'd a been in his place, it would a pissed me off too, but I wasn't thinking of it that way. Besides, if they was all that concerned about it, they should a locked the damn door.

"Get out of here, you silly little shit," the hairy bastard said.

"I just want to talk to Sherry for a minute," I said, and I could actual feel my face a blushing some.

"Not now, Kid," Sherry said. "Go on downstairs. I'll come find you in a bit."

"Sherry," I said, "I want you to get dressed and pack up your things. I'm leaving these parts, and I want you to go with me."

"What?" she said, and she looked some amazed at what I had just said to her. I was concentrating on Sherry, so I hardly noticed when the big nekkid man reached for his revolver what was hanging on the corner post of the bed. I seed it, though just as he jerked it up and cocked it, and it was pointed full at me. I reacted quick then, and I pulled my own Colt, cocking it as I pulled it, and squeezing the trigger all at the same time, and the blast a my Colt filled the air a that little room and set my ears to ringing. Then ole Sherry started in to screaming. The big hairy bastard never made no sound 'cept only whenever his nekkid body thudded down onto the floor. His hairy chest was covered over with blood. He was still and dead. I put my Colt away.

"Calm down, Sherry," I said. "It's okay. It was self-defense for sure. He pulled down on me first. You

seed it. Listen to me now. Calm down, darlin'. I want
you to get yourself ready to ride. I got me some
money, and I'm moving on out of these parts."

Well, she quit screaming all of a sudden, and she
give me the hardest, meanest look I guess I ever got.
"Go with you?" she said, and it was like she was
spitting them words out at me. "Why the hell would
I want to go with you? You're a nothing. You're a
dime-a-dozen cowhand and gunfighter. And you just
quit your job. And you're just a baby on top of all
that. Get the hell out of here. Get out."

"Sherry," I said, not hardly believing what I was
hearing. Hell, I was in love with her, and I believed
that she just had to be in love with me.

"Get out. Get out," she screamed.

I turned and run out of there. I hadn't never heared
that kind a shrieking before. Well, for sure there
weren't nothing left to hold me in Ass Grove after
that, but about the time I got to the bottom of the
stairs, ole Sherry, wrapped up in just a sheet with one
titty a hanging out, was standing at the landing up
above, and she was screaming again.

"Stop him," she yelled. "Stop Kid Parmlee. He just
murdered Harley Hook. Harley was nekkid in my
room, and Kid Parmlee just walked in and shot him
down. Stop him. Come on up and see for yourself.
He's laying nekkid and bloody on the floor."

Well, I figgered that I should be a scooting on out
a there, but I tuck me a quick look around the room
first, and there didn't seem to be no one planning on
making no moves at me, so I slowed down and
backed my way on over to the door. Just as I was
about to go out, I seed Sandy just a setting there at a
table. I give him a look.

"You'd best hightail it, Kid," he said. "Hooks ain't even with the Snakes outfit. This ain't our fight. It's just only yours. And Hooks has got brothers and cousins and friends all around the place. Here."

He stood up and pulled a wad a bills out a his pocket and shoved them at me, and I tuck them.

"I was a leaving anyhow," I said to him. Then I went on outside and mounted up on ole horse and rid out of town real fast. I never looked back at ole Ass Grove neither.

Chapter Six

Well, for the third time now in my young life, here I was a running off from what had been serving me as home 'cause I'd gone and kilt a man, and I come to realize then that folks really was a looking at me like as if I was a hardened killer and a real bad-ass gunslinger. I never looked at it thataway myself though, 'cause, in the first place, I had just hit that first one, that ole Pigg, in the back a the head with a ax handle. He never even knowed it was coming. That weren't the way no bad-ass gunfighter kills a man. But then, I guess I had gone on from there and shot it out fair enough with them other two, and with the one whose left ear I had shot off, but I never done none a them killings out a meanness nor even to build me up a reputation nor even for money. Other than the bastard what had shot Farty, they was all a trying to kill me first, and I was just either faster or maybe luckier than they was, that's all.

So here I was, just only seventeen year old was all, and for the third time in my short life, I was headed out for I didn't have no idea where to. This time, though, I headed straight west, on deeper into New Mexico. I ain't real for certain why. And that land was sure flat and bone dry. I rid all day long,

and then I settled me down for the night with a hel-
lacious growling stomach. You see, I had lit out awful
fast after I'd shot that nekkid Hook up there in
Sherry's room. So I was just laying on my back on
that hard ground, and it a getting cold too, and I was
hungry, and I was thinking about my lost first love.
Now you might recall that I said I had never keered
about nothing but ole Farty, and now here I am talking about my lost love and all.

Well, I thought about how I had felt about her and
about how she had did me dirty in a crucial moment
a my young and tender life, and so I just up and told
myself, hell, she's just a damn bitch is all she is. She
ain't no better than my ole maw what slapped me up
beside the head whenever I got myself into trouble,
just only younger and better looking is all. And that
don't mean nothing. She ain't going to stay thataway.
So you see, I was able to shove her right clean out a
my mind.

Now, I ain't never been able to do that with ole
Farty. I never could. Why, I can't even think about
putting ole Farty out a my mind. I don't want to neither. I still think about Farty most ever' day, and
what's even more than that, I guarantee you this—
that if it had been ole Farty with me 'stead a that
damn Sherry whenever I shot ole Hook, well, by God,
ole Farty would a been right by my side a running
like hell out a Ass Grove. He'd a lit out with me, and
he'd a stayed with me. Me and him was pardners for
good and bad and forever, as long as we was both
alive. I sure did miss that ole dog. I cried some that
night too, thinking about all a them sad and pitiful
thoughts.

* * *

I rid on half a the next day, and by and by I begun to think that I had picked me the road straight to hell, but I fin'ly did come to some water, and me and ole horse, we drunk water till we might near bursted our guts. We was both trying like hell to fill up our bellies with water and trick them into thinking that we wasn't hungry. But it never worked. Not for me, and I'm pretty sure it didn't work no better for ole horse neither. I mounted up again, and we moved on though. Weren't nothing else to do.

But having made up my mind by that time that I was for real on the road to hell, I decided to turn north and head for Colorady instead. I figgered it had to be some better than hell, and I knowed there was mountains up there somewheres, and I had heared tell that some of them had got snow on their top all year long. With the hot sun a baking the ground all around me and cooking me and ole horse both, and me convinced that I was on my way straight to the bottomless pits a hell, them snow-topped mountains seemed mighty inviting. I didn't have no idea how far off they was nor how long it would take me to get to them. So I was just a riding along real slow and easy like and kind of daydreaming about building me a snowman and throwing snowballs at someone and sliding down a long hillside in the snow on my ass, and such as that, and then suddenly I seed me a little antelope up ahead and off to my right just a grazing away real unconcerned. He either hadn't seed me nor nosed me, or else I was moving along so slow and easy like that he didn't think I was nothing to worry about.

Well, I didn't have no rifle, so my heart commenced to thumping real hard with worry that I might miss my one only chance to keep myself alive in this

wicked world. I didn't make out to ole horse like
nothing had come up, but only just kept moving along
real easy, hoping that we'd get close enough for a
shot from my Colt before that critter tuck a mind to
make a break for it. We kept a moving, and he just
kept a grazing, and pretty soon, by God, I thought I
might could make me a shot, and so I whupped out
my ole Colt in a flash, the only way I knowed how
to use it, and I blasted that pretty little thing. I
dropped him dead with just one shot. I just couldn't
hardly believe my own good fortune, even though I
had some time back got to where it was usual just
one shot what I needed to get the job did. Ole horse,
he was a little startled at the sudden loud noise, but
he recovered hisself right quick like.

"I'm sorry 'bout that, ole horse," I said, "but I
didn't have time to give you no warning. That little
ole critter might a got away from me."

I give ole horse a pat on the neck and rid him on
over there and looked down on that antelope. It was
real still. I put my six-gun away, dismounted and
pulled out my knife. Then I commenced to cutting
that critter up. I felt a little guilty that I was fixing to
have me a real good meal, and I didn't have nothing
special for ole horse, but then I seed that he had
started in a grazing right there just where that antelope
had been a grazing, so I guessed that he'd be all right
after all, and then it come to me that the little critter
had tuck keer a both me and ole horse. Pretty soon I
had me a fire going, and I had me some choice pieces
of meat roasting over it. It sure did put off some fine
and tantalizing smells. Well, there wasn't no fooling
the belly this time. I et myself plumb full. I overdone
it somewhat. I tried like hell to eat that whole damn

antelope. 'Course I couldn't, but I sure did try.

Well, it weren't late yet, but I sure didn't feel like climbing back on ole horse what with my belly all that full, and I looked at ole horse, and he was just a grazing on them clumps a whatever it was that antelope had been eating on. I figgered I was living on the stuff too, 'cause that was what had made that little antelope fat, and I had done et a bunch a him. Anyhow, I reckoned that we'd just lay around fat and sassy for the rest a that day and all through the night. Hell, I didn't have no idea where it was we was headed for nohow, so I reckoned a little leisure time wouldn't hurt no one. I was also thinking that I might ought to really try to eat up all that meat before it was to spoil on me.

So I unsaddled ole horse, spread out my blankets and stretched myself out there on the ground. It felt pretty good, and I was staring up into the hot sky and thinking about dozing off when ole horse kinda snuffled. I knowed that snuffle. Something was a bothering him. I looked over at him, and he was standing stiff with his head high and his ears pricked up. He had seed or heared something that made him take note like that, and he thunk that I had oughta do the same. I set up and looked off in the same direction ole horse was a staring, and I had to kind a squinny up my eyes all right, but then I seed something moving a ways off over there. I couldn't hardly make out what it was at first, but I kept a watching. It come closer. Pretty soon I could make out it was a man walking alongside a burro. That's how come him to be moving so slow.

I decided that it was going to be a good while before he come near enough for me to worry about him, so I just told ole horse to relax and keep on eating, that it was all right, and then I stretched myself back out. Ever' now and then I'd roll my head over and take another gander to see how close he was a getting, whoever he was. When he fin'ly looked might near close enough to holler at, I set up. When he come even closer, I got up on my feet, and I kinda stood there with my arms crossed over my chest and my head cocked over to one side. He waved and yelled at me then.

"Howdy, you there in the camp," he said. "Do ye mind if I come in?"

"Come on in," I said.

"I seen your smoke from way off yonder," he said. "I see you got yerself antelope meat a cooking. Enough for two?"

"Help yourself," I said. "I've done et."

"I got some coffee," he said.

That perked me right on up. "You do?" I said. "Well, let's boil up some of it. I was just laying here wishing I had me some coffee, 'stead a just water to wash all that antelope down with."

"By gum, we'll get 'er going," he said. And damned if he didn't set right to work. I just let him take on over, and I watched him. He was a short feller, not hardly no taller than me, and back then I was just only about five foot six. And he weren't much heavier than me neither, I bet you. I'd say he weighed maybe a hunnerd and twenty-five pound was all. But he was at least twice as old as me. Hell, more than that. Maybe three, maybe four times. His face was all wrinkly, and his hair and beard was mostly gray. His clothes was all rumpled up too and dusty and patched, and his boots was wore out some. He had on an ole slouch hat that looked to me like as if he'd wore it constant since back when he was my age.

"What do they call ye, young feller?" he said.

"They call me Kid Parmlee," I said, and I waited to see if the name meant anything to him, but I reckon he'd been in the mountains for so many years that he hadn't heard no news since ole Tom Jefferson was President. "What's your name?" I asked him.

"Zebulon Pike," he said. "You heard of me?"

"Well," I said, "I don't guess I have."

"Why, hell, boy," he said, "they named a mountain after me."

"A whole mountain?" I said.

"Well, at least the top of it," he said. "It's over by old Cripple Creek, and they call it Pike's Peak."

"Pike's Peak," I said with some wonderment.

"Yep," he said.

"Is there usual snow on it?" I asked him.

"Most all the time," he said.

"I'd sure admire to go see it," I said.

"Well, it just sets there," he said. "Anytime you get there, it'll be waiting."

He was eating some of my antelope meat by that time, and from the looks of it, he was really enjoying it. And the brew he had set on was starting to smell like coffee too. It sure flung a craving on me. In just a little while then, he had gone and dug two tin cups from out of the pack on the back of his ole burro, and then we each had us a cup a hot steaming coffee. By then the desert was starting in to cool off for the evening, and that coffee sure did taste real good.

"Mr. Pike," I said, but he interrupted me.

"Call me Zeb," he said. "Just ole Zeb."

"Zeb," I said, "which way are you a headed?"

"Ah," he said, "any way the wind blows. Where my nose sniffles gold, that's where I head. I mean to make a big strike and build me a mansion. Mebbe I'll build me a opry house like some of them others has done and hire in some flimsy-dressed female singers. Maybe even some of them Shakespeare actors, you know."

"No," I said. "I don't know about them things."

"Well, it don't matter none," he said. "But I bet you know about getting rich."

"I worked on a ranch once," I said, "where the owner had hisself a real big house—two stories tall it was, and it had a porch with a roof over it what went all the way around on all four walls. And his front gate had a big arching thing over it what you had to ride underneath it to get on into his property, and it had the name of his ranch writ right up there on it for ever'one to see it when they come in or even just passed by."

"Ah, well," he said, "to folks like me and you, that seems rich all right, but it ain't near like the kinda rich I'm talking about. I'm talking about getting rich enough to buy that there big ranch you worked on with just my pocket change. I'm talking about traveling around the whole damn world first class. Maybe buying my own railroad and riding in a private car. Drinking champagne all day long. Having three or four pretty little blondes hanging on my arms ever'where I go. Buying me a whole damn town and running it the way I want it to be run. Getting drunk as I want to get and never getting throwed in jail. How's that kind a rich sound to you?"

"I don't know," I said. "I ain't never thought about nothing like that. Hell, all I want is just a good job where I can have me some money in my pockets at least most of the time. A place to sleep and three good meals a day. That's all I want."

I reached over and poured myself another cup of ole Zeb's hot coffee. He was still gnawing on my fresh meat.

"You out a work then, are you?" he said.

"Yeah," I said, "for right now. But I've worked on two big ranches, and I can get me another job, all right, just anytime I take a mind to."

"Where you headed for, Kid?" he asked me.

"I don't know," I said. "I was just kind a headed north. I might like to go see that there mountain a yours. That Pike's Peak. Is there any big ranches close by?"

"Ah, you might find one or two thereabouts," he said. "This is good meat, boy. I don't see no rifle gun. You take this down with just that six-gun you're packing?"

"I sure did," I said.

"You must be pretty good with that thing," he said.

Well, I figgered he was working his way around to calling me some kind a gunfighter, and I was more than just a little bit uneasy about that, so I just said, "I get along."

"I bet you do," he said. "I bet you do. Hunting with a six-gun. Ain't many can handle that. Say, do you mind if I camp here with you tonight? You'd have yourself some coffee in the morning. Coffee's real good first thing in the morning. I got the makings for biscuits too, and I can make them. Good'uns. We'd still have plenty of your meat."

I shrugged, and then I said, "I don't mind."

Actual I was more than glad to have the old man's

company. Much as I had did it, I didn't like being out
on the trail all by my lonesome. So I was real glad a
his company, for one thing, but for another thing, I
sure did like his coffee, and biscuit for breakfast
sounded pretty good to me too.

Well, old Zeb was up early the next morning, way
before me, and whenever I come awake, he already
had them biscuit going and the coffee too. It sure did
smell good, and I was tickled to death that I had let
him stay with me in my camp. Whenever I rubbed
my eyes and set up, he looked over at me and grinned,
and I seed then that he had a few missing teeth in his
head.

"I was a wondering if you was still alive," he said.
"Coffee's ready. Help yourself."

"Thanks," I said, and I poured me some. It sure
was good having it first thing in the morning like that.
Anyhow, we et antelope meat and biscuit and drunk
coffee till we was good and full, and then we set and
jawed a bit. All that time ole horse and ole Zeb's
burro was gnawing at whatever it was they was a
gnawing at. I reckon they got good and fed too. And
ole Zeb made sure they each had a good drink a water
too. Fin'ly I got up and started in to pack up my stuff.

"You fixing to head out?" Zeb said.

"Can't stay here forever," I said.

"You say where you was headed?" he asked me.

"Don't rightly know," I said. "I'm just kind a moving north, I guess."

"You could string along with me," he said. "Turn
west. We'll head out for them Rockies. You wanting
to see snow? You'll see snow on them for sure. We
might even work our way on up to ole Pike's Peak

thataway. Hell, you don't need no job on no ranch. I lived out in them mountains for months at a time. I got a few supplies here. We'll pick up some more along the way. Anything else we need, we can find it out there. And you can get us fresh meat whenever we need it with that six-gun a yours. What do you say?"

"What'll we be doing?" I asked him.

"Hunting for gold a course," he said. "Sniffing out the yella. Ain't nothing else in this life worth the doing."

"Hunting for gold," I said, just kinda muttering to myself. "I don't know nothing about that."

"You don't need to know," Zeb said. "I know ever'thing that's to be knowed about it. I been at it longer than anyone else alive. I'm the world's greatest expert at hunting and finding gold. I'll teach you ever'thing you need to know. Well?"

"I don't know," I said.

"We strike it rich, we'll split ever'thing halfway down the middle. Fifty-fifty," he said. "We'll be pardners. What do you say? Hell, you ain't got nothing else to do. Have ye? You ain't got no coffee neither."

Well, I set back down on my saddle. I hadn't throwed it up on ole horse yet, and I reached in my pocket for the makings and rolled myself a smoke. Ole Zeb, he got all excited. "You never told me you had none of that," he said. I handed it over to him, and he rolled one for hisself. We each lit up and tuck a puff or two. I was thinking real hard. Fin'ly I said, "Zeb, I got to tell you something."

"What's that?" he said.

"No one ever asked me to be his pardner before," I said. "No one. I got to tell you something. You might not want me for a pardner. I got to tell you that I done a few killings. The first one I done, I done it because some ole bastard shot my dog. I was just only fourteen year old back then. I got real mad. I sort a seed red whenever he kilt my dog, and I hit him in the back a the head with a ax handle. Kilt him dead."

"Did you do it a purpose?" Zeb asked me. "I mean, did you kill him a purpose?"

"I never had time to think that far," I said. "I was just mad as hell 'cause of what he done, and I hit him with the first thing I could get hold of. But when I knowed for sure he was dead, I weren't sorry for it. I ain't going to lie to you 'bout that."

"Well, hell," he said, "any man hurt my Bernice Burro there, I'd kill him for it too. I'd do it a purpose. A man what would hurt a dumb animal like that, he ain't worth a damn. You said you done some killings. What about the next one?"

"It were two years later," I said. "A kin a his come looking to kill me 'cause a what I done, and I shot him first. He was drawing down on me though."

"That's all right then," he said.

"I lost my job over it though," I said.

Then I told him about shooting ole Hook while he was nekkid, but even though he was nekkid, he had got hold a his revolver and had it cocked and aimed right at me, and I added that I had lost me another job over that one. When I was all done with all my confessing, ole Zeb, he tuck a deep draw on his ci-gareet and then let the smoke out real slow. He looked like he was cogitating real hard.

"Kid, it sounds to me like you never had no choice in none of them killings," he said. "You never done

no deliberate murders. Is that all it was you was wanting to tell me about?"

"There's more," I said.

"I'm a listening," he said.

"I shot off a man's left ear one time," I told him.

Chapter Seven

Me and ole horse and Zeb and his Bernice Burro headed west, and we moved on into some desolate country, I can tell you. But I had sure as hell picked me the best pardner for it, 'cause I'm damned if ole Zeb didn't know where ever' water hole was located at along the way. We et jackrabbit and rattlesnake and now and then another antelope as we made our way towards them mountains, and ever' day I longed more and more to see that snow up there, but I begun to wonder if it was all just a dream and ole Zeb was just a crazy lying old coot. Then fin'ly one day we seed them.

It was like as if a great jaggedy wall was stretched out across the whole entire world out there in the distance in front of us, and they was kinda purply except way up on top, sure enough, they was white. I seed that snow. I wanted to run ahead and climb up on there, but Zeb, he told me that they was still some days off the pace we was a moving at. And he told me that we sure as hell wouldn't climb up on there in no hurry neither. I had to have me some patience. It sure was hard to be patient though, for I had never in my whole life seed a sight such as that. It like to tuck my breath away. I almost believed in God just then, and I figgered that maybe he lived up there in that snow.

We kept on and kept on, and after a couple a more days a slow traveling, I begun to wonder if we'd ever get there. I thought that maybe it was all some kinda great big trick on ordinary folks. You know, like you can see it, but you can't have it. Something like that. But by God, we eventual got there. We got to them mountains. But there was a little town there kinda down at the base of the mountains. Ole Zeb told me that it was a mining town. Most ever'one there was a looking for gold or else they was making their living off the ones that was looking. He didn't keer too much for them last kind, but he opined as how he guessed they was sort a necessary. After all, he said, we had to get our coffee and tobaccy and that sort of stuff from somewhere.

I never seed nothing like it before. There was some buildings, a course, but there was also a whole mess a great big canvas tents, tents the size a buildings. There was smoke coming out of all the chimbleys. But the thing that struck me the most was how many people and dogs and horses and mules and burros was crowding the street, which was nothing but a long mud hole. Why, it was all you could do to keep from running over someone or to keep your own self from getting runned over and to keep from getting stuck in the mud. I bet my eyeballs was opened as wide as a couple of cow pies, well, at least as if they was just dropped by yearling calfs.

Well, the first thing we done in that town was we looked up the first saloon we could find, and we hitched our critters up outside and went on in. It sure was crowded in there, but we managed to belly on up

to the bar and order us some good whiskey. I paid
for it, and me and ole Zeb commenced to putting it
away. It was just a little bit after that when a couple
a gals come a rubbing on us, and the one that was
petting on me put me in the mood right away, I can
tell you. I never thought that ole Zeb would a had it
in him no more, but he surprised me, so we both went
out the back door and into a couple a little shacks
with them two gals, and we had us a hell of a good
time. At least I did, and judging from the possum grin
on ole Zeb's face whenever he come outa that shack,
I'm pretty sure for certain that he did too.

Anyhow, I paid both gals, 'cause ole Zeb, he didn't
have no cash, and I did. Well, I rolled me a smoke,
and I handed ole Zeb the makings, and then I struck
a match on the ass of my britches the way I'd seed
ole Sandy do it, you know, and me and Zeb both lit
our cigareets off of it. We strutted back through the
rear door a that saloon like two old bulls what had
just made some new calfs on a couple of heifers, and
we went back to the bar and had us some more whiskey.

"What'll we do now, Zeb?" I asked him. "Get us
a room for the night?"

"Hell, no," he said. "Not in a place like this here.
We'd wake up in the morning with our throats cut
and all your money gone for good and ever. What
we'll do, see, is we'll just have us all the whiskey we
want, which is likely just one more drink after this
here, and then we'll buy us up some more coffee and
beans and tobaccy and such and shuck this town."

I didn't argue with him none, 'cause I reckoned as
how I had me a lot to learn yet about the ways a the
world, and ole Zeb, he'd been around some in all his

years. We had us one more whiskey each, and then we bought us a bottle to take along with us. We found a store just down the street, after dodging all kinds a rifraff and dogs and such, and we stocked up on all the stuff we might need once we got our ass out away from civilization, if you could call it that. Then fin'ly we headed on outa town and up into the mountains. I was sure anxious to get up to all that snow up there.

Ole Zeb knowed all them mountain trails, but I tell you what—it was steep going, and it was slow, 'cause, a course, Zeb was walking and leading Bernice Burro, and so I wouldn't get ahead of him, 'cause I sure didn't have no idea where we was going, well, I just naturally had to walk along and lead ole horse. Ever since I had run away from home on ole Swayback, I had rid horses most ever'where I went, and only since I pardnered up with Zeb had I been walking again. But we had walked enough already that I begun to get used to it again. But not walking near straight up like heading up for that snow. Oh, my legs was a hurting me.

I did notice, though, that the air was getting kinda thin and crisp and cold, so I figgered that we really was sure enough going to find that snow. I was thinking that the first thing I'd do was I would get me a handful of it and eat it. After that I thought that I'd prob'ly roll around in it some. I was sure getting anxious, but we still hadn't come to it when Zeb said that we had oughta stop for the night. We had come to a place where there was a kinda wide and sort a flat spot there beside the trail.

"Ain't no other good camping site for a ways," he said, "and we don't want to be climbing this trail after dark. Folks have fell off the side of this here trail and never been seed again in this world."

I tuck his word for it, and we made us a camp. We had a nice little fire, and we cooked up some beans and brewed some coffee. We et hardtack for bread and chewed on jerky for meat. I was just settling down for the night a sipping myself another cup a hot coffee, when ole Zeb kinda leaned across the fire and near whispered to me.

"Don't look around, Kid," he said, "but I think we got uninvited company a coming."

Well, I kinda stiffened up at them words, but I tried to stay cool. "Who?" I said.

"I ain't for sure," he said. "My guess is someone follered us outa that mining town after they seed us spending your cash around."

I stammered a bit. "Well, what'll we do?" I said.

"Just kinda casual like," he said, "you get up and get yourself over against them rocks in that shadder. You see?"

"Yeah," I said, and my voice sounded nervous and quaky. I could tell. "Now?"

"Now's as good a time as any," Zeb said, so I tuck me another sip of coffee, then put the cup down by the fire. I stood up and hitched my britches, casual like, the way he'd said, and I strolled away from the fire. I got in that dark shadder against the rock, and I just leaned back there against the cold rock wall and tried to be ready for most anything that might come up. Ole Zeb, he built the fire up some, more than what we needed, and then he moved away from it, and I lost sight a him in the dark. By and by, he come back, and he tossed something into the fire, more twigs, I guessed. Then he wandered off again.

I was beginning to think he was crazy when I heared the noise of a couple a horses a riding up the trail coming toward us. It was kinda late for anybody to be riding up that mountain trail, like ole Zeb had tole me earlier. I got nervous then, and I could feel my ole heart a pounding in my chest. Pretty soon two riders come up to the fire and stopped. They looked around some. Then one of them yelled out.

"Hey," he said, "you. We're a couple of travelers a looking for coffee and grub. You got any? Are we welcome here in your camp?"

I didn't say nothing, and neither did ole Zeb. I wondered for a bit if he had fell off the side of the trail.

"Say," the visitor called out, "anybody home at the camp? We can smell your coffee."

"Clinch," said the other one, keeping his voice kinda low, "they're here all right. Unless they left a foot." He pointed at Bernice Burro and ole horse. "They're just hiding out on us is all."

"Come on out," said Clinch. "We're just looking for a little hospitality is all. Some hot coffee on a cold night."

"What you doing riding this mountain trail after dark?" Zeb said, and I couldn't tell where his voice was a coming from. Clinch and his buddy couldn't neither. They looked all around real surprised like.

"We're just traveling," Clinch said.

"Where to?" Zeb asked. "Ain't nothing up there. You looking for gold?"

"Well—well, sure," Clinch said. "Ain't ever one?"

"You ain't outfitted to do no prospecting," Zeb said. "I think you're just a prospecting for someone to rob. Ain't you? That's what I think."

"Now, wait a minute there, old timer," Clinch said. "You got us all wrong. Why don't you show yourself? Come on out and let's set a spell and have us some coffee together. Get acquainted."

"I seed you in town," Zeb said. "You seed us too, didn't you? You seed my pardner spend some cash money. You figger we still got some, and you're aiming to kill us and ride out a here with it in your pockets. Well now, I recommend real strong that you two turn around and get your ass back down that trail, if you can do it without falling off the edge in this dark. Get going now. To answer your question, you ain't welcome here."

"Now wait a minute there, old man," said Clinch.

"You can't run us off a this mountain," Clinch's buddy said.

"I reckon my pardner kin," Zeb said. "You likely heard about him. They call him the Kid. Billy the Kid."

"Billy the Kid?" said Clinch. "I ain't heard nothing about him being in these parts."

"Well, you don't hear ever'thing, now do you?" Zeb said.

Now I was getting tired of all this talk, and I had been standing there in the shadder long enough to calm down some and to get a look at who it was I might have to deal with. They didn't look none too dangerous to me, not after the men I had already kilt and that ear I had shot off. I decided it was time for me to talk up.

"I don't believe that you're pardnering with no Billy the Kid," Clinch said.

I stepped out of the shadder.

"Here I am," I said.

Clinch and that other one kinda jumped a setting there in their saddles. They looked around at me. From where they was on the other side a the fire from me, they most likely never got a real good look. They was kinda silhouetty to me too, but at least I had been standing there looking at them for a spell, and I was used to it. I seed their outlines real good, and I figgered that was all I needed to see.

"You Billy the Kid?" Clinch asked me.

"Find out, chicken shit," I said.

Both of them would-be road agents went for their guns at the same time, but I whupped mine out faster. I tuck Clinch with a shot in the head, and with my second shot, I hit his buddy right smack in the heart. They both tumbled outa their saddles and fell hard on the cold mountain trail just on the other side a the fire from where I was standing at. Their horses nickered and stomped around a bit, but then they settled down. Ole Zeb come a running out of the shadders a giggling like a crazy ole fart, which he sorta was.

"You tuck 'em both," he said. "You tuck 'em both. Hot ziggity. Hot damn."

He danced a kinda little jig all around them two bodies for a spell, a carrying on like that. "Hot ziggity damn. Hi ho." And then he'd give a little silly giggle. "Heh, heh, heh." Kinda like that. Fin'ly he stopped dancing and talking silly and giggling, and he went over and dropped down on his knees beside ole Clinch. He went all through Clinch's pockets a taking out ever'thing of any kinda value whatsoever. He tuck a pocket knife and a few coins. He tuck the gun and gun belt. When he seed there was nothing more to take, he dragged ole Clinch over to the far edge of

the trail and just dumped him right off the side. I
never even heard him hit bottom.

Then ole Zeb commenced to doing the same thing
with the other one. When he had stole ever'thing they
had and dumped them both off the side, he went on
over to their horses and pulled the blanket rolls and
the saddles off a them. Then he put the two horses
over with our own critters.

"What're we going to do with them horses?" I
asked him.

"Take them along," he said. "Take them along."

"What if someone finds them two dead men," I
said, "and then finds us with their horses?"

"Hah," he said. "Ain't no one what ever fell off
that there trail ever been found. Like as not they fell
all the way down to hell. Or China."

He was unrolling the blanket rolls and checking to
see if there was anything in there he wanted. I went
on back over to the fire and set down again. I picked
up my coffee cup, but the coffee had got cold. I
pitched it out and poured me another cup. Whenever
Clinch and that other feller had rode into our camp,
I had been about ready to go to sleep, but after killing
them and watching ole Zeb go through them antics, I
was wide awake again. Fin'ly Zeb quit poking around
in stuff and come back to set by the fire with me
again. He was still a cackling like an old hen though.

"Zeb," I said. "Don't do that no more. Will you?"

"What?" he said. "Hell, boy, if you hadn't a did
what you did, they'd a killed us all for sure."

"Not that," I said. "I didn't mean that."

"What then?" he asked me.

"Don't go around telling folks that I'm Billy the
Kid," I said.

"What's wrong?" he said.

"I ain't no cold-blooded killer," I said, "and I just don't want it going around that I'm Billy the Kid, 'cause I ain't. That's all."

Ole Zeb give his silly giggle, and then he said, "Kid, what I said just a while ago to them two road agents sure as hell ain't going no farther, is it? Not unless they spread the rumor around hell. Or China. Wherever they might a landed at."

"Well," I said, kinda pouting, "just don't do it no more. That's all."

"All right, Kid," Zeb said. "I won't never call you that no more. But damn me if you didn't take them two slick. Slicker'n owl shit it was. It was just pretty to watch. Hell, it was downright bee-ootiful. Pow. Pow. Two shots. Just like that. Pow. Pow. Two of them down and dead. You're good, Kid. You're real good. Do I know how to pick me a pardner or what?"

"Is that how come you tuck me on?" I said. "Just so I could do your fighting and killing for you?"

"No," he said. "Hell no. I like you, Kid. Hell, you fed me antelope. That's how come me to take you on. But you being able to shoot like that, why, hell, it's just icing on the cake, now, ain't it? It's a little something extry in a pardner. Ain't nothing wrong with being happy about it, now is there? Listen here, we got us twelve dollars and thirty-seven cents off them two, and we got two extry horses and saddles. We got two more six-guns with belts and holsters. We got us a Winchester and a Henry rifle, four blankets, and—"

"I didn't kill them to rob them," I said.

"I know you didn't Kid," he said, "but listen to me now and listen good. You got to stop being so stiff-necked about this sort a thing. Listen. Two men rid in here to our camp after dark. They come to kill us and rob us. You kilt them first. Ain't nothing wrong with that, is there? Now, once they're dead, why waste the stuff they has on them? Why not take it and make use of it? Hell, if we was to just dump it over the side with them that'd be wasteful. Now wouldn't it?"

Well, I couldn't come up with no argument for all that, so I reckoned that he was right after all. I hadn't never been no good at philosophising myself, and when he put it all like that, it did kinda make me feel better about the whole thing. You see, I hadn't really toughened up as much as you might think. I could kill a man all right, but I still figgered I ought to have myself a real good reason for it. And after ole Zeb had finished in telling me all that, well, I reckoned I was still okay. I'd had me a good reason for the killing a them two after all, and ole Zeb, he'd had hisself a good reason for going through their pockets and all the way he done. Well, I finished off my coffee, and I rolled out my blankets, but I really weren't terrible sleepy just yet. Not after all that excitement I had gone through for the evening.

"Hey, Zeb," I said.

"What is it, Kid?" he said.

"How about we have us a drink a whiskey before we turn in?" I said.

"By God, Kid," he said, "that's a hell of a good idea. I knowed all along that I liked you for some reason. Yes sir. Let's just have us that little drinkee."

Well, we popped that cork and poured us each a snort. After I had drunk about half a mine, I begun to feel a little drowsy.

"Zeb," I said.

"Yeah?" he said.

"When we gonna reach that snow up there?" I asked him.

"I'd say two more days a climbing," he said. "We'll get to it then."

I tuck myself another drink. My belly was warm, and my head was beginning to feel some light.

"Zeb?" I said.

"What?" he said.

"Where's Pike's Peak?" I said. "I'd kinda like to see that Pike's Peak."

"It's some north of us," he said. "Maybe we'll work our way up to it. Yeah. We'll work our way on up there, and I'll show it to you. It's got a regular sign down at the bottom. Says Pike's Peak on it, it does. We'll climb up to the top of it. I know the best way. Hell, I was the first man to ever go up there. First white man leastways. That's how come it to be named after me. We'll climb right on up to the top."

"Yeah," I said. "That'll be nice. I'd like to do that. Zeb?"

"Uh-huh," he said. "Well, we'll do her."

"Are we going to strike it rich, Zeb?" I asked him.

"Kid," he said, "we're going to be so rich we'll have to open us our own banks. One for me and one for you. Ain't no way we could carry all that richness around with us. And there ain't no way one bank could handle it. 'Course, we'll carry us around maybe a million each for pocket spending money, but we'll leave the rest of it in our banks for safekeeping. We'll hire us a small army a gunfighters, most nearly as good as you, just to guard our banks. We'll go plumb all the way to New York City just to buy our clothes.

We'll even buy us our own railroad car and ride in it from New York to San Francisco. We'll have cooks and servants and pretty gals all around us. We'll—"

I don't know how much more he said about what we'd do whenever we got rich, 'cause right about then, I just kinda drifted off to sleep. Whenever I woke up the next morning, I was under two blankets. I guess ole Zeb had put an extry one over me, 'cause it got kinda cold that night way up there on that ole mountain.

Chapter Eight

Fin'ly we got plumb up to where that cold, white snow was at, real high up that mountainside, and I guess I musta acted like about five times a damn fool or at least a dumb kid. I got down off ole horse, and I just run right into that stuff, but it was slick, and I weren't ready for that, and my ole feet just come a flying right out from under me, and I landed smack down on my ass. Ole Zeb, he laughed like hell, a rocking back and forth in his saddle. I stood on back up again, laughing myself, and then I slipped and fell down again, and he laughed all the harder and me too. Fin'ly he quit though and caught his breath.

"Now, listen here, Kid," he said. "You watch out just where you go to sliding down like that, 'cause you could real easy slide your young ass right on down off the side a this here mountain. I sure don't want to lose you thataway."

I recalled then about them two corpuses ole Zeb had tossed over the side, and that was even down lower than where we was at, and I hadn't never heared them hit bottom. I looked around me then real keerful like to make for sure that I weren't no place where that could happen to me, and then I tuck and commenced to just rolling over and over in that cold white stuff. It ain't that I hadn't never seed no snow before. I'd saw it, a course, several times, but this here was smack in the middle a hot summer, and it was more snow than I had ever saw at once even in the wintertime. Well, I stuck my face down in it, and I made snowballs, and I even rolled up some great big snowballs and made me a snowman up there. Zeb, he got to shaking his head like as if he didn't quite know what to make out of me.

"I hope no one comes along," he said. "I don't rightly know how I'd explain you to them. Likely they'd want to take you down below to one of them nuthouses over in Denver or some such place and lock you up in it for the rest a your natural life."

Eventual, I got tuckered out, and then I just set there till I started in to feel my britches butt getting cold and soggy. I decided I better get up and stop playing like some little kid, but to tell the truth, I reckon I wasn't much more than that really. I was just a snot-nosed kid what had kilt me some men and shot a feller's ear off, and that's how come some of them went to trying to make me out to be some kinda Billy the Kid, but like you already know, I always done my best to try to put a stop to that kinda foolish talk ever' chance I got.

Then Zeb went and said that we had ought to go on back down the mountain a little bit. He had only just brought me up that far 'cause he knowed I wanted to see that snow so bad, but it weren't no place to be camping for the night, he said. So we turned around and rode back on down a ways, and then we made us a little camp, and right then's when I realized just how much of a fool I was, 'cause I was starting in to chill more than just a bit from my cold and wet clothes, but pretty soon we had us a camp and a fire, and while ole Zeb commenced to fixing up our meal, I sidled myself on up to that fire and changed my clothes—ever' stitch. Well, I felt all right again after that, with dry clothes on and that fire a warming me, and I was just as glad that I had gone on ahead and had myself a fine romp in that there pretty white snow.

We et that evening and sipped a little whiskey, and then we spent the night at that camp, and in the morning we packed up and mosied on back down lower on the edge of the mountain till we come to a place where the trail almost become a road, and it meandered alongside a real pretty, fast-running, cold-water mountain stream. I seen that ole Zeb was a moving slow and squinting his eyes and craning his neck, watching that stream real close like. I wondered what the hell he was up to, but I never asked him no questions. Then he spotted a gravel bar out in the water, and he stopped.

"Right here we'll make us some pocket money," he said.

"How?" I said.

"Set up camp," he said, not answering my damnfool question. "I got work to do."

I set up the camp while ole Zeb went out to the bar with a shallow pan. I tried to watch him while I was a working, but I tripped over a rock and fell on my face, so I decided I'd best mind my own business and let Zeb mind his. When I fin'ly had the camp all set up and the fire built and nothing else to do, I went on out there where he was at. He was squatted down on his haunches a swirling water and sand around in that little pan of his. I squatted down next to him and looked at the swirling water in his pan for a bit. Then, "What the hell are you doing?" I asked him.

"Ain't you never panned for gold?" he said.

"No," I admitted, feeling somewhat ignorant. "I ain't. I done told you I don't know nothing about this gold-hunting business, didn't I?"

"Never even seed it done?" he asked me.

"I guess not," I said. "If that's what you're a doing, I ain't never seed it before this."

"Well, looky here at this," he said, and he held that pan over for me to look in it, and I seed that fine gold dust just a shining down there on the bottom of the pan.

"Is that there real gold?" I said, and I think that my eyeballs was kinda popping out at the sight of it. "Real gold?"

"It ain't no fool's gold," he said. "Do I know gold when I see it? Why, hell, I don't need to see it. I can smell it. It's real, all right. It's the most real thing in this whole world. There ain't nothing on God's earth more real than gold."

He went on then and explained to me how the gold dust and little bitty nuggets gets washed down the stream from somewheres up on the mountain, and then they get caught up on sand and gravel bars like the one we was a squatting on. That's how come him to stop us there in the first place. If you get a panful a that sand and gravel and water and swish it around the way he was doing, he told me, the sand washes out and the gold, what's heavier, settles down in the bottom a the pan.

So I went and got me a pan, and I joined him there. I wanted to get me some a that gold, just the way he had did it. I watched him real close and done my best to do it just like he was a doing it, and it weren't long till I got the hang of it all right. Well, we panned up a fair amount that first day. Then we put it away in little sacks what ole Zeb had brung along with him for just such a purpose, and we stashed it all under a big rock. We et us a good meal that evening, drank us a little whiskey to celebrate our good fortune, then slept the night there in our little camp. After breakfast the next morning, we went right back to panning. After a few days of that and several full bags of gold dust, Zeb said that was enough.

"Pocket change," he said. "That's all you'll ever get that way."

He told me that he reckoned that we had us a couple thousand dollars in them bags. That sounded awful good to me, and I wondered why we didn't just stick around and get us a few more thousand. It seemed like easy enough work for that much money, but ole Zeb, he weren't interested. Now that some time has gone by since them days, and I look back on it, I think that he just plain got bored with it. I believe that for him, the finding of it was the most important thing, or leastwise, the most fun. And all that talk about getting rich, why, hell, I think that if ole Zeb had owned the whole entire wide world, he would still a gone wandering off into the mountains with his ole Bernice Burro a hunting for gold.

Anyhow, he said that the dust we had panned was just only for pocket change, but what we were really after was a great big vein, a mother lode, he called it, something where we would have to get out the picks and hack great huge chunks a gold right out a the side a the mountain. And we wouldn't be able to pack it off in little bags like what we was a doing with this dust, he said. The sacks a gold from out a the mother lode would be like big old tater sacks, and a burro like Bernice wouldn't be able to haul but one or two of them at a time.

"We got two extry horses," I said.

"They ain't no good for nothing but 'cept to ride on maybe," he said. "No sir, whenever the time comes, we'll go down off a this mountain and buy us up a whole damn string a burros. Then when we ride down with all our gold, it'll be just like a caravan. A caravan a gold. It'll look like the King of Egypt is a coming down off a the mountain. Then maybe we'll take and buy Denver. I ain't quite sure if I really want it though. Too many folks in it."

"I don't rightly know what I'd do with it," I said, "if I had it."

Well, for the next several weeks, I ain't really sure for how long, me and old Zeb just rid them mountain trails. We done placer mining and crevicing. We panned out or dug out a little color most ever'where we went, 'cause ole Zeb, he really knowed his line of work. He just knowed if there was gold somewhere, so we never even went to work where there weren't none. I begun to believe that he really did smell it. But it was all just only pocket change what we found, as he said. We never did come across that bonanza that he was a looking for, that mother lode.

All that time, we lived mostly on beans and flapjacks and sourdough bread. That old man was a hell of a good cook too. Now and then we'd come across something that I could shoot so we'd have us some meat to eat. I'll never forget the first time I seed one a them bighorn sheep. I hadn't never seed nothing like that before, but Zeb said to shoot it, and I did, and be damned if it didn't taste pretty good all cooked up. It kept us in meat for a few days.

Then we was fin'ly getting low on coffee and beans and flour and such, and ole Zeb said it was time for us to go down amongst them again, much as he hated to, so we went on down, and where we come out was at another one a them mining towns, but only this one was bigger and more substantial than the last one I had saw. It was full a more people and horses and burros and dogs too. The first thing when we got there was we cashed in our gold, and sure enough, we had us a few thousand dollars for all our work. Ole Zeb's pocket change made me feel pretty rich.

Then we hunted us up a good place to eat. That was prob'ly the fanciest and finest meal I had ever et in my life, I can tell you. Ole Zeb had to tell them what to fix for me, 'cause I never even knowed what all them names meant. When we'd had our fill a that fine food, we walked on down the street to a saloon and gambling place. We had us a few drinks, and ole Zeb went to playing cards. I didn't want to lose my money like that, so I stayed out of it. Besides, I had never played cards in my whole life, and I didn't want to look ignernt, so I was just standing at the bar with a glass of rye whiskey when a pretty little redhead come up beside me.

"Buy me a drink?" she said. I give her a quick look, and she weren't bad.

"I don't mind," I said, and I held up my hand to get the barkeep's attention. While I was waiting for him to get around to me in that busy place, I tuck me a good look at the little gal. She was a cute one all right, but she did look to me as how she had been rode hard and put away wet, and not just one time neither. That was all right by me though, me what had kilt men and shot off a ear and been fired from two cowboying jobs.

"What's your name?" she said.

"They just call me Kid," I said. "That's all. What's yours?"

"Red," she said.

I looked at her hair.

"Yeah," I said. "I reckon."

The barkeep come up just then, and she told him to bring her usual. I wondered what that might be, but I didn't say nothing. When he brought it, whatever it was, I had him pour me another shot of whiskey. We drank them drinks down and had us each another. She was holding on to my arm all the time, so that if anyone else should take a notion on her, he would see that she was occupied.

"You want to go upstairs?" she said, and the suddenness of it kinda shocked me. Oh, I knowed what she was, but it still kinda tuck me by surprise. I hesitated, 'cause it brought to mind ole Sherry Chute and the effect she'd had on me and the way she had did me that time. I didn't want to go through all that again. Then I said to myself, hell, I ain't going to fall for no whore again, so why shouldn't I have myself a good romp in her bed?

"Let's go," I said.

She pulled on my arm and led me up the stairs and down a hallway to a room at the far end. We went inside, and she locked the door. Then she walked over to stand beside the bed and commenced to taking off her clothes. Well, the more nekkid she got the better looking she got, and I told myself, you be keerful now. You don't want to go falling in love and getting all calf-eyed again.

So this time I clumb nekkid in bed with the right attitude, and I had myself a hell of a good time on ole Red, and her on me too, I think. If she didn't, she sure as hell knowed how to act like it, but I think that she really did have most as good a time as me. I had such a good time that I decided to pay her for the entire night, and we sure did romp away most of it, not getting us much sleep.

The next morning I got up and offered to buy her a breakfast, but she said that she'd just as soon sleep a while, so I left her there and went a hunting ole Zeb. I couldn't find him nowhere, and I was getting awful hungry, so I went to a hash house for breakfast. I ordered up eggs and ham and taters and biscuit and gravy and coffee, and I et myself real full. I felt good. I felt good, but I was still kind a worried about ole Zeb. 'Course, he had got hisself old all right without me along to fuss over him, so I ain't sure how come I was feeling thataway, but anyhow, I was.

I was finishing up a last cup a coffee when I kind a recognized a feller setting across the room from me. He was a real slick one, with a dark suit and a fancy hat. Fin'ly I recollected that he had been at the card table the night before where ole Zeb had set in on the game. I finished my coffee and paid for my meal, and then I walked over to where this feller was setting.

" 'Scuse me, sir," I said, "but I'm looking for my pardner, ole Zeb Pike. You was playing cards with him last night, and I was just wondering if you'd maybe saw him somewhere this morning."

"No, I haven't," the man said. "You mean that old sourdough that came in the game late?"

"That'd be him," I said.

"What did you call him?" the man said.

"Zeb Pike," I said. "He's the one what got a mountain named after him. After he clumb up it. You know, Pike's Peak."

The slick feller looked at his buddy what was setting across from him, and the two of them laughed, not real raucous like, but pretty clear at my expense.

"What's wrong?" I said. "You ain't seed him, have you? You said you ain't."

"Sonny," Slick's pardner said, "that old lying fool has been pulling your leg. In the first place, Zebulon Pike never even climbed the peak that carries his name. In the second place, he's been dead for years. Hell, Pike was dead before you were born."

Well, I was flat embarrassed, and I was plumb humiliated too. I didn't know what to say. I stood there looking dumb for what seemed to me a long damn time. Whenever I could bring myself to say something again, I just said, "Well, thank you, sir," and I turned and walked out a there as fast as I could. If I coulda found ole Zeb, or whoever the hell he really was, just then, I reckon I'd a knocked the shit right out of him. I was calling him all kinds a names for making such a fool outa me. But I was too mad to go looking anymore. I was so mad I couldn't think a doing nothing but just maybe getting drunk, early as it was, so I went on back to the saloon and bellied up to the bar.

It was early, like I said, so there was just only a few customers in the place, but I bought myself a whole bottle a rye whiskey and tuck it and a glass over to a table and set down to commence on accomplishing my intention. I poured me a glass and drunk it pretty fast, and then I realized that if I was to do that again, I'd likely be falling down on the floor. So I poured me a second glass, but I just only kinda sipped at that one.

In my mind I was meeting up with ole Zeb again, and I was going over just what I would say to him whenever I seed him. Zeb Pike, I'd say. So you come back out a the grave to try to make a fool outa me, did you? You never even clumb that ole peak, you dirty old lying son of a bitch. Are you a lying son of a bitch, or are you just plain crazy? Do you really think you really are ole Zeb Pike? Well, damn it, you old bastard, you just find somebody else to do your lying to, 'cause I'm off on my own. I ain't running around the damn mountains with you and letting you tell lies to me no more.

That was the kind a speech I was making in my head and telling myself that I'd say to him just as soon as I seed him again. Then I got to wondering again, just where the hell could the old fart be anyhow. I tuck up my bottle and left the glass there on the table, and I walked on outside. The air was kinda crisp in the morning, but it weren't nearly as cold as on up in the mountains.

I went down the street to where we had left our horses and ole Bernice Burro the night before. They was all there all right. I asked the man if he'd seed ole Zeb, but he said he never. I walked the streets then, going into damn near ever' place what didn't have its door locked a looking for ole Zeb. I was beginning to worry something fierce. When I had finished going up and down the main street, I started on a side street to go over to the next row a buildings, and about halfway down, I glanced down the alley, and I seed someone just a laying there like as if he was dead. I run down there, my heart a pounding.

I dropped down on my knees and rolled him over, and sure as hell, it was ole Zeb. I was about to think that he had passed out drunk, and then I seed all the blood on him. I lifted up his head and held it on my thigh.

"Zeb," I said. "Zeb. You ain't dead are you? Zeb?"

I laid my head down against his chest listening for a heartbeat, and fin'ly I heared one. He was still alive, but I couldn't make him wake up. I even tried pouring a little whiskey in his mouth, but it just only dribbled out on his chin. I capped the bottle back and stuck it down in my coat pocket. Then I heaved ole Zeb up and got him onto my shoulder. I never thought the old bastard would be so damn heavy, but I managed to stagger back out to the main street.

Well, I attracted some attention out there like that, and some feller kindly directed me to the doc's office. He never offered to help me lug my load though, but I got ole Zeb over there, and I was sure relieved when the doc said that he'd be all right. It appeared, the doc said, that Zeb had got hisself some drunk last night, and then someone had stomped on his ass a bit. He had some cuts and bruises and maybe a busted rib or two, but that would all mend.

"He'll wake up and come around," the doc said, "when he's slept it off. Likely he'll have a hangover, and his ribs'll hurt like hell. But like I said, he'll get over it all, and he'll be all right."

I thanked the doc and paid him, and then I went out and found us a room in a real hotel, not no whorehouse, and I had ole Zeb hauled over there and put to bed. I figgered we'd be in town a spell while he mended, and we might just as well be comfy. I set in the room with him for a time, and when I fin'ly decided that he was for real okay, and he was just only sleeping off a drunk, I got to thinking again about the lies what he had told me, and I almost said that he deserved to get his old ass beat up like that for what he done to me.

Then I had me another thought come into my head, and I got up and went over to the bed and checked his pockets. His cash was gone. Ever' bit of it. Either he had lost it in that card game, or most likely, someone had seed him in the game and knowed that he had money and follered him outside, whopped him and tuck it. I wanted to know who it was that might have did that to my ole pardner, 'cause even though I had been thinking about knocking the shit out of him my own self, I sure didn't want no one else a doing it. I was wishing that he'd come around and hoping that maybe he had got a look at the culprit.

I meant to even things up for ole Zeb.

Chapter Nine

Well, ole Zeb, he fin'ly come on around, but his poor ole ribs was sore as hell, he said, and he couldn't hardly set up or do nothing. He was grouchy as hell, just a setting there in the bed and being waited on and all, but I fetched him over a bottle of good whiskey, and that calmed him down some. I thought about accusing him a lying to me and making a fool outa me, but somehow I just couldn't bring myself to getting on to the ole son of a bitch about that Zebulon Pike and Pike's Peak business. Just then it all seemed kinda silly. Besides, I figgered that if his name weren't really Zeb, then that meant he had to have some other name, like maybe John, or Charlie, or even Melvin. I didn't think that I'd be able to call him by any name other than just ole Zeb, so I let it lay. I did ask him, though, if he'd got hisself a look at whoever it was that clobbered him.

"I seed them all right," he said. "Slick bastards, they was. Two of them. I knowed them too. Played cards with them."

"Did you lose all your money in the card game?" I asked him.

"Lose?" he said, real loud and indignant like. "Lose? Hell, boy, I won. I won big too. That's how come the slickery shits to come after me. Bad losers, they was, them two. A man can't afford to lose his money hadn't ought to play cards."

"So they was two of them," I said, "and they jumped you 'cause you won their money. Do you know their names? Or what they look like?"

"All I caught was just first names," Zeb said. "They was called Asa and Clell. I never heared no last names. Asa and Clell. Asa, he was a slick dresser. Black suit and fancy vest. String tie. Had all the look of a gambler about him. You know? He sure ain't got the right disposition for it though. A man can't lose, he hadn't ought to gamble. Sorry no-good son of a bitch."

Well, I couldn't help it, but whenever ole Zeb described Asa to me, I thought about that feller in the eating place what him and his pardner laughed at me for believing that ole Zeb was really Zeb Pike whenever the real Zeb Pike was long dead. I had saw them two in the game anyhow. I remembered them. I figgered that he must be Asa. I wondered if his buddy was Clell. It seemed likely.

"What'd the other'n look like, Zeb?" I asked. "The one called Clell. What'd he look like?"

"Not so fancy as Asa," he said. "Still slick-looking, but he weren't wearing no suit though. Just a shirt and vest. No tie. Them two looked kindly alike in the face like they might a been brothers or cousins or some damn thing like that. Only thing is, Asa has black hair and Clell's is yella."

"By God," I said to Zeb, "I seed them. I seed them together the next morning. The morning after they beat you up. Hell, I even asked them if they had saw you around that morning. They even laughed at me

'cause—Well, never mind that. I'll get them for you,
pardner. I promise you that."

"Well," he said, "if I was a big enough man, I'd
tell you to forget it, but I ain't. I want you to get
them, and I know you can handle them too. Only
thing, just be careful. I don't want nothing bad happening to you."

Well, that might near brung tears into my eyes, and
I didn't keer no more about ole Zeb's name. Not a
bit. By God, if he said he was Zeb Pike, then he was
Zeb Pike, and them others just only thought that he
was dead. Hell, maybe he was old as the hills. And
maybe he had gone back to that ole peak and clumb
it when no one was around to see. And I swore to
myself that the next man what told me that ole Zeb
was a liar and a fool, well, hell, I'd just kill the son
of a bitch. That's all.

I made sure that ole Zeb had ever'thing he needed,
and then I went out a looking for Clell and Asa. I
spent the whole rest of that day wandering around that
town, but I never seed them. Now and then I checked
back on ole Zeb, and I made sure that he had his
meals whenever he got hungry, and I made damn sure
that he had plenty a good whiskey. Late that evening
I was back in the same saloon where I had original
met up with ole Red, and I was looking around for
Asa and Clell, and damned if ole Red didn't come a
sidling back up to me. To tell the truth, I was kinda
glad to see her again.

Well, to cut this short, me and her had us a drink
and went on upstairs and had us another good time,
and when we was done, she got kinda quiet. She was
kinda setting up there on the bed, and she looked to
me like as if her mind was off somewheres else. That

didn't set real well with me, 'cause my mind weren't nowhere except on her pretty nekkid body and what all we had just did with one another.

"Something wrong, Red?" I asked her. I just come right out and asked her that. She waited a minute and then she looked at me.

"Kid," she said, "is your last name Parmlee?"

That kinda surprised me. I didn't recall that I had ever said nothing about my full name in this damn town, and I sorta wondered how come her to have heared it and where it was or who it was from that she had got hold of it like that.

"Yeah," I said. "Matter a fact, it is. How come you to ask me that?"

"Did you kill a man named Hook a while back?" she said.

"How'd you know about that?" I said. I was astonished.

"Did you do it?" she asked me again. She wouldn't answer none a my questions. She just kept on a asking her own questions to me.

"Yeah," I said. "I did. I come in on him and my sweetheart. Well, I thought she was my sweetheart, but I guess she weren't really. She was just no good. Anyhow, I wanted her to go away with me, and I didn't even get mad when I seed her with him, I just only told her to get ready to go away with me, but he got mad as hell, and he jumped right up outa bed nekkid and grabbed his gun and was about to shoot me, so I just shot him first is all. Then she went to screaming and all like that, and I got the hell outa town. That's all they was to it."

"Well," she said, "he had a brother and a cousin, and they're in town looking for you. They was asking around if anyone knew you. I thought maybe it was you, but I didn't say nothing about it."

"How'd you happen to hear about all this?" I said.

"Well, you know," she said, giving a little shrug of her pretty nekkid shoulders, "I hear lots of things in my line of work. But I like you, Kid, and I thought I'd best tell you about them."

I thought about ole Sherry Chute and how she had turned on me in a real crucial time in my young life, and then I just went real soft on ole Red for looking out for me. Right then I learned that just because women is whores don't mean they're all alike. It come to me that if it had a been ole Red in that bed 'stead a Sherry when I killed that Hook, ole Red would a run off with me. I believe she woulda.

"Thanks," I said. "I surely do appreciate that, Red. Them two fellas, is both their names Hook?"

"Yeah," she said. "Clell and Asa Hook. Be careful, Kid. They're mean ones."

Well, that set me up, I can tell you. Clell and Asa. So they was looking for me. Well, by God, I was a looking for them too. This here was shaping up to be a showdown to my liking. Yes sir. I jumped right up outa bed then and started in to pulling on my britches, and I guess ole Red tuck it the wrong way.

"I can help you sneak out the back way," she said.

"Hell," I said, "I ain't sneaking nowhere. Them's the same two what beat up my ole pardner and robbed him a all his money. They don't want me near as bad as I want them. I done spent all day till I come in here to you a looking for them two. Are they still in town, do you reckon?"

"I think so," she said. "I think they're just down the hall. Not in the same room, though. They each come up a while back with one of the girls."

"Do you know what rooms they'd be in?" I asked her.

"No," she said. "I don't know."

I finished pulling on all my clothes and then I strapped on my fine Colt. I was ready for them. I was craving some action. For the first time since I had busted that ole Pigg with a ax handle, I was really wanting to kill someone. I wanted to kill them two, not 'cause they was Hooks and was after me, but I wanted to kill them 'cause of what they had did to ole Zeb, and I guess just a little bit 'cause of the way they had laughed at ole Zeb and at me and that being after they had done beat him up. I was in a killing mood, I can tell you. I was a wanting to make their blood run. I was a smelling blood. Well, I stuck my hat on my head and went for the door, but ole Red kinda stopped me.

"What're you fixing to do, Kid?" she said.

"I'm fixing to find them two bastards," I said, "and when I find them, I mean to kill them deader'n hell."

"You can't just bust into all the rooms looking for them," she said.

"The hell I can't," I said.

"Wait," she said. "Listen to me."

I stopped and turned around to look at her.

"What?" I said.

"Wait for me," she said. "I'll get dressed, and we can go downstairs. Whenever they get done up here, they'll come back down the stairs into the saloon. Likely they won't both come down at the same time. We'll see them one at a time when they come down. We know who they are, but they don't know you."

I puzzled over that for a bit.

"Okay," I said. "That sounds like a pretty good plan. Go on and get dressed then. But while I'm a waiting for you, I'll step out in the hall and watch, just in case one of them bastards should come out right away."

I opened the door and sidled on out there. I looked up and down the hall, and it was mostly dark and it was empty, 'cept only for just me. By and by, ole Red come out of the room all dressed, and me and her walked together down to the end a the hall and then on down the stairs. I got us a bottle and two glasses from the barkeep and found us a table where we set down together and had us a good view. Both of us just stared at that stairway while we sipped whiskey. I had finished me one snort and was getting some impatient. I picked up the bottle to pour me another one when ole Red put a hand on my arm. I looked up then and seed him right up there at the top of the stairs. He was sure a looking smug too.

"Be careful, Kid," she said.

I put down the bottle and stood up. I hitched my britches a bit and then walked on over to the foot of the stairway, real casual like. I stood right there at the bottom step like as if I was blocking his path, which I woulda been if he had come on down, and I looked up at him. He seed me all right.

"Asa Hook," I said.

"That's me," he said. "Who might you be?"

"From what I hear," I said, "you been a looking for me. You and your cousin Clell."

"What's your name?" he said, and now he was looking real curious.

"What you don't know," I said, "is that I been a looking for you too. I been a looking for you 'cause you and Clell stomped on my partner, ole Zeb Pike, and robbed him a all his money. You likely thought you'd killed him, or maybe you just thought that he never seed you out there in the dark alley, but he seed you all right. It takes a couple a sneaking cowards to beat up a old man like that."

"I remember you now," he said. "So you're that old fool's pardner, huh? Well, sonny, we never touched him. If he said that, he's a crazy old coot. Go to the law and see if you can prove anything on us. Better yet, be smart and just forget the whole thing."

"You done forgot one thing," I said. "I told you that I heared you was looking for me."

"Who are you?" he said.

"Some folks has called me a regular Billy the Kid," I said. "I'm knowed as Kid Parmlee, and I kilt ole Harley Hook while he was nekkid as a mole."

Well, that done it all right. Asa Hook went for his shooter just as fast as he could, but it weren't fast enough. I whupped out my Colt just as slick as you please, and I got off the first shot. Shooting up high at an angle like that, I weren't near as accurate as I usual was. If he had been down on the floor and level with me, I'd a got him in the chest, but shooting up the stairs like that, my bullet caught him right under the chin, and when it come out the back a his head, it brought a bunch a his brains out with it.

His finger went ahead and squeezed the trigger, but the shot went down harmless into one a the steps. His knees buckled a bit, but he didn't fall right off. He just sort a sort a stood there with his head a wobbling on his shoulders, and then a kind a shudder went all through his body, and fin'ly he pitched head first down onto the stairway. Then he just laid there still. He was dead all right. I felt some satisfaction, but mostly I just wanted to shoot the other'n.

"Asa went for his gun first," ole Red cried out, and then there was some other voices that joined hers and agreed with what she had said. I figgered I was okay. I reloaded the empty chamber in my Colt, holstered my gun and walked back over to set down again with ole Red and wait for Clell to come down. I figgered that maybe the shot woulda brought him out, but it never.

"Someone go get the sheriff," the barkeep said.

I never bothered to look, but I guess that someone did, 'cause in just a little bit, the sheriff come in. He was carrying a sawed-off shotgun. He didn't mean to take no chances. I seed him stop by the bar, and the barkeep said something to him and motioned to the corpus up there on the stairway, and then he nodded at me. The sheriff come a sauntering over to where I was setting there with ole Red.

"What's your name?" he said to me.

"They call me Kid Parmlee," I said.

"Did you just kill that man up there?" he asked.

"I surely did," I said.

"What was it all about?" he said.

"Well," I said, "it was two things. First of all, him and his cousin beat up my ole pardner and robbed him. I was a looking for them for that. Then I come to find out that they was a looking for me all along, 'cause I had killed a kin a theirs down at Ass Grove."

"You mean Ash Grove," he said.

"That's the place," I said.

"What was the name of the man you killed down there?" he said.

"Harley Hook," I said.

"I heard about that," he said. "There was some down there wanted to charge you with murder, but Hook, naked as he was, had a gun in his hand."

"That's right," I said. "I never kilt a man that weren't trying to kill me first."

He nodded to the bloody body on the stairway.

"Who was that?" he said.

"His name was Asa Hook," I said. "He was after me 'cause of Harley."

"Asa went for his gun first," ole Red said, jumping right into the conversation. She sure was a whole world different from that ole Sherry. I was proud to have her a setting there beside me.

"That's right," said a man at the next table. "I seen it all."

Then again, several other voices agreed.

"Why don't you do me a favor, Kid?" the sheriff said. "Why don't you do your best to keep out of any more gunfights while you're in town? I got a mess to clean up here and a bunch of paperwork to do."

I give a shrug.

"I promise you I won't start nothing, Sheriff," I said.

"Hell," he said, "I guess that's the best I can hope for."

"Sheriff," I said, "if that man's got any money on him, it belongs to my pardner, ole Zeb Pike. Him and his cousin beat ole Zeb up and robbed him."

I told him where ole Zeb was laid up, and he said that he'd see about it. I couldn't see why he couldn't just take the money out a the dead bastard's pockets and go on and give it back to Zeb, but he told me that things just didn't work that way. There weren't nothing I could do about it, so I just let it go. All the while this was a going on, me and ole Red both kept a looking up them stairs wondering when Clell would come out and show hisself. We never seed him. Fin'ly the sheriff left the place, and after that someone come and dragged the body on down the stairs and hauled it out a the saloon. There still weren't no sign of Clell.

Then one a the gals come down, and she spotted ole Red and come right on over to where we was at. She set down beside Red and sidled up to her. She acted a bit nervous the whole time. Then she said, "What happened down here, honey?"

"You mean the shooting?" Red said.

"Yeah," the other one said. "I was up there at work, you know, with Clell Hook, and when we heard the shot, Clell pulled on his britches and sneaked out the door to take a look. When he come back in the room, he got dressed real fast. He never even tucked his shirttail in. He grabbed up his boots and his hat and climbed out the window. I told him it was a long drop down there, but he just went on and jumped out into the street. What happened?"

"His cousin got killed," Red said.

"I done it," I said. "I was waiting here for Clell to come down too, but he outsmarted me, I guess."

I tossed down the rest of my whiskey, but I shouldn't a did that, 'cause it made me somewhat dizzy. I had got to where I could drink some whiskey all right, but if I drunk too much or drunk it down too fast, I'd still get real woozy. I stood on up anyhow.

"Where you going, Kid?" Red asked me.

"I got to find Clell," I said.

She must of seed how I was a bit wobbly from

tossing down that drink, 'cause she said, "You can't face him like that, Kid. Sit down."

My head was kinda spinning then, and I knowed that she was right. I set back down. Damn it, I thought, if only ole Clell had come on out 'stead a jumping out the damn winder, and that before I had tossed down that whiskey, I could a tuck keer a him too. Now there weren't no telling where the bastard had gone to or when I'd get another chance to come up on him. Woozy as I was, I poured myself another drink. Hell, I told myself, at least I got one of them. I knowed I'd get another chance at Clell. I'd get him one of these days. But I sure did wish that I had got my shot at him that night. I wished that I could go over and tell ole Zeb that I had kilt the two of them for him.

Well, I sipped at that next glass full real slow, and after I had done drunk it all down and calmed down some, I asked Red if she'd walk with me on over to the room so I could tell ole Zeb what I had did for him that night. She agreed, and me and her left the saloon together. She was a holding my arm, and likely she kept me from falling over. She was sure a fine gal. I thought again, if it had a been Red in that room when I shot ole Harley Hook 'stead of Sherry, why, ole Red would a left town with me for sure. She'd a stuck with me just like ole Farty would of. But somehow things never seems to work out right. You know?

Chapter Ten

"I kilt that Asa Hook, Zeb," I said. "He was one of them two what robbed you and beat you up. I shot him right under his chin and blowed some brains out the back a his head."

"Good," Zeb said, but sideways he eyed ole Red real suspicious like. "Who's she?" he asked me.

"Oh," I said. "Zeb, this here is a friend of mine. She helped me out a watching for them Hookses. They call her Red. Red, this is my pardner, ole Zeb Pike."

Zeb and Red kinda shuck hands, and then Zeb looked back at me. "How'd you do it?" he asked me. "I mean, was it legal and all?"

"He went for his gun first," I said, "and there was all kinds a witnesses. I done had me a talk with the sheriff. 'Course, he wants me to leave town anyhow."

"What the hell for?" Zeb protested. "It was self-defense, weren't it?"

"Aw, hell, Zeb," I said, "it don't matter, 'cause the other'n, ole Clell Hook, he got away, and I think he's done skipped town, so I got to leave anyhow to track him down and kill him. It ain't just for you, ole pardner. Come to find out, these is the brothers or cousins or something of the Hook I killed back in Ass Grove.

118

Hell, they was hunting me meaning to kill me. So it was self-defense two different ways."

"Yeah," Zeb said. "Any way you look at it."

"So I got to leave town, Pard, and get after Clell," I said. "I hate to leave you all stove up like this, but, well, here."

I shoved my hand deep down in my britches pocket and come up with almost all a my cash, and I had a fair amount too. I still had most a my money from my last cowboying job along with the extry what ole Sandy had give me whenever he told me to get the hell out a town, and I had my half a the gold money what me and ole Zeb had split up too. So I sure weren't leaving him strapped. I wouldn't do that if I could help it. I figgered with that much money, he'd get tuck keer of real good all right. Well, I made sure he had plenty a whiskey for the night, and then I tuck ole Red and we left out a there. I figgered even that ole sheriff wouldn't make a man ride out a town with night coming on, so I went back to Red's room with her.

I kinda figgered that we owed one another a real good farewell, and she seemed to agree with me, so we really and truly did have us a grand ole fling that lasted most all night long. In the morning I really didn't feel like hitting the trail, but I figgered that my welcome in town was done wore out, at least with that damn sheriff.

"What's his name anyhow?" I asked Red.

"Jim Chastain," she said. "Ever hear of him?"

"He's got a kinda reputation," I said. "Yeah, I heared of him, all right."

I give ole Red most of the little cash what I had kept, and I asked her to check up on ole Zeb for me now and then. She promised me that she would do that, and then she made me promise that if ever I was to come back through them parts again, I would for certain come and see her, and I assured her that I would do just that very thing. Hell, it wouldn't of tuck no swearing to make me want to see her again. She was just about the nicest thing that I had ever knowed, 'cept for ole Farty and ole Zeb, a course.

I didn't bother going to see Zeb again to tell him good-bye 'cause I had did that the night before, and besides, I reckoned that he would still be asleep what with all the whiskey I had left with him. I paid for my room, and then I went on down to the stables and paid out my ole horse. I told that stable man that the burro and the two extry horses in there belonged to ole Zeb and to take good keer of them, and he promised me that he would. I sure felt like I was riding away from a whole bunch of unfinished business whenever I rid out a that town, but then there just didn't seem to be nothing for it but to just go on and get.

I had also asked that stable man about ole Clell, what he was riding on and which way he had rid out, but if he knowed anything, well, he played dumb and said he didn't know. I figgered the shit had rode north, so I headed thataway. I had done been down south of there anyhow and didn't really see no sense in going back. On my way outa town, I seed a little kid playing with a stick.

"Say, boy," I said, "you don't happen to know who ole Clell Hook is, do you?"

He said that he reckoned as how he did, and then he said, "You the man that shot his brother dead?"

"Yeah," I said, "but he went for his gun first."

"I know that," he said. "Ever'one in town's talking about it. They say you're a regular Billy the Kid."

"That's what they're a saying, is it?" I said.

"All of them's saying that," the boy told me. I decided to get back to the point.

"You don't happen to know where ole Clell went, do you?" I asked him.

The kid pointed north. My guess had been right.

"You going to kill him too?" he asked me.

"Why you ask?" I said. "Is he a friend a yours?"

"No," he said. "The son of a bitch kicked my dog."

I seen an old hound laying back over against the wall of the building behind the kid, and I nodded at it. "That your dog?" I asked him.

"Yeah," he said.

"Is he all right now?"

"Yeah," the kid said. "He's okay, but that don't make it all right that Clell kicked him that time."

"You're right about that," I said. "Ain't no good reason for a growed man to go kicking no dog. Tell you what. When I find Clell, if he draws on me the way Asa did, I'll kill him."

"You think he'll draw on you?" the kid asked me.

"He will," I said. "I guarantee it."

Well, I rode on out a that town with a third reason in my head for killing ole Clell Hook, and that was that he had kicked that kid's dog. It brung me in mind of ole Pigg, that first man I had kilt, and it brung me in mind of ole Farty and the way I had walked all the way home a bawling and carrying his bloody body. I like to of cried again right then and there just a thinking on it, but I sure did feel good for that kid back there that Clell hadn't killed his dog or even hurt it too bad. Anyhow, I was dead set on killing Clell then.

Now I didn't have no idea where the next town would be, for I was total unfamiliar with that whole damn country, but the road I was a riding seemed like it was well traveled, so I guessed that there must be one somewhere up north of me, and further, I figgered if I was to keep on a riding, I'd eventual come to it. So I kept on a riding, and for company, I talked to ole horse, and now and then, it seemed like to me that he'd answer me. The trouble was that I couldn't understand his horse talk. I wondered then if horses was smarter than men, 'cause they can understand our talk, at least some of it, and we can't understand theirs.

You know, dogs is thataway too. Why, hell, ole Farty understood might near ever'thing I ever said to him. If ever I called out to him, he'd come a running. He'd fetch a stick or he'd fetch a squirrel after I'd shot it. If I told him to sit down and keep quiet, why, he'd do that too. I swear he could understand people talk, and sometimes I could understand his dog talk, but not near all the time. So anyhow, I ain't at all sure who's the smartest a the critters, horses or dogs or folks. And then there's ole Zeb's burro. Bernice seems to know a whole lot a people words too. I tell you what, it's a downright puzzlement.

Anyhow, I got me a little antelope and had me a fair meal, but I wished that ole Zeb had a been along to cook it 'stead a me. I cut up and packed along all the meat that I could, 'cause I never did believe in wasting nothing. Besides, I knowed from personal experience what it was like to be on the trail without nothing, not even water. I rode that whole day without seeing a single solitary human person, and that night I found me a good campsite off the road so that no one would come a riding along in the middle a the night and run right over me by mistake, and I set up my camp there. I built me up a little fire, ole Zeb had learned me not to build them up too big, and I fixed me some coffee and seared me up some more of that antelope meat. I et myself full, and then settled in for the night.

And then I couldn't help myself, but I got to wondering about the smarts of a antelope. I wondered if maybe one a them critters could understand people talk too, like dogs and horses and burros. They might, you know. I never knowed of a human person a trying to talk to one a them. I thought that maybe if I was to ever get the chance and I weren't too hungry, I might just try talking to one and find out, but then I changed my mind, 'cause I sure did like to eat that antelope meat, and if I was to find out that he could understand my lingo, why, that would just spoil it for me. It'd make me feel like a cannibal to go and eat one after that. I decided to leave it alone.

Next morning I woke up just a shivering. It had got downright cold overnight. I hopped around some and got the fire built back up as quick as I could, and I huddled myself around it for a spell. After a while, I cooked myself up the same kinda meal for breakfast what I'd et for supper the night before, but I didn't mind that none. It was good, 'special out there in that cold mountain air. When the sun went and got a little higher up in the sky, the air commenced to warming some, and I started in to clean up after myself and pack my stuff up again. I figgered I'd best be on my way.

But then a strange feeling come over me. It was kinda eerie like. I couldn't pin it down to nothing

neither, and that was just what made it so weird. I
just of a sudden got this feeling that someone was a
watching me from my back trail, maybe follering me.
I looked all around behind me and never seed nothing
though. Then I looked in ever' direction, real slow
and keerful. It appeared like as if I was the only living
human critter within yelling distance or a rifle shot or
even farther, hell, within human eyesight. I couldn't
get shuck of that feeling though that someone was
back there a dogging my trail, and that begun to
bother me something fierce.

I packed my horse up, put out the fire and swung
myself up into the saddle. I give another look back
over my shoulder. I couldn't help myself from doing
that, and then I rode on, but ever' now and then, I'd
look back. I still couldn't see nothing back there. I
was so dead set on looking back and seeing whatever
it was that was a giving me that feeling, that I damn
near rid right over the sign that someone had camped
along the road not too awful much ahead of me, but
I did see it. I couldn't find no evidence a who it
mighta been though, but I figgered that maybe it was
ole Clell, and he weren't too far off. I studied his
campsite for a spell, looked back down my trail again,
then headed on north.

I come up on a pretty good rise a little after that,
and I kinda moved to the side a the road and snugged
up against the rock wall there and set still. Ole horse,
he didn't understand, so I talked low to him and
shooshed him and done what I could to keep him
calm. I was just a waiting to give whoever it was back
behind me time to catch up and let me get a glimpse
a whoever it was, but I waited a spell, and I never
seed no one. Then I told myself that if there really

was someone back there, and he really was a follering me, why then, he was some kinda expert at the tracking and follering business. Fin'ly I moved on. Then in a bit, I come down in a kinda valley, and I done the same thing again. I sidled off to the edge a the road and waited and watched the horizon behind me. This time I waited even longer than the time before. I rolled me a cigareet and smoked it full. No one ever come up on that horizon. Fin'ly I rid on again.

Well, here I was in some kinda predicament. I knowed for pretty sure that ole Clell Hook was ahead a me 'cause I was tracking him, and now it sure as hell seemed to me that someone was on my trail and being real keerful about not letting me see him—or them. I didn't know of no Hookses other than the two I had done kilt and ole Clell what was up there ahead a me. Nor I couldn't think a no one else what might be after my young ass just then neither.

Then for the first time for real I begun to sort out my real and true situation in this here life. I had kilt me a couple a Piggses, the first one with just only a ax handle, but the next one in a for-real gunfight. I had kilt me two Hookses in face-to-face fights, even though the first one was nekkid at the time, and I had shot the ear off a ole Cutter. Now I didn't know a no more Piggses or Hookses, but that didn't mean that there weren't none out there somewheres just a itching to get at me for what I done to their kin.

And friends too. So I had me two families, the friends and relatives a each a which was possible all out to get me for what I done to their kin. Why, hell, there might not be no end in sight. There might not never be no end to it. The monumentalness of it all sunk into my head of a sudden. You know, when someone makes you fighting mad and you lash out at him without thinking about the consequences beyond just the winning or losing a the fight, why, you just never know what kind of shit you might be a piling up on yourself for years to come, maybe for the rest of your natural life.

And then on top a all that, there was the reputation that I was a getting from all this stuff that had been a happening to me. I never asked for it nor looked for it, and it wasn't none to my liking, but that didn't seem to make no difference. I was a getting it. Hell, I was being called "a regular Billy the Kid" most ever' time I turned around, even in a new town. I had tried a time or two to put a stop to that kind a talk, but it didn't do no good. Even ole Zeb had used it, and I had kinda chastised him, you might say, over it. Then I had gone and did it my own self. Just before I shot that Asa Hook, I had said it my own self just to kinda shake him up a bit. I reckon it worked too, 'cause I sure as hell blowed him away there on that staircase. But there was other folks around too that time, and they heared me, what I said. I had went and promoted the saying a that saying what I had been trying to put a stop to it. I had did it myself.

So I had me this reputation all of a sudden, and what that meant what I had never before give no thought to, was it meant that there would be bastards a gunning for me just for the hell of it. Why, if I was "a regular Billy the Kid," then what might the feller that gunned me down get to start in calling hisself? Maybe he'd be "a regular Wild Bill Hickok" or something, and there would be a plenty of them out there just itching to make that kind a reputation for theirselfs, and it wouldn't bother them none at all if they was to have to make it by blowing my young ass away.

So I thought again about who it might be what was back there behind me on the trail, and even though I still hadn't really seed no one back there, I just knowed that it was someone a follering me. Like I said before, I could just feel it. Anyhow, I thought again about who it might be, and then I said to myself, hell, it could be just anyone, anyone at all. It could be a friend or a relative of a Pigg or of a Hook or it could be just some young shit just a wanting to kill hisself "a regular Billy the Kid."

Then I had me another thought. I didn't think that it could be so, but what if it was the law? What if, because of one or another a them scrapes I had got myself into, what if some kinda charges had been filed on me and I didn't even know nothing about it, and there was a lawman, or a posse even, a coming up on my trail? What about that? Well now, to my mind, that was the worst thought a them all. That one final thought a coming into my head made the hairs on the back a my neck stand up and wave around and tickle me, I can tell you. I really didn't want no law dogs on my trail, and I hated to think about being caught and throwed in jail and then getting my ass hung up by my neck.

Someone once told me that whenever they hang a man, he shits in his pants. And, you know, there's always a big crowd around a hanging. Folks thinks it's good entertainment, you know, and there's some that thinks it's a good lesson for the kids to see. They watch a hanging, then they won't go out and get theirselfs into no trouble. At least that's what some folks thinks. But I sure can't think a nothing more embar-

rassing than to get hung out in front of a big crowd
a folks and then to shit in my pants right there with
all of them a looking on. So I was worrying about
that lawman back there behind me. And I was thinking how if I'd a knowed what would be in store for
me later, would I have bashed ole Pigg in the back a
the head with that ax handle? I don't know, but I think
that likely I would of. I never really had no time that
time to think on it anyhow.

You see that's what's wrong with that there theory
about hanging, I mean the one where they thinks the
kids'll learn from it and then keep outa trouble. When
a feller goes to kill someone, he don't stop and think
about hanging. He don't think about getting hisself
caught. He don't think about is it right or wrong what
I'm fixing to do, or is it against the law, 'cause he
ain't really thinking none at all. He's just blind mad,
'cause someone done him something, and he means
to do it back and worse. The thinking all comes later.

The thinking comes like when you're alone riding
a trail a follering after someone you want to kill who
also wants to kill you, and then you sense that someone's coming up on your own back trail. That's when
the thinking comes, and that's just what I was a thinking. Fin'ly I told myself to lay off that deep thinking.
It wasn't going to do me no good, and it was a keeping me from thinking about what I had ought to be
thinking about, which was to find out for once and
sure just who it was coming at my back.

If I was for real right in between two different
parties, both of which had a sincere desire to make
me into a youthful corpus, I had best get to scheming
on the most likely way to survive the situation. Well,
I said to myself, it didn't make no sense to go racing

ahead after ole Clell for a number a reasons, the first and most obvious a which was that I'd wear out ole horse. So I decided that I'd oughter first concentrate on the probable danger to my rear. I had already tried watching the trail from high and from low, and I hadn't seed nothing either time. I was going to have to try some other trick to smoke that smart feller out.

Just then I seed a real narrow trail turn sharp to my left off a the main road, and it run through a narrow gap, really just a kinda slit in the rocks. I didn't stop to think about it. I just turned ole horse real sharp into that there narrow passageway and let him pick his way along and up the mountainside. There weren't no need for guiding him along neither. There was only one way he could go. The onliest thing I could do was to just stop him whenever I decided it was time to stop. Hell, if I'd a changed my mind and wanted to go back, there wouldn't a been no way, just 'cept to back him out all the way back down. So I was what you might call committed, but that was all right too.

Well, ole horse poked his way through that there channel till we come onto a kinda peak. That is, we come out the other end on a wide flat rock up high over the main trail what was now down below. I stopped him then and patted his neck and told him he done good and clumb down off a his back. Then I went on over to the edge and looked over it down onto the road down there, and I could see it all right. I kinda laid low though, 'cause I didn't want no one looking up and seeing me up there. I looked back the way I had come from, and I still didn't see no one. So I decided to just settle in for a spell and really wait him out this time. I made up my mind I weren't going nowhere till I knowed for sure and certain if there was someone back there, and if there was, then who it was, exact.

I went back over to ole horse and unsaddled him. There weren't much for him up there, but I did find him a little patch a grass, and so I led him on over there, and then, by God, I spotted me a little round pool of fresh water up there too. So ole horse, he was in luck. I left him there, and, taking my rifle and my blanket roll along with me, I went back over to a spot near the edge. I built me a comfy little place there where I could lay down and get snug and still watch the road. I figgered this would be my camp for a spell, but I didn't build no fire. I wanted to find the other feller, not him find me. I settled down and I watched.

I checked my rifle and I checked my Colt. They was both clean and loaded and ready for action. I knowed they would be, but it was something to do while I waited there. I got kinda hungry after a spell, so I unpacked me a tin a beans and opened them up and et them cold. I washed them down with water out a my canteen. Then I guess I musta dozed off for a spell, 'cause all of a sudden I kinda jerked my head awake, and I could see that the sun was real low in the western sky. I kinda flew into a little bit of a panic then. I jerked up my Winchester and looked all around, but I didn't see no one, not up on top with me and not down on the road below. Then I asked myself, what if I had gone and let him slip by me down there on the road while I was a snoozing? I called myself nine kinds of a fool then.

Well, then I thought on it some more, and I guessed that it wouldn't be too bad after all if I had let him slip by. 'Cause then I'd be behind him 'stead

a the other way around, but then, how would I know
if that was what had really happened? I couldn't figger that one out. Fin'ly I sorta calmed myself down.
I settled back to watch the road. The sun had gone
clear down by then, and the sky was a getting black.
I decided that I could risk having myself a smoke, so
I rolled me a cigareet and lit it. I was just laying back
and enjoying my smoke when I seen a flicker down
below, and I seen more smoke. But this here smoke
was a coming from a campfire down on the road.

Chapter Eleven

Well, it was dark a night, and I sure didn't want to go creeping back down that narrow craveese like that. But I also weren't at all sure that I wanted that feller down there, whoever he might be, to get between me and ole Clell. I did crave to know just who it was though and whether he was for real on my trail. But there didn't seem to be nothing for it but just for me to wait out the night. So I tried to settle down and get me some sleep, but it didn't work too good. I dozed off a little ever' now and then, but mostly I just tossed around all through the night. I sure did have me a lot a things on my mind, and I never had been too good at thinking.

I had Clell ahead a me and someone unknown behind me. I had ole Zeb laid up hurt on down the road south and ole Red a looking over him for me, or at least I thought so. I had give away most all a my money, so I needed to get this business with Clell tuck keer of and start in to worry about my own pockets again. I had me what had begun to seem like a endless supply a Hookses and Piggses a trying to even up family scores with me, and I had my unwanted reputation as "a regular Billy the Kid" and ever'thing what that brung along with it.

Well, I weren't too fresh in the morning, I can tell you, and I didn't want no more cold beans, so I just packed up without no breakfast and got myself and ole horse ready to move on out, but first I decided I'd take me another last look over the edge and see what I might could see down there. What I seed was smoke a coming up from his campfire again. He was a cooking his own breakfast, I reckoned. Well, that kinda pissed me off, 'cause here I was doing without on account a him. I decided though that I'd take advantage a his cooking and eating time, and I'd get a start on him. I headed back down to the main road.

After we had crept back down through that narrow trail and got ourselfs back on the road, I rid ole horse along at a pretty fair clip for a spell, and he enjoyed it some too. I could tell. I come to another place where someone had camped real recent, and I figgered, like the last time, that it was likely ole Clell. I also figgered that I was a catching up with him. But then, I weren't keeping my mind on my business with him neither, 'cause I was still a looking back over my shoulder real regular like. I decided that I had to do something about that. I commenced to spying along the sides of the road for a good spot for an ambush.

I hadn't never shot no one what weren't trying to kill me first, but then I figgered there's got to be a first time for ever'thing, and this here seemed like a good time for the first time. That man on my trail was annoying me all to hell, and so I had good reason for stopping him dead. Anyhow that's what I told myself. If he was a lawman and fixing to get me hung up, why, in a sort a peculiar way, it'd be self-defense. If it was some friend of a Hooks or a Pigg, or if it was some gunslinger out to make hisself a name outa killing me, then it'd be the same thing.

It musta been a couple a hours on down the road before I seed what looked to me like a good location for such a thing, a big bunch a round boulders what looked like they'd rolled down the mountainside a good long time ago, and I rode back around behind them. I tuck ole horse a good ways back and hid him well outa sight, and then I went back and found myself a likely spot. I was up just a little off the road and not very far back. I wouldn't be seed right away by no one a coming along from the south, but I'd see him all right. I'd get the drop on him before he had a chance to even be surprised. I settled in real good then and got my rifle ready, and I waited.

I waited a while real anxious, but then of a sudden I got to asking myself just what the hell I thought I was going to do when whoever that was back there actual come a riding up. What if it was a total stranger to me? It could be a total stranger a coming after me, that was for sure, but then it could also be just a total stranger, someone who didn't know me from Big and Little Harp. So what would I do? Shoot him down anyhow? And what even would I do if I was sure he was after me? I'd killed me a few men, that's true, but I hadn't never shot no one from ambush nor in the back. I weren't that kinda killer. I know I had said that this here might be the time for it, and I had made all kinda excuses about self-defense and all, but I was having me some real serious second thoughts on that.

Well, them questions and them second thoughts worried me some, I can tell you, but I stayed right there and kept right on a waiting, 'cause the one only thing I was damn sure about was that I wanted to know if someone was really dogging me, and if so just who the hell was it. So I stayed, and I couldn't even make myself a smoke, 'cause just a little smoke even from a cigareet would a give away my hidey-hole there. I just waited and kept asking myself them annoying questions.

It musta been near about noon when I heared the horse a clomping along the road. It was coming from the south, so I figgered that it had to be my man. I checked my rifle, but I knowed that I had already chambered a shell and was ready to shoot if such was called for. I set the Winchester into my shoulder, and my heart was a pounding something fierce. The air was still cool, but I begun to sweat. Fin'ly that horse and rider come around the bend, and it weren't no one I had ever seed before in my whole life, not that I could recollect, but I reminded myself that a stone stranger could be a follering me, hired by someone, or trying to build hisself a reputation, or maybe a friend or a relative of them Hookses or Piggses. I let him come on a little more. He didn't see me nor suspect nothing, and he rid just a little past me.

"Hold it right there, mister," I said.

Well, he sure stopped right then, and he kinda raised his hands out to his sides to show me he weren't thinking about going for no kinda weapon nor nothing like that. He just set there still and quiet, and then it come to me that I didn't know what the hell to say to him next. I felt pretty damn foolish.

"Well," he said fin'ly, "you mean to rob me, or you just want me to set here like this all day?" In secret, I was kinda grateful to him for starting the conversation.

"What's your name, mister?" I said.

"I'm Bill Rice," he said, "out of Texas."

"Texas is a fur piece," I said. "What brings you up here to these parts?"

"Business," he said.

"What's your business?" I said.

"You sure are full of questions," he said. "If I drop my gun belt, can I put my hands down and get off this horse? We could have us a civilized conversation then."

"Just set right there where you are, Mister Bill Rice from Texas," I said, "and tell me what's your business."

"Well," he said, "I'm a lawman, and I'm trailing someone, but I'm also out of my jurisdiction. So to tell you the truth, I guess I'm on what you might call personal or unofficial business."

"Was you trailing me?" I asked him.

"I ain't even seen you," he said. "I don't know who you are. How can I answer that?"

"Well, drop your gun belt then," I said, and he did, and then I said, "All right. Climb down offa that horse, but climb down on the other side from where you dropped your gun."

He swung on down, and then he turned around and got a look at me from where I was a holding my rifle on him. He motioned to the other side of the road from where I was at. There was a clear flat place over there.

"How about I build us a little fire and boil up some coffee?" he said. "I don't believe you had any this morning."

I set my jaw to look real mean, and I said, "How come you to know that?"

"It ain't no big deal," he said. "I didn't see no

campfire smoke up ahead of me. That's all."

Well, I guessed that he weren't lying to me, 'cause I had seed his smoke, and I had figgered that he was having his breakfast and his coffee. So it made sense for him to figger I never 'cause he never seed no smoke from me. I eased myself down and around that boulder so I was standing facing him on level ground. I moved over and picked up his gun belt, and then I pulled his rifle out a the scabbard on the side a his saddle.

"All right," I said. "Go on ahead."

Taking his guns along with me, I went back and got ole horse and brung him out with the rest of us. There was some grazing and a little stream a running along the side a the road on the same side as where the Texas lawman was a building the fire, and I tuck ole horse down there. Then I tuck the Texan's horse down there too. It weren't nothing against the horse what his rider might a been up to against me. I waited for that Texan to say something about me messing with his horse, but he never said nothing. 'Course, I was doing good by the horse, and I did have all the guns.

Anyhow, he put the coffee on to make, and real soon, it sure did smell good to me. I was kinda glad he had made that suggestion, but I didn't smile none nor let on that I was glad for nothing. I just kept a scowling at him. I found me a spot and set down with all my guns and all a his, and I was eyeing him from across the fire. I didn't say nothing, nor neither did he till the coffee was all did, and he had poured out two cups of it. He brung one over toward me, but I stopped him cold.

"Just set it down right there," I said, "and then go

on back around there where you come from."

He set down the cup for me and kinda grinned, and then he went on back around to the other side a the fire and set his own ass down to sip his coffee. I waited for him to be set clear down before I got up and went for my cup. Then I tuck it back with me to where I had been a setting with the guns. I tuck me a sip and like to blistered my lips and tongue, but I never let on, and damn, it sure did taste good in that cool mountain air.

"Well," he said, "what else do you want to know from me?"

"I believe you been tailing me," I said.

"That ain't a question," he said, "so I can't answer it."

"All right then," I said, "have you been a tailing me?"

"Well," he said, and he tuck another sip a coffee just to make me wait a little longer for my answer I think, "let's just say that maybe I thought you were headed in the right direction for me."

"You mean you been follering me, but I been like a guide?" I said. "Is that what you mean?"

"Kinda like that," he said.

"That's pretty far-fetched, ain't it?" I said. "What part of Texas you from anyhow?"

"West Texas," he said.

"Yeah?" I said. "Well, me too. Some years back. Little place called Sneed. You ever hear tell of it?"

"I've been through there," he said.

"You wouldn't be a dogging a kid what kilt a man name a Pigg, would you?" I said. I figgered it was about time to quit all that shilly-shallying around and get right to the point. "Meaning to take him back to hang?"

"I know about Pigg, all right," he said, "and I know about the kid who did it. Melvin Parmlee, his name was. Oh, it was murder, all right. Plain and simple. The kid hit Pigg in the back of the head with an ax handle. Pigg never knew what hit him. The kid ran off. But then, no one in Texas ever thought it was worth following up. The kid was just a kid, like I said, and Pigg was a worthless scoundrel. We just never got the goods on him to put him under arrest. So I guess the local law just figured to let it all go and chalk it all up to some kind of natural justice. 'Course, if I was that kid, I wouldn't go back into Texas. On the other hand, I wouldn't worry myself over it as long as I was out of the state. Texas ain't going to pursue him. I'm pretty sure of that."

Well, I kinda mulled all that over in my head a wondering if he was telling me the truth of it, or if maybe he was just trying to catch me off guard. He didn't say nothing more about it, and fin'ly I said, "Do you know who I am?"

"They call you 'Kid Parmlee,' " he said, " 'a regular Billy the Kid.' "

"I ain't no Billy the Kid," I said. "Whenever I hear that kinda talk, I try to put a stop to it. I've killed me a few men, but they was all a gunning for me. They all pulled their irons first too. And I shot a ear off a man."

"I heard about that one," Rice said.

"So you know that a kid named Parmlee killed that Pigg feller," I said, "and you know my name. We both come from West Texas, and you been a dogging my trail, and you want me to believe that you ain't after me to take me back to Texas? I could kill you right now. You know that?"

"You could," he said, "but you don't kill like that, do you?"

"Pigg was hit in the back a the head," I said.

"That was different," he said.

"It was," I said, and I thought about ole Farty, and tears come into my eyes, but I blinked them back.

"Listen to me, Kid," he said, then he paused a bit, and he said, "I take it you don't go by Melvin anymore?"

"I never did like that name," I said, "and if you ever say it in front a any other human person, I will kill you, front or back."

"I won't ever say it again," he said. "Now listen to me. Texas law wants a man named Clell Hook for rustling cattle and for murder. They want him so bad that I was sort of sent out here on my own to bring him back to Texas. That can't be official, of course, so I'm really out here on my own as a bounty hunter, you might say, looking to catch me a wanted killer for the price on his head. When I catch him, I'll take him back to Texas. Then I'll make it official and put him under arrest and take him on in."

"You're a hunting Clell Hook?" I said, and I can tell you, I was astonished.

"That's right," he said. "And I heard that he was looking for you, so I decided to follow you, hoping that you might lead me to Hook."

"You shoulda come on a little sooner," I said. "I come on to Clell and Asa back yonder, and I kilt Asa, but Clell got away."

"I know," Rice said. "I heard about it when I hit town."

"And you mean to take him back to Texas alive?" I said.

"That's right," he said.

"Well, I can't let you do that," I said. "I mean to kill him."

"What's the difference if you kill him or if he hangs?" Rice said.

"One difference is it'll make me feel some better if I kill him," I said, "partly because I made a couple a promises."

"Tell me about it," he said.

Well, I just set quiet for a spell and sipped me some coffee. I had been talking so much that I had let the coffee in my cup get cooled down too much, so I just gulped it on down and then went to get myself a fresh hot cup. Rice never made no move at me nor nothing. I set back down and I sipped hot coffee. Then I put down the cup.

"I got a pardner back yonder," I said. "Ole Zeb Pike." I waited to see if Rice would make fun a me or of ole Zeb 'cause a that name, Zeb Pike, but he never, so I went on. "He's a old man. Them two Hookses, Asa and Clell, they beat him up and stole all his money. They beat him up pretty bad. I promised ole Zeb that I'd kill them for it. I've only did half the job."

Rice waited a minute, and then he said, "You said two promises."

"There's a kid back there," I said, "what told me that Clell kicked his dog."

Damn if I didn't start to get teary-eyed again, and this time I think that ole Rice seed it, but he never let on. I believe though that he knowed the whole story a why I kilt that first Pigg, and I think he kinda understood what was going through my head. Anyhow, I quick like gulped some hot coffee, and then I put the cup back down and made like that coffee was so hot and burned my gullet so bad that it teared up my eyes, and then I wiped them out.

"Another reason is that ole Clell's been wanting to kill me," I said. "I just figger it makes good sense for me to kill him first."

"Sounds like you have all kinds of reasons, Kid," Rice said. "Is that all of them?"

"There's one more," I said.

"I'm listening," he said.

"Sometimes the law lets them a loose after a trial," I said. "I've heared tell a that happening. I let you take him in alive, he might not ever hang, and I can't just set and wait for the trial to be over and then get him if they turn him a loose, 'cause you already done told me to stay outa Texas."

"All right. Well, I'll tell you something else, Kid," Rice said. "This ought to give you a big surprise too."

"What's that?" I said.

"The Pigg brothers and some of their cousins rode with the Hooks gang." he said. "They're all one big bad bunch."

That like to of knocked me over in the dirt. Here I'd had trouble dogging me from two families and come to find out it's all one outlaw gang. I just didn't know what to say or what to make of it.

"I'll be damned," I said.

"What do you say we join forces?" he said, after he give me a little bit to recover from the surprise.

"You mean, me and you go after Clell?" I said.

"There's liable to be more than just Clell," he said.

"I expect he's headed north to join up with what's left of the gang."

"There's more?" I said.

"I'm afraid so," he said.

"How many?" I asked him.

"We're not exactly sure about that," he said. "There's at least one more Pigg, Stanley, and there's Jody and Eddie Hook. There was someone else back in Texas that we never quite pinned down, but we don't think he was a relative, just another member of the gang. That's at least five that we know of. 'Course, I don't know how many of them he'll manage to pull together either."

Well, now, I had thought that I was just a hunting down ole Clell Hook to kill him for what he done to ole Zeb and to that kid's dog and partly because a the fact that he was a hunting me, but of a sudden now I was liable to find myself facing a whole gang a outlaws, five maybe. Maybe more. 'Course if I was to take up with ole Rice like he suggested to me, then it would be two against five. That still didn't sound too good to me. I wondered if maybe I had ought to just forget the whole damn thing and head for Californy or some such place.

Then I thought about Zeb again, and I give some more thought to that kid and his dog, and I recalled ole Farty and how come me to even be out here in this kinda pickle. But fin'ly it come to me that 'cause I had done kilt me a couple a Piggses and a couple of Hookses, them other five or so what was left would all be a wanting to kill me and would come a hunting me sooner or later. I figgered then that I'd be a hell of a lot better off with this here lawman siding me than if I was to have to deal with them all by my lonesome. I didn't want to give in that easy though.

"Let's just ride along together for a spell on ole Clell's trail," I said, "and see what happens to come up."

I laid down my rifle and stood up. I picked up Rice's rifle and his gun belt, and I walked over to where he was a setting and handed them to him. Then I turned my back on him and walked back over to my own spot. I never even looked over my shoulder. Then I set back down and picked up my coffee cup and tuck a sip. Then I eyeballed him over the top of the cup. He was just a setting there.

"That sounds good to me," he said. "For now."

"If we stick together though," I said, "eventual we're going to have us a problem."

"What's that?" Rice asked me.

"Whenever it comes to a showdown, and we got ole Clell right there in front of us," I said, "you're going to be a wanting to take him back to Texas alive, and I'm going to be aiming to kill him dead. Whenever that time comes, if we still disagree real strong on that point, we might just have to fight it out betwixt the two of us."

Chapter Twelve

So me and ole Bill Rice, we traveled on together. We stopped at noon or thereabouts to fix us another meal and some coffee and to feed and water and rest our horses. Then we moved on some more. We kept on a watching ole Clell's tracks all along the way. At least we both thought they was Clell's. It seemed like as if we was getting closer to him all the time, and I felt just like as if I couldn't hardly stand to wait till we come up on him.

"He must not think he's being followed," Rice said. "He don't seem to be worried none."

"Or else he knows he's being follered all right," I said, "and he's just a waiting to lay in a ambush for us somewheres."

"Naw," Rice said, "I don't think so. If he had that in mind, he's already passed by a couple of real good spots for it. I think he feels safe."

"Maybe so," I said, feeling a little burned like as if he'd showed me up to be some kinda greenhorn, which I guess I really was compared to a real veteran manhunter like what he was. Still, I didn't like having it pointed out to me like that. Well, we rid on through till suppertime, and then we stopped again. We fixed us up another meal, and this time we set and smoked some after we was done eating.

"Why do you and me have to fight it out, Kid?" he said. "When we catch up with Clell, why won't watching him hang be good enough for you?"

" 'Cause it'll take too damn long," I said. "Your way, there'll be a trial and sentencing and then fin'ly the hanging. And that's all after we catch up with him, and after you take him all the way back to Texas. If ever'thing goes right. He might get off. They sometimes do. Even if he don't get off, though, I don't want to wait all that long to see him dead. Hell, I thought we went all over all this before."

"You sure are impatient for such a young fellow," he said.

"Well," I said, "there's something else too."

"What's that?" he asked me.

"I ain't so sure that you told me straight," I said, "whenever you said that no one wants me back there for killing that Joe Pigg with a ax handle. For one thing, you also said I'd oughta stay outa Texas."

"Well," he said, and he kinda shoved his hat back to scratch his head, "it's all the truth, but I can't really say I blame you for being suspicious about it. I sure am going to be sorry to have shoot you, though, when the time comes."

"Don't be so damn sure it won't be me what shoots you first," I said. "You know I am—"

"A regular Billy the Kid," he said.

"Yeah," I said. "It might be good for you to keep that in your head."

We had us a few more hours of daylight, so we decided to make use of them, and we rid on down the trail. Whenever the sun got way low in the west, we started in looking for a place to camp the night. We found us a nice little place beside a stream in a grove of trees, and we fixed ourselfs up there. The horses had good grazing and plenty of water. I think we all slept good that night, and in the morning we had us a good breakfast. We drunk all the coffee we wanted, cleaned up and headed on out. It was about mid-morning I'd guess whenever ole Rice stopped his horse to study tracks on the road.

"Uh-oh," he said.

"What is it?" I said.

"He's left the road," he said. "Right there. See?"

He pointed out to me a place just ahead of us where some tracks took a sharp turn to the left a going up a narrow trail that led higher on up into the mountains.

"How do you know them are his tracks?" I said.

"I don't know for sure," Rice said, "but they're the tracks you've been following all along. I just followed after you. Remember?"

"That's the same horse I was follering?" I said.

"That's right," he said.

"And he's headed up that mountain trail," I said.

"Yep," said Rice.

"Well," I said, "just what the hell are we a going to do now?"

I was thinking that it might not be too bright to foller ole Clell up that narrow trail, 'cause just any-place along it, he could be laying in wait up above us with a rifle aimed right down our throats.

"I don't know," Rice said. "I'll have to study on it for a spell. I never figured him to do anything like that. I figured he'd ride right on into the next town.

There's nothing up there but snow. Why the hell would he go up there?"

"To lay a trap for us," I said.

"You could be right," said Rice. "Maybe he did figure out he was being followed."

"Well?" I said, feeling some kinda smug.

"Well," Rice said, "I say we don't follow him up there. I say we don't fall into that trap. What do you say, Kid?"

"I ain't going to argue with that," I said, "but then, what do we do?"

Rice kinda stood up in his stirrups and looked around some. The road we was a riding still wound along at the foot of the mountains and still had a little meandering stream running along on its other side. The stream was mostly tree-lined.

"I say we make us a camp right over there," he said, pointing off toward the trees and the stream, "and wait it out. I bet he won't want to stay up there for too long. It gets cold up there, especially at night."

So we done what ole Rice suggested and made us another camp. Like I think I done said, it was only 'bout mid-morning, but ole Clell was up the mountain, and we wasn't about to foller him, so we didn't really have us no place to go. We agreed that there wouldn't be no fires, 'cause we didn't want to give ourselfs away, so when noon come around, we et cold. We et cold again for supper. I was thinking, it was going to be a cold damn night, too, without no fire, but then I thought about ole Clell up on the mountain. It would be worser for him, and that give me some comfort. But along toward dark, I looked up the mountain, and I seen smoke.

"Well, God damn," I said. "Would you looky there at that?"

Ole Rice looked, and he seed it too.

"The bastard's built him a fire," I said. "He's cozy and prob'y eating hot food and drinking coffee."

Rice just stared at it for a bit, and then he said, "Yeah, and what's more, I think his fire's in a fireplace or a stove. That smoke looks to me to be coming out a chimney."

"The son of a bitch," I said. "Him in a warm house up there and us a shivering down here. I can't hardly wait to kill his ass."

"He must have known there was a house up there," Rice said. "He must have been headed for it all along."

"What's that mean?" I said. I was really feeling stupid about then.

"I don't know," said Rice, and that give me some comfort. "Let's sleep on it. Maybe we'll come up with something by morning."

We put down our blankets, but I was thinking that I sure didn't have near enough of them for what the night was going be like without no fire going, but I piled them up on me and soon got warmed up enough to start getting drowsy, and just as I did, I heared the pounding of horses' hoofs. I set up quick, and in the moonlight, I could see that ole Rice was already up. He was a watching the road from behind a tree. I set still for fear I'd make some fool move and give our ass away.

Pretty soon come four horsemen riding along the road from the north, and damned if they didn't turn off just where ole Clell had turned off. They headed up that trail right after his ass. I waited till Rice watched all he wanted to, and when he come walking back toward our little cold camp, I said to him in a real low voice, like as if them riders might could still hear me even though they was getting well up that trail, "It looks like we ain't the only ones after ole Clell."

"Could be," Rice said, "but what I think is more likely is that those four were part of his gang. We didn't catch up with him soon enough. Now we'll have five of them to fight. Or more."

"More?" I said.

"Someone could have been up there already," he said, "waiting for him."

"We can't fight no army," I said. Now I know that ole Rice had told me earlier that there might be five or more, but I didn't really hardly believe it nor think about it till I actual seen them four ride by. Of a sudden now, it seemed pretty damn real. "Just the two of us? Can we?"

"Not without some pretty careful planning," Rice said. "Let's get some sleep."

Well, I guess he did, but I sure never. It was too damn cold, and I was thinking about that damn gang of outlaws up on the mountain in their warm cabin. I was wondering what the hell me and Rice would do whenever they come back down. I wished that he would get us a plan and tell me about it, but at the same time, I realized that I was sure damn glad that he was along with me and we was in it now together. If it was just me by my lonesome, I don't know what the hell I'd a did. I wanted to kill ole Clell bad enough that I might of did some fool thing like take a shot at him and just take my chances on getting away from the rest of them. You know, kinda shoot and run. But

I also knowed that such a move would be pretty damn stupid.

I never thought that I'd be glad to be in the company of a lawman, but I sure damn was. 'Course it helped some that he was a West Texas lawman, and we was in Colorady, so he couldn't arrest me nor nothing like that. Not legal anyhow. He had admitted to me that he was planning on capturing ole Clell and taking him back to Texas so he could arrest him. Now I didn't have no use for Clell, as I think you already know, and somehow that plan of ole Rice's just didn't seem fair.

It didn't really matter though, 'cause I didn't have no intention of letting him carry it on through. Like I had done told him two or three times, I meant to kill Clell whenever I laid eyes on the son of a bitch. It had seemed kinda simple. I'd have to deal with Rice in order to kill Clell, but somehow I didn't think that ole Rice would kill me just so he could take Clell back to hang. But now with four more outlaws, maybe more, in the picture, the whole thing was a bunch more complicated. It would be me and Rice trying to stay alive through a fight with all them bastards.

Whenever we got up the next morning, I was still a shivering, and I sure did want me a cup a hot coffee, but we et cold again, and I felt like a damn soldier in the middle of a war or something, being deprived like that. I wondered just how long this situation was going to last, and if it was to last much longer, I wondered how long I would last. But lucky for me, them outlaws come on down the mountain later that morning. They come on down, and there was seven a the bastards.

Me and Rice, we stayed right with our horses to keep them quiet while that gang rid by, and what they done was they turned back south whenever they got down on the road. They turned south, and I was a worrying about ole Zeb and ole Red, but then the outlaws turned a ways downstream and crossed over the water and headed out east onto the Colorady flats. I give ole Rice a look.

"They're up to something," he said. "We'll let them get a ways ahead, and then we'll follow them."

We tuck advantage a the situation and built us a fire, and the first thing I done was I put on some coffee. It sure did taste good that morning, I can tell you. We went on ahead and we et us a good hot breakfast and drunk us some more coffee, and when my belly was good and full and I weren't shivering so much no more, I rolled me a cigareet and smoked it. Fin'ly ole Rice said that we had ought to get going, so we cleaned up our campsite, packed up our things and crossed the stream to foller them outlaws east.

"You reckon they're planning on some kinda raid?" I asked him as we rid along.

"They're sure up to something," he said.

"We going to just let them do it and get away with it?" I said.

"What can we do?" he said.

"We could try to warn folks up ahead," I said.

"We can't get around them and ahead of them," he said, "and even if we could, we don't know what they're planning to do."

He was right, a course, and it burned me up again, him showing me to be so dumb like that. I wished just once that I could figger things out ahead a him and get the best a him and show him that I had some brains too. But he was a old guy. I reckoned him to be maybe thirty-five, and he'd had him a lot of experience with chasing outlaws and such. I figgered that if I was to ever live so long, why, maybe I'd have me enough experience by then that I'd be smart like him too. But right then I wasn't good for much of nothing. I could do ranch work, most all of it, 'cept for the paperwork, and I could do gunfighting, but that was about all. And I didn't really want to be knowed for the gunfighting.

The more easter we went the flatter and drier that Colorady got, and it was so flat that we could most see them outlaws. Not quite. We could see their dust, though, sometimes. We was follering their tracks, and it was real easy, there was so many of them. But they was a good ways ahead of us, and it weren't likely that they knowed we was on their trail. Rice seed to it that we hung back far enough to keep them from taking note of us. Toward noon, he stopped us.

"What?" I said.

"Look ahead," he told me, and I did, and I seed the smoke from a couple a fires. "Campfires," he said. "They've stopped to eat. We might as well do the same thing."

We et again and drunk some more coffee and smoked some more cigareets. By and by the smoke of their fires had stopped, and ole Rice figgered that they was on their way again. We cleaned up and packed up and follered. I begun to wonder if we was going to foller them all the way to the other side of the country and right into the ocean out there, but I never said nothing. I did want to kill ole Clell, but I sure hadn't never thought that it would turn out to be this much trouble.

"Say," I said, riding along, "we ain't going back into Texas, are we?"

"If they keep on the way they're headed," Rice said, "we'll wind up in Kansas, but my guess is they'll try to pull something right here in Colorado. It's a long ride on into Kansas."

"It's done been a long ride," I said, and he kinda laughed at me. I tell you what, sometimes I actual kinda liked that man, but other times I just wanted to ride off in some other direction from where he was headed and hope that I wouldn't never set eyes on his ass again. We follered them outlaws the rest a the day, and come nightfall, ole Rice, he said that he thought that we oughta just keep a going. He figgered that they'd stop for the night, and if we was to just keep riding, why, we might just ride right on around them. It seemed to me that I had suggested something like that earlier and he had made me feel like a fool for it, but I kept my mouth shut about that.

You know, there's times when a feller oughta take advantage of a situation and say I told you so to another feller. If you was right in the first place, why, it'd make you feel some better to say that. But then there's other times when it seems like as if the best thing to do is to just not say nothing and let it ride. 'Cause it might not be worth the little bit a pleasure you'd get outa saying it to mess up something else you got going.

Well sure enough, them outlaws stopped, and so we went and made us a wide swing around them, moving slow and keerful in the dark, but we just kept on a riding all night, so by morning, we was well ahead of them. I weren't for sure just what ole Rice meant for us to do, now that we was out front like that, but pretty soon we seed us a sign that said a town was just up ahead. Lowry it was. We just kinda looked at each other, and we rid on. I was just about to fall asleep in my saddle, and I figgered that ole horse was pretty damn tired too. But we rid on into that town, and Rice, he found the law right away.

We pulled up at the hitch rail there in front of the Lowry sheriff's office, and Rice clumb down and headed for the door. He stopped and looked back at me.

"I'll just wait here," I said.

He went on in and pretty soon he come back out.

"I told him who's coming," he said. "He told me they've got a bank here with a lot of money in it. We're going to get ready as if we know they mean to rob that bank. Just in case. Come on."

"Where we going?" I asked him.

"We're going to climb up on top of that hotel over there," he said. "The sheriff said there's a staircase out back. Come on."

As we headed across the street, I seed the sheriff come out of his office and go running down the board sidewalk. I figgered he was on his way to round up some a the citizens to get ready for this bank robbery that maybe was about to happen. Me and ole Rice rid on around behind the big hotel he had pointed out to me. We tied our horses back there, unpacked our rifles and all our extry ammunition, for rifles and six-guns, and clumb up the stairs on the back a the building. We got ourselfs up to a upstairs landing thataway, but then we had to stand on the rail a the landing to grab hold of the roof overhang.

Rice done it okay. He got up there. But whenever I got my hands on the edge a that roof, and my feet come off a the railing, I was just a hanging there and kicking my feet around in the air. I just knowed I was going to fall all the way back down to the alley and break myself all to pieces, and I had a funny and scared feeling that hit so far down deep into the pit of my stomach that I felt it clear into the end of my pecker.

"Rice," I yelled. "I can't do it. I'm going to fall."

He come over and reached down and tuck hold a my wrists and pulled me right on up onto the roof. He had him some strong arms, I can tell you. I crawled on all fours till I was a few feet away from the edge. I was trying to think a what I had ought to say to him, but he just turned and headed for the front a the building. "Come on," he said. I stood up on uneasy legs and follered him over to where the top of the building front made a kind of a wall for us to hide behind, but we could stand up and see over it and shoot over it all right. I looked west, but I never seed nothing a coming.

What I did see was I seed all kinds a citizens on the rooftops a the other buildings, all with guns: rifles, shotguns, revolvers. Pretty soon it seemed to me like as if ever' man what lived in Lowry must a been out there somewheres with his guns. And the womenfolks and the kids had all disappeared into houses or something. The town looked most near deserted. There was a couple a stray dogs wandering around sniffing things, but that was about all. Then I seed the sheriff again. He was walking along with three other men, all armed to the teeth, and they was a looking west just the same way like I had did. He pointed a couple a times in different directions. Then two a the men went across the street and inside a building over there, and the sheriff and the other feller went on into each a the buildings on either side a the bank.

I hadn't never seed a town look like that before, and it was kinda spooky like. It was real quiet, and the streets was empty. Them two dogs was all that was moving. Well, there was some horses tied at the rails here and there, and they was switching their tails and such, but there weren't no people. Then Rice punched me on the shoulder and pointed west, and I looked, and I seed the cloud a dust that was a follering that outlaw gang. I knowed that's what it was. It couldn't a been nothing else. I got ready to kill me another Hook.

Chapter Thirteen

Well, sure enough, they was a coming our way. 'Course, they didn't know it was us they was a coming at. They just thought they was a coming at the unsuspecting town a Lowry to do whatever it was they was a planning to do. Rich figgered it was to rob the bank, and the local law didn't disagree none with him on that issue. There was men on rooftops, including me and ole Rice, men in doorways, men peeking outa winders. There was men ever'where, and most all of them with rifles. Some had shotguns, and some others had only handguns, but they was all armed. Them outlaws didn't have no idea a what kinda trap they was riding into. I was just a hoping that no one would kill Clell before I got me a shot at him.

Well, the sheriff a Lowry had passed the word that no one but just only him was to fire the first shot, and so when them bastards come a riding on into town, ever'thing still stayed real quiet like. All of us gunmen in town kept ourselfs hid and waited. It was all I could do to keep my head down, I wanted so bad to raise it up and get a look at Clell to see where he was at. Anyhow, they rid on in kinda slow and easy, and sure enough, they stopped their horses right in front a the bank. I managed to take me a sly sorta peek.

You could see them looking around kinda edgy like, and you could see them heft their six-shooters to make sure they was sliding easy in their holsters. A couple of them was carrying rifles. Then you could see them all look toward the bank. They each but one pulled sacks outa their saddle bags, and then it come total clear what they was up to. All of them but that one started walking toward the bank. The one was left to watch the horses. The sheriff didn't wait for them to get to the bank. He stepped right out and faced them.

"Hold it right there," he said. "You men are covered from all over town. Stop where you stand and drop your guns."

They stopped all right, and then they just stood there for a minute or so or maybe just for a couple a seconds, but it sure seemed a long time, like they was thinking it all over. Then three or four of them at once blasted the sheriff, and he went crashing back'ards through the big front winder a the store he was standing in front of. He was hit plenty. You could see the blood splatter each time a bullet tore into him. That broke all hell loose.

I seed three outlaws just tore to pieces by bullets coming at them from ever' whichaway. They jerked and twitched, and it seemed almost like it was only just the bullets a hitting them that was keeping them from falling on over dead. I don't know how come ever'one in town seemed to shoot at the same three outlaws, but they did, 'cause the other four made it in between buildings or around to the back a the buildings or something, and they headed out in four different directions.

I never even got off a shot, and I sure felt like a greenhorn. I had killed me some men, as you well know, but I hadn't never seed nothing like that battle in the main street a Lowry. It musta been the way it was to be in a real war. I was just so astonished by the whole thing that I just set and stared. Well, when them four outlaws lit out in four different directions, what with the sheriff killed and all, why, different ones a the town folks jumped on horses and just tuck their pick on which one they was going to foller. My head fin'ly started to clear, and I seed ole Rice stand up and head for the back a the building we was on.

"Did you see where Clell went?" I said.

"Come on," he said. "I'm going after him."

We clumb down offa that roof, and I fell on my ass when I dropped down to the landing, but I scrambled right back up again. Rice was already halfway down the stairs. By the time I got down in the alley to where ole horse was a waiting for me, Rice was riding out, headed kinda northeast. I kicked ole horse into a fast run and tuck out after him. We rid hard for a ways, and I was fearful that ole horse might give out underneath me. We passed by where one a the town folks had got shot down. Going on a little farther, we passed two more town folks what had decided to give up the chase and go on back home. We kept a going.

Far as I could tell there wasn't no one left between us and ole Clell. He was ours. I figgered the showdown between me and ole Rice was just around the bend. Of a sudden, Rice slowed his horse down, and so I slowed ole horse under me, but not too much before I rid myself on up alongside a Rice. I give him a look, but he never noticed it, or if he did, he made out like he never.

"What're you doing?" I said.

"You see that line up there?" he asked me. He had a bad habit a answering a question with another question. That was another thing about him that annoyed the hell outa me. But I didn't say nothing about it. Instead I just answered his question.

"Yeah," I said. "I see it."

"That's a riverbank," he said. "Hook has gone down that bank. I doubt he's trying to cross the river with that tired horse. More likely, he's resting his horse and waiting to try to pick us off from behind that riverbank. I figured we'd slow down. Rest our horses a bit too."

"Yeah," I said, "but what happens when we get close enough for him to get a good rifle shot at us?"

"Well," he said, "in just about another minute, we'll spread out wide. Try to keep out of his range. When we reach the riverbank, we'll go on down and then come at him from two sides."

"If I get to him first," I said, "I'll kill him."

"I figured that," he said. "But if I get to him first and have him in my sights, you back off."

I rid on a ways a thinking about that one before I give him a answer.

"Well," I said, "all right."

"Let's spread out," he said, and he turned his horse to the right and started out at a sharp angle to the riverbed. I turned mine to the left and done the same thing. My heart was a pounding with anxiety, I wanted to kill ole Clell so bad. I even hurried ole horse a bit, hoping that I would get to Clell first, but then I slowed down again. I got to questioning whether or not I really wanted to get down behind that high riverbank all by my lonesome and try a sneaking up on ole Clell without Rice coming at him from the other side.

It seemed like a real long ride, and I kept expecting to hear a shot ring out from down there where he was a hiding and waiting, but maybe ole Rice's plan was working. Maybe we was keeping well outa his range. When I fin'ly reached the bank, I had lost sight a Rice, but I figgered that he was prob'ly there too. It was a steep bank and a fair ways down, so I eased ole horse down in there real easy like. I looked quick to my right, but I didn't see no one. Then it come to me that I'd have a easier time a sneaking up on ole Clell if I was afoot, so I clumb down offa ole horse's back and give him a pat or two. I pulled out my Colt and started walking slow and keerful, watching ahead, stopping now and then whenever the river tuck a turn and peeking around the curve in the bank.

I knowed it was going to be a long walk, 'cause I had rid a ways off to the left, keeping outa his rifle range. 'Cause I had rid at a angle, if the riverbank had been straight, it woulda been a shorter distance to go, but it weren't. It was crookedy as ole Farty's hind leg. I just kept a creeping and a watching, ready to shoot anything what moved. Then I seen him of a sudden, but he had his back to me, and he had his rifle up to his shoulder ready to shoot, but before he could pull the trigger, there was a blast, and he twitched. He stood a wavering for a second or two, and then he fell over on his face.

"God damn you, Rice," I yelled, and I went running on ahead. "You said you wasn't going to kill the son of a bitch."

I got up to where the body was just a laying there on its face, and I seen Rice a standing there, six-gun still in his hand. He holstered it.

"He didn't give me any choice," he said.

"Damn you," I said.

"Roll him over and look at him," Rice said, "before you cuss me out any more."

"Huh?" I said. I dropped down and tuck hold of the man's shirt and rolled him over on his back. "That ain't Clell," I said.

"No," said Rice. "It ain't."

"Well," I said, "you said we was follering Clell. You said you seed where he went."

"I thought I did," Rice said. "I was wrong."

"Ain't no telling where he's went to by now," I said.

"There were four of them," Rice said. "There'll be four trails out of town. Come on. Let's load this one up and head back."

"You load him up," I said. "You kilt him."

We didn't talk none on the way back to town. I was a pouting, and I reckon ole Rice just didn't figger I was worth talking at just then. But whenever we got back, we found folks in town still a running around and talking all excited about what had tuck place there. They was glad to see that me and Rice was bringing in one more a the outlaws. There was a small citizens posse in front a the sheriff's office. They had caught their man too, and they had kilt him, just like Rice had did. Then Rice and some a the other men there went inside the sheriff's office and commenced to looking through a stack a dodgers to see could they find out who all it was they had kilt. Rice come back out to find me in a bit.

"We got a reward coming for that fellow," he said.

"I ain't got nothing coming," I said. "You kilt him."

"We were in on it together," he said. "You'll get half the reward. What are you pouting about anyhow? It wasn't Clell Hook I killed."

Hell, I knowed that, and so I started in trying to figger out just what it really was that I was pouting about, but I never figgered it out. I guessed that maybe I had oughta cut it out.

"How much reward we got?" I asked him.

"Five hundred dollars," he said. "The man was Leiland Hook."

"Ain't there no end to them Hooks?" I said.

"Not so far," he said. Then he changed the subject. "The men that followed the other two trails came back empty-handed," he said. "The trails will be easy enough to follow, but we won't know which one is Clell."

"Well, Rice," I said, "you're all the time telling me what we're going to do next, so for once I'm going to tell you. Here's what we'll do. You foller one trail, and I'll foller the other'n."

"You sure?" he asked me.

"It'll be just one on one either way," I said.

"Okay," he said. "But let's wait till morning. We'll get our reward money here in town. Get us a good meal and a good bed for the night. Start out fresh in the morning."

I thought that one over for a minute, and I couldn't see nothing wrong with the plan. It was already a bit late in the day to go starting off on a chase like that. "Okay," I said. Well, we did get our money, and so where I had been near broke from giving near all my cash money to ole Zeb and to ole Red, as you might recall, I had me another two hunnert and fifty bucks in my pocket. I also had a evening and a night to kill.

I went and et me a supper in a pretty nice eating place with ole Rice, and then I went out on my own and hunted up a good-looking saloon. I went inside and had me a glass a whiskey, and I was kinda looking around at the gals in there. They had some gals in there all right, and a couple of them was kinda rank-looking, like as if they'd been rode a time or two too many, but there was also a couple a kinda cute ones.

Well, I waited till a little blonde was looking my way, and I pulled out my roll a bills and made sure that she got a look at them. Sure enough, the little blonde come a sidling my way in pretty short order. She come right up close and made sure that her bare nekkid arm was pressing against me.

"Hi," I said.

"How do," said she. "You just ride in today?"

"That's right," I said.

"You help fight them outlaws?" she asked me.

"I was out there," I said, so I never lied about it.

"You likely need a little relaxing," she said.

"You meaning to help me do that?" I asked her.

"I bet I could," she said.

"Well," I said, "let me get us another glass to go with this here bottle, and let's just take our ass upstairs, you and me. Oh, is this bottle all right with you, or do you like something different?"

"What you got there is fine with me," she said. I

liked her for that, and I waved at the barkeep who come over right away. I paid him for the whole bottle and got another glass from him. Then I headed for the stairway with this blonde a hanging tight onto my arm. I guess I was kinda swaggering. Whenever we got upstairs and into a room just the two of us, she commenced to taking off all her clothes. I poured us each a drink, and then I done the same thing. We set nekkid on the edge a the bed and drunk whiskey, and then we got after it. When we was all done, she set up and looked kinda like she was deep thinking on something.

"Are you all right?" I asked her.

"Are you staying in town?" she said.

"Me?" I said. "Naw. I'll be pulling out first thing in the morning."

"Will you take me with you?" she said.

Well, now, that surprised the hell outa me. It was the last thing I expected to hear from a whore.

"What for?" I said.

"I want out," she said. "I got enough money for stage fare, but Alf, he won't let me go. He says I owe him, and till I can pay him off, he owns me, he says. I got to get out of here. I can't stand it no more. Oh, I like you all right, but some of the others I have to be with—well, you just wouldn't believe it."

"I reckon I know what you mean," I said. "But I'm riding outa here early in the morning. I'm traveling horseback."

"I can ride a horse," she said.

"But do you got a horse?" I asked her.

She dropped her head and looked real sad. "No," she said. I couldn't hardly stand seeing her like that.

"Hey, wait," I said. "I got a idea."

That perked her back up. "What is it?" she said.

"Never you mind," I said. "You don't got to know. 'Specially if it don't work out. Be best if you don't know. You stay here and make like I'm buying the whole night with you. I'll come back before daylight."

I pulled on my clothes and went out the winder, and when I dropped to the ground, I fell on my ass. She was looking out the winder and seen me fall down, and I wished that she hadn't saw that. Anyhow, I got up and dusted off my butt, and then I went around a hunting for ole Rice. I fin'ly found out that he had checked into a room at the biggest hotel in town, and I went up and knocked on his door. He opened it with a gun in his hand.

"What are you doing here, Kid?" he said.

"I got to ask you something," I said.

"Well," he said, "what is it?"

"You know that feller you kilt today?" I said. "What's going to come a his horse?"

"I'm not sure," he said. "Usually it would go to a sheriff's auction. What do you want?"

"I want the horse," I said.

He scratched his head and thunk a bit. "I don't know," he said. "Without a sheriff in town, it ain't likely that anyone would notice. You want it, I'd say go ahead and take it. You planning on leaving here before morning? Trying to get a head start on me?"

"It ain't that," I said. "I just need that extry horse, and I don't need no one in this here town asking no questions about it. That's all."

"Well, like I said," Rice told me, "just take it. You know where that one trail headed back west?"

"Yeah," I said. "I think so."

"Why don't you follow that one," he said. "The fourth one headed northwest. I'll take it. First one of us gets his man, no matter who it is, cut across and look for the other. Agreed?"

I agreed and thanked him and felt kinda funny about it. Then I left. I went down the street to where the stable was at and found that horse and its saddle. I put the saddle on the horse and then led it around to the back side a the saloon where that blonde gal was, a waiting for me. I hadn't even thought of it till just then, but I never even had asked her name. Anyhow, I put the horse there, and then I went and got mine and brung him around. Then I tried to figger out how I was going to get back up in that room without no one seeing me, 'cause I meant for them to think I was up there all night, you know.

Fin'ly I led ole horse around to the winder where I dropped down from, and I stood up in the saddle and reached for the winder. I couldn't quite get to it, but while I was stretching for it, that blonde gal come and looked out the winder and seed me.

"I got you a horse," I said. "Can you get outa there?"

"I can get out just like you did," she said, and she clumb right out that winder and down onto my shoulders, and the both of us went tumbling offa ole horse's back and fell into the street. We sorted ourselfs out and got up and dusted off some.

"You ready to go?" I asked her.

"Like this?" she said, and she called my attention to her working-girl outfit what she had on.

"Well, what do you mean to do?" I said.

"Just go by my room and let me get some clothes," she said. "It won't take but five minutes."

Chapter Fourteen

Well, I got that little ole gal's clothes all bundled up and loaded on that extry horse, and the two of us got all mounted up and rid out a town in the direction what Rice had told me to go, so I was a helping that gal to get away and at the same time I was a trailing one a them last two outlaws. 'Course I was hoping that I was on the trail of ole Clell. I figgered that things had actual worked out pretty good for me. If ole Clell, or whichever one it might be, was to spot us on his trail, why, he wouldn't be near so suspicious of a man and a woman a traveling together as he would a just a man a riding along by hisself.

Then if my luck was to hold up then maybe I would find out that I was for sure a trailing Clell, then I could just go on ahead and kill him before ole Rice even knowed that I had caught up with him. Thataway I wouldn't have to fight Rice over him. That's how I was hoping things would work out. I hadn't yet worried about just what I was a going to do with that yella-haired gal, but I did get to thinking after we had rid a ways outa town that maybe I had ought to at least know her name.

"I'm Kid Parmlee," I told her as we was riding along side by side. "What's your name?"

"I'm Sally Goodin," she said.

"Well," I said, "you are too. You're just that."

"What?" she said.

"You're a good'un," I said. "Sure enough."

She laughed a little at that and kinda ducked her head.

"Do you mean that?" she said.

"Oh, yeah," I said. "I mean it. I never say nothing 'less I mean it. I'm kinda keerful with what I say and with my words and all."

"Well," she said, "maybe you just ain't had much to compare me to."

"I've had me a few," I said, and I guessed that I weren't lying too much when I said that. I guessed a couple was the same thing as a few, or close enough anyhow, and to tell the truth, ever' time I got myself with a gal like that, I thought it was the best thing I had ever had. I reckon if I had been able to get back with ole Red right at that very minute, why, I'd think she was the best again. Even ole Sherry Chute back in Ass Grove. That's just the way I was about that business. Whatever I was a getting into at the time seemed like the very best in the whole wide world.

"Kid," Sally said, "where are we headed for?"

"Aw," I said, "we're just kinda headed generally away from where we was at. You said you wanted to get away from there, and you never said where it was you wanted to go. Well, we're headed kinda west."

"Okay," she said. "Are there towns out there?"

"Oh, yeah," I said. "Lots a towns."

I begun to feel a little guilty then, 'cause I never told her that I was actual tracking a killer and wasn't really headed for no town, not unless he was to lead me into one. And I give some thought too to the kinda

towns we might run into, them rough-and-tumble
mining towns, and I thought that if it was just any
old whore I was taking along, well, she prob'ly
wouldn't mind them kinda towns. But Sally was running away from her whore life, and she most likely
would ruther find herself some nicer kinda place than
them kinda towns. I didn't know nothing about them
kinda places, though, and I weren't at all for sure just
what it was I would wind up doing with her.

Well, we rid along slow and easy through the
night, and come morning I checked around to make
for sure that I was really on that outlaw's trail. I found
it all right without too much trouble. I told myself
then that I didn't need ole Rice around to help me
track no outlaw. Sally seen me a poking around like
that, and she asked me what I was a doing.

"Oh, just checking the trail," I said, and she didn't
say nothing more about it, but I don't see how she
coulda been satisfied with that kinda answer. We
moved on, and in a little while she complained that
she was getting hungry for breakfast. I watched out
then for a good camp spot, and when I found one by
some water, I stopped us and made a little camp. I
brewed up some coffee and fixed us a little meal. It
weren't much, but at least we didn't have to go on
hungry. She never complained neither. She even
thanked me for the feed. Ole Sally, she had a real
good disposition. I cleaned up and packed up, and we
headed on out again.

We made good traveling time, I guess, 'cause I
kept thinking that the trail I was follering was a little
fresher the more we went on. The sun was up over
our heads whenever we come to the river. I don't
know what its name was, and it weren't very deep,

but it was clean and running along real nice. I told Sally that it was a good place to stop and eat, and it was about the right time for it too, so we stopped, and I begun going through the little ritual a setting up a camp again. I was just getting a little fire a going when I looked up and seed ole Sally a stripping off all a her clothes.

'Course I had seed her like that before, but even so I couldn't hardly take my eyes offa her. I for sure had never seed no woman strip nekkid right out in the middle a the wide world like that. Well, it kinda wrought me up, if you get my meaning. There weren't nothing I could do about it. I throwed a little more wood on the fire so it wouldn't go out on me, and I run right over to the water. She had done waded in. I tore off my clothes and follered her right on in there. Pretty soon I had grabbed onto her, and it was really something being all wet and hugging and feeling a wet woman. I hadn't never done nothing like that before neither.

Well, there weren't nothing else for it but to just go on ahead and do it right there in the water, and we did too. When we was all done, I was feeling somehow guilty, and I guess I musta showed it in my face. She put her hands on my cheeks and kissed me real nice and sweet, and then she said, "Is something wrong, Kid?"

"Maybe I shouldn't oughta have did that here in the water," I said. "Someone else might come along after us and want to drink some a this water."

She laughed at me then, and I got kinda embarrassed like.

"Fish live in this water, don't they?" she said.

"Yeah," I said. "I reckon."

"And how do they make more fish?" she asked me.

I thought about it for just a short spell, and then I grinned wide. I felt all right again.

"Yeah," I said. "And turtles. They do it in the water too, don't they?"

"And cows and horses and ever'thing else walk right out in it to get a drink," she said, "and sometimes they just pee right in it."

"Yeah," I said. "I seen that happen sometimes."

I felt so much better about what I had did, that I pulled her close to me and kissed her real good and long, and then we went and done it all over again. Oh my, she was good. Just then I was sure glad that I had her company along that trail. I thought about ole Red back there a keeping watch over ole Zeb for me, and I felt just a little guilty about that, but it passed. Well, we fooled around at that noon camp a spell longer than what we prob'ly should of, but I didn't keer about that too much. I figgered that trail was still warm, so pretty soon we went ahead and got dressed and et, and then we started out again.

It musta been a couple a hours on down the trail when I heard a shot up ahead. It was a good ways off, I could tell. I figgered that outlaw must a shot something for his supper, or at least tried to. Whenever Sally asked me about it, that was what I told her too. I didn't say outlaw though. I just told her that likely someone up there somewhere was a hunting. We kept a going, and in a while I seed smoke, a thin wisp like from a campfire. I started in looking for the highest spot a ground around. Whenever I did find it, it weren't very high, but I tuck to it anyhow. I was a squinting real hard trying to make out something

about the campfire ahead, and Sally was right beside
me puzzling over my actions.

"You trying to spy on that camp up there?" she
asked me.

"Yeah," I said. "I'm kinda curious."

"I've got some opera glasses in my stuff," she said.

"Opry glasses?" I said. "What's that?"

She went and dug them out and brung them to me,
and it was the sissiest pair a looking glasses I had
ever saw, but I used them, and they worked pretty
good. I could make out the campfire, and I could tell
a good-sized hunk a meat was roasting over it too. I
had been right about the gunshot. I seed a horse standing by, and I seed the man, but I couldn't make out
was it Clell or not. I studied on the situation some,
trying to figger my next move. As flat and bare as
that damn country was, there sure wouldn't be no
sneaking up on the man. I decided that we could just
hang out and rest a bit before follering him anymore.
Let him get his meal did and start out again. Then
move on after him. What I didn't know was that Sally
had been a studying on me too.

"We're following that man up there," she said.
"Aren't we?"

I looked at her, and she was giving me a real serious hard look. Well, I just couldn't lie to her, and
since she had gone and asked me direct like that, there
weren't nothing more for it but to just go on ahead
and tell her the whole truth.

"Yeah," I said. "We are."

"How come?" she said.

"He's one a them bank robbers from back there,"
I said. "There's likely a reward of some kind on him.
There was on the others. We got all but two of them.

That one up ahead and one other one. My pardner's on the other'n's trail."

"Is there going to be some shooting?" she said.

"Most likely," I said. "I guess I shoulda told you, but the reason I was so ready and willing to get you outa town is just 'cause I knowed I was going to be getting on after him anyhow. I woulda waited till morning to foller him if it hadn't a been that you was wanting to get out right away. I guess maybe you wouldn't a wanted to come along with me though if you'd a knowed that I was on a manhunt."

"Well," she said, "I do wish you'd've told me, but then, I guess it wouldn't've made no real difference. I'd've come along with you anyhow. I sure did want to get away from that Alf. He thinks he owns me. I couldn't've stood it much longer. I think I'd've killed myself."

"Oh," I said, "I wouldn't a wanted you to do a fool thing like that. If things was all that bad, I'm sure as hell glad that I come along when I did."

"I'm glad too," she said, "and I ain't mad that you didn't tell me about trailing after this guy, whoever he is."

Well, she had me going so that I just couldn't help myself. I went and told her the whole rest a the story 'bout how Clell and that other'n had beat up my partner, ole Zeb, and tuck all his money, and how I come to find out that them Hookses was after me anyhow, and I had kilt one of them but ole Clell had got away, and that was how come me to be after him in the first place. I told her how I come to be a riding with ole Rice too, and how I meant to kill ole Clell but ole Rice meant to take him alive back to Texas.

"Kid," she said, "are you a gunfighter?"

"I reckon I am," I said. "I been trying to tell myself that I ain't. I been trying to just say that I can handle myself pretty good, you know, and that I got myself into a couple a scrapes is all. But trying to be truthful with you here, I guess I got to say that I am a gunfighter. 'Course, I don't hire out to kill no one. I ain't that kind. My jobs has all been working on cattle ranches."

"I'm glad you told me all that," she said.

We hung around there for a spell, and then that outlaw up ahead fin'ly put out his fire and mounted up. We got back on·our horses and follered after him real casual like. I knowed that just heading back west the way we was going, the country wasn't going to change much till we come to that mining town back there, so I was studying on just how I might deal with that feller up there. I hadn't come up with nothing when I seed that he was stopped. He weren't going nowhere.

We was moving slow and easy, so I just kept us a-going at that same pace. As we got closer, I seed that his horse had come up lame on him. That was how come him to stop like that. He pulled the saddlebags off a the animal and throwed them over his own shoulder, tuck a rifle in his hand and started to walk. He just left that lame horse to take keer of itself. I knowed that whoever he was, he weren't much of a man. I figgered that I'd take keer of the horse whenever I come up on it.

Well, the outlaw never seed us behind him, so when I come up on that horse and checked him out and found out there wasn't no hope for him, and I went on ahead and shot and kilt the poor thing, that outlaw looked around. I didn't notice him but Sally did.

"He heard your shot," she said. "He's looking back at us."

"He's got eyes," I said. "That's what they're for. Let him look."

I was plumb mad at the son of a bitch for leaving a horse like that. I was sure hoping that it would turn out to be ole Clell, 'cause now I had me one more reason to kill him.

I mounted back up and we started in riding again. For a while, the outlaw kept a walking. Ever' now and then he'd turn around and look at us a coming after him. Then he just stopped. He was a waiting for us to catch up to him. I figgered he only had two things he could do. One was he could ask us to give him a hand. Let him ride double with one of us till we come to someplace where he could get hisself another horse. But the other was the most likely. Likely he'd just look for a chance to kill me and steal my horse and whatever else I had that he might find useful. I figgered he'd think that Sally would be some useful to him. I had to start thinking clear, and I wondered what ole Rice might come up with for such a situation.

When we come within rifle range, I begun to feel somewhat nervous. It seemed to me the easiest thing he could do was to try to pick me off before I come any closer. I kept a moving slow right towards him, but I was ever' minute expecting him to raise that rifle to his shoulder. He never. I glanced over at Sally.

"That man's a bad outlaw," I said. "He's liable to try something to get at least one of our horses. If he takes a shot at me or something like that, you ride

like hell off in some other direction. Even if he was
to hit me, it would take him some time to catch up
to ole horse here."

"All right," she said.

Anyhow, whoever it was up there, he weren't stupid. He guessed what was a running through my
mind, 'cause he dropped his saddlebags on the
ground. Then he laid his rifle on top of them and
walked well off to one side. He was a trying to tell
me that he weren't meaning to be no threat to us. I
looked over at Sally again.

"Remember what I said," I told her. Then I said,
"Come on," and we rid on at a gallop till we come
in close to him. We was close enough for a good man
with a six-gun to hit his mark, and I figgered that he
weren't meaning to start nothing, when of a sudden,
he made a dive for where he had dropped his rifle.
That sure enough caught me by surprise.

"Ride," I yelled to Sally, and she turned her horse
sharp and headed south. At the same time I throwed
myself off the left side of ole horse, but I hung on. I
was hiding behind ole horse, so the bastard couldn't
shoot me, but then I couldn't shoot neither. My right
hand was a holding tight to the saddle horn. I done a
total turnaround with ole horse and headed back east
to get outa his rifle range. He fired off a shot, and I
heared it whistle over my head. He could easy have
tuck ole horse down, but I figgered he wanted ole
horse alive and healthy, and he wouldn't do that.

I got out a ways and turned around again, and this
time I stopped ole horse and slid on down to the
ground. I pulled out my own Winchester and laid it
across the saddle, taking keerful aim at that outlaw. I
knowed already that he weren't Clell. He fired again,

and ole horse jumped a little, but he settled down again. I knowed now that I had a big advantage over my foe, for I had a clear shot at him, and he didn't have no clear shot at me, not without taking a chance on killing ole horse, what he was wanting awful bad.

I sighted in on him real good, and I pulled the trigger. He jumped and hollered, and I knowed that I had hit my mark. When he come down from his jump, he fell on over on his back, and he didn't move. I knowed that he might be a playing possum trying to trick me into riding in close again, so I tuck me another keerful aim. I shot him in the leg while he was just a laying there, and he kicked and yelped. He got up onto his feet again and commenced to hopping around and howling, and I tuck one more shot and laid him down again. This time I was pretty sure he was done for.

I mounted ole horse and rid back over there. The outlaw never moved. I was holding my rifle ready though, just in case. I tuck ole horse so close that he would a stepped on the man if he had tuck one more step, and the man never moved. I was looking right down on him. He looked dead enough to me, and besides, he weren't in no position to grab up a gun real quick. I got down and checked him real close and for sure. I had kilt him all right. As I was a straightening up, Sally come riding back in.

"You got him," she said.

"Yeah," I said. "I did. He shot first though."

"I know he did," she said. "Is it the man you were after?"

"No," I said. "He ain't."

"Well," she said, "what now?"

"I'm thinking on that," I said. "I don't rightly

know. Ole Rice said the first one of us to get our man should ride across to pick up the other'n's trail. But right now I'm thinking that these guys is mostly worth money, so I can't just leave this one here and still collect no reward. If we go looking for Rice, this corpus ain't likely to keep. It's getting cold up in them mountains, but I ain't felt no sign of cool down here on these flats."

I was thinking on something else too. I was thinking that since my man weren't ole Clell, then Rice had to be on Clell's trail. Could be he had him already. That would mean that I was going to have to fight ole Rice over him after all. But Sally brung me back to my more pressing problem concerning the corpus what was just a laying there.

"Where do you need to take him?" she asked me.

"The closest town with a law office in it," I said. "It's too far to them mining towns out west."

She never said nothing right then, and I knowed what she was a thinking. The closest place would be right back where she had just run away from, and I knowed she didn't want to ride back there.

"Let's make us a camp and sleep on it," I said.

Chapter Fifteen

Ole Sally didn't cotton too much to sleeping real close to that there corpus what I had just kilt, so I moved us off a little and made us a camp for the night. I kind a thought that we might have us a little fun that night, but she weren't in a mood for it. I guess the killing done that too. Just then I was some sorry that I had kilt the feller. I thought, if I was to have to kill the son of a bitch, why the hell couldn't it at least a been ole Clell. Damn it all to hell. There I was in the middle a nowhere with a good-looking whore, and I had gone and messed up the chances just by killing a damned ole outlaw. It just didn't seem fair.

Under the circumstances, it tuck me a while to get off to sleep, but I fin'ly done it all right. I musta been sleeping like a rock too, 'cause Sally woke me up by shaking on me and whispering in my ear. "Kid," she said, "someone's coming." I shuck my head some and rubbed my eyes and started in to sit up.

"What?" I said.

She shooshed me by clapping her hand over my mouth.

"I said someone's coming. Listen," she said.

I heared her plain that second time, and what she

181

said kinda cleared my head. I tuck a grip on my Colt and sat on up and listened. Sure enough, I could hear a horse a coming. In another minute I could tell it was two horses. The fire was most nearly out, but even so I told her, "Move away from the fire," and I got up and follered her away from it. I wanted to make sure that whoever it was riding up wouldn't see us in the light, what little there was of it. A few feet out into the dark, I put Sally behind me and waited. Two horses with riders come up into the camp. I thumbed back the hammer a my Colt.

"Just set easy there," I said.

"Kid?" come a voice. "Is that you?"

"Rice?" I said. "Who's that with you?" and I come on up to the fire. Getting closer like that, I could see that he had a prisoner a setting on that other horse, but it weren't Clell, and the man I had kilt weren't Clell either.

"It's the outlaw I trailed," Rice said. "He ain't Clell Hook though."

I tossed some more fuel on the fire to build it up some and get a better look at the bastard Rice had brung in alive, and I was never so surprised in my whole young life as I was when I recognized him. I reckon he was about as dumbfounded as me, but the both of us had enough horse sense about us to keep our mouth shut. But I'll be dipped in shit if it weren't my own ole paw a setting on that horse with his hands tied.

I couldn't think a nothing to say. I never was so speechless in the whole history a my life. I realized right off though that I had myself a hell of a problem. If ole Rice knowed what he was a doing, and he usual did, then my ole paw was one a them outlaws, and what was worse, Rice had him captured. And I was pardnering with Rice. Well, likely you know already that I didn't have no overabundance a love for my paw, but still in all, the bare true fact a the matter was that he was my paw. I knowed that I couldn't just let Rice take him in to get tried and maybe hung up by his neck. He had give me a dime for candy and then after I had splitted ole Joe Pigg's skull, he had give me ten dollars and a old swaybacked horse. I guessed that I owed him something.

"What about the other one?" Rice asked me. "You still on his trail?"

"I ain't trailing him no more," I said.

"He killed him," Sally said.

"Was it—"

"It weren't Clell," I said. "It was some other feller, and he didn't give me no choice. He started in blasting away at me, so I kilt him. That's all. He's over yonder a ways. I been trying to figger out what to do about the reward. Back to Lowry's the closest place, but I kinda hate to take little ole Sally back there after she run off from that Alf what thinks he owns her."

"If we've got a body on our hands," Rice said, "we'd better get it turned in as quickly as possible. We'll go back to Lowry. Whoever this Alf is, miss, he won't bother you with me and the Kid alongside you. You game for it?"

"I guess," she said.

"Or, better yet," he said, "when we get close, you and the Kid can stay outside of town, if you like. I'll take the body in and claim the reward, if there is one. Would that be better?"

"Yes," she said. "I think so."

"It sounds okay to me," I said. "Then we'll head back for Lowry in the morning?"

"Early," said Rice. He walked over to where Paw was still a setting on top a that horse, and he reached up and tuck hold of him. "Come on down," he said. I couldn't tell if he pulled ole Paw down or helped him down, but anyhow Paw was soon standing on the ground. I rolled him out a blanket close to the fire.

"You can sleep there," I said.

He give me a look right in the eyes. "Thanks," he said, and he stretched on out on the ground. His hands were still tied behind his back. I turned away from him right quick.

"Rice," I said, "if you trailed after this feller here, and I trailed after that other one, the one I shot, where the hell is ole Clell?"

"That's what I'd like to know," Rice said. "He gave us the slip somehow. I thought we had all but two of them, but we got those two and neither one is Clell."

I turned back to ole Paw where he was laying. "How about it, mister," I said. "Where'd ole Clell go?"

"I don't even know no Clell," Paw said, "and I don't know how come this ranny to track me down and hogtie me like this."

"We was chasing bank robbers," I said.

"Well," said Paw, "I never robbed no bank."

"No," I said. "None of them did. We opened up on them first before they had a chance to go in on it."

"Well," he said, "I don't know nothing about it. Nothing at all. And I don't know no Clell. Why don't you just leave me get some sleep?"

I didn't see no advantage in pursuing the question with ole Paw. He was always stubborn as hell, and being all trussed up like that didn't seem to make no difference. Likely he didn't keer none for me talking to him like that neither. But we was both playing like, so I really didn't have no idea how to take the way he was acting. I decided to just let it go.

"I couldn't get anything out of him either," Rice said. "Not even his name. When we go back into Lowry, I'll just turn him in there. Let them worry about him."

Well, we all bedded down shortly after that, and what with Paw and Rice both right there with us, I decided that it was all for the best that me and Sally hadn't got nekkid together after all. I was wide awake though. I was thinking about ole Paw. I was wondering what would become of him, him being caught by ole Rice for one a the bank robbers. I figgered too that he likely was one of them, 'cause I never had knowed where it was that he went off to ever' now and then, and he would come back home with groceries and whiskey and maybe even a little cash money.

I sure didn't want to see him hang or even know that it was fixing to happen. I wished that I had never saw him again in my whole life, 'cause if I had never saw him, it wouldn't a been no worry a mine what might a become of him. Damn it, I was sure mad at him for having rid along with ole Clell on this here bank job, what with me riding along with ole Rice and tracking Clell. It was all a real unfortunate mess what he had got me into. I told myself that I would never forgive him for all that as long as I might live even if I was to live to be a hunnerd, which, a course, weren't likely. Not the way I was a going.

Anyhow, eventual I drifted off to sleep again, and this time I slept till morning. When I come awake ole Rice was already cooking up our breakfast and done had the coffee made. We said our good-mornings all around, and me and ole Paw was a giving each other strange looks. Rice never said nothing. If he noticed, he likely just thought that I was giving ole Paw the eye 'cause he wouldn't tell us about Clell. I poured Paw a cup a coffee and give it to him. I had to let loose his hands first. He thanked me, and then I give one to Sally, got one for myself and set down beside her.

"I'm sorry 'bout having to go back to Lowry," I said.

"Oh," she said, "it'll be all right. At least I'm away from Alf."

"Yeah," I said.

Pretty soon ole Rice dished us all out some grub and we et. Then we cleaned up our camp and packed up our horses. We loaded the corpus onto Sally's horse, and she clumb on behind me and we headed back toward Lowry. Nothing much of any interest happened along the way. I guess there was some little small talk, but that's about all. The only one a them outlaws left out there was just ole Clell, and he weren't likely to come on us. Prob'ly he was doing his best to avoid us. Maybe even heading for Mexico. Anyhow, it was near dark when we come on Lowry again, and we stayed out a town and made us another camp.

"I think I'll ride on in with our two outlaws," Rice said.

"Just take in the corpus," I said. "I don't think this one here's worth nothing nohow."

"You don't know that till you search through the dodgers," Rice said.

"Well," I said, "you keep all the money for the dead one. Leave this one here with me. You can go on ahead and search through them dodgers and look for him and let me know if you found his picture in there when you get back. Just leave him here for now. Okay?"

Rice give me a real curious look then.

"How come?" he said. "What do you care about this one?"

"I don't keer nothing about him," I said, lying like hell, "but I want to talk to him some more. See if I can find out something about ole Clell. That's all."

Rice scratched his head the way he done sometimes, and then he said, "All right. Maybe you can get something out of him, but I doubt it."

He headed on into town a leading the horse what was toting the corpus on it, and I'll tell you what, it was none too soon to be getting shuck a that. Anyhow, whenever he was outa earshot, Paw turned on me.

"I never thought to see you again, boy," he said.

"Well, I sure never thought to see you," I said. "Special not out thisaway."

"You turned into some kinda gunfighter?" he said.

"I can handle myself all right," I said.

"I'll be damned," he said. "I can't hardly believe it. Me and your maw, we wondered from time to time if you was even still alive. And traveling with a lawman too."

"Me and him was just after the same feller," I said. "That's all."

"Clell?" Paw asked me.

"Yeah," I said. "Ole Clell. Only thing is, he wants to take him in alive, and I mean to kill him."

"How come?" Paw asked me.

I told him about how Clell and them wanted to kill me 'cause I had kilt one a their kin, and I told him about how Clell and that other Hook had beat up my ole pardner and robbed him, and I even told him about Clell kicking that kid's dog.

"Get my chaw outa my pocket, will you?" Paw said. His hands was tied up again by then. I pulled out his chaw for him and held it up for him to bite, and he bit off a chunk, and I tucked the rest back into his pocket. He chawed on it a bit and spit. "You never will get over that damn Farty," he said. "I knowed you wouldn't."

"Farty ain't got nothing to do with this," I said, but actual, I reckoned that Paw was at least some right about that.

"So you got to get Clell, do you?" he said.

"I sure as hell do got to," I said.

"Well," Paw said, "ole Clell, he never left town when the rest of us did. As we was hightailing out a town, I seed him duck in a doorway."

"You mean he's right there in Lowry?" I said.

"Naw," said Paw. "Not likely. All I said is that he never rid outa town with the rest of us. Likely he waited a spell and then slipped out in another direction. That's what's likely."

"Well, where would he go?" I asked.

"If I was to have to guess," Paw said, "I'd guess

that he headed back for his hidey-hole in the mountain."

"Cabin up in the mountains?" I said.

"Yeah," Paw said. "How'd you know that?"

"Never mind how I know," I said, "but I do know."

Paw spit again. "You going to let that man take me in to hang?" he said.

"You said you never robbed no bank," I said.

"Well, now," he said, "you reckon them fine folks is going to believe anything I tell them?"

I looked at him, and I figgered I sure as hell wouldn't, but I never answered him. Just about then, ole Sally poked herself into the talking anyhow and kinda saved me from having to answer that question. She had been a watching and a listening all this time, but from some little distance, and I had noticed earlier that she was real curious.

"You two know each other?" she said.

I sure didn't want to give her no details.

"We knowed each other a while back," I said. "We ain't seed each other for some years though."

Then I seed ole Rice a coming back, and he was by his lonesome. I give Sally a look. "Don't say nothing to Rice," I told her.

"All right," she said.

Then I seed her eyes open kinda wide and her hand go up to her mouth, and I could see that she was a looking in the direction a town, and so I looked too. There was a rider coming along behind ole Rice.

"What's wrong?" I asked her.

"It's Alf," she said. "He's coming after me."

"Just you take it easy," I said. "He ain't a going to get you."

Rice come on in then, and before his feet hit the

ground, I said, "You bring Alf along, did you?"

"Alf?" he said. He looked around and seed Alf a coming. "No," he said. "I didn't bring him."

Me and Rice stood a facing Alf and waited for him to ride on in. When he come close, I seed that he was a slick one. He had the look of a gambling man and maybe a smooth gun hand too. He pulled up his horse, and he looked right past me and Rice, right at Sally.

"Come on," he said.

"No," Sally said. "I ain't going back with you."

"You got no choice," Alf said. "You owe me. Now come on before I get mad."

"You heard the lady," said Rice. "She's not going back with you."

"You stay the hell out of this," said Alf. "That's my property."

"She ain't your property," I said. "This here's a free country, ain't it? And Rice, you just do like old Alfie says. You stay outa this. It was me what tuck Sally outa town. This here is between me and Alfie. You going to set your horse and fight, Alfie, or you wanta get down?"

Ole Alfie smiled at me, and he swung down offa his horse real casual. Then he kinda flipped back the long tails a his black coat. He was wearing a six-gun on each hip. I wondered which one he'd go for, or if he'd go for the both of them. I set myself for action.

"You sure you want a part of this, boy?" Alf said. "She's just a whore, but she's my whore. She ain't worth you getting yourself killed over."

"It might not be me what gets kilt," I said. "You don't know who you're a facing, do you?"

He smiled again, like as if he didn't really give a shit, but he said, "Who are you, boy?"

"They call me Kid Parmlee," I said. "They say I'm a regular Billy the Kid."

Alf reached fast for his left-hand gun, but my Colt was out faster, and when it blasted, a hole opened up in Alfie's chest. He never even pulled the trigger. He looked real surprised. He stared right at me for a few seconds, and then he looked down at that hole in his chest and the blood a running down his white shirt-front. He wobbled a bit. He looked up at me again, and then he just pitched forward and landed hard on his face in the dirt. Rice run over and knelt down beside him and checked him. Then he looked up at me.

"He's dead," he said.

Sally went to crying. I holstered my Colt and walked over to her and put a arm around her shoulders and kinda hugged her to me. "It's all right now," I said. "It's all over. He won't never bother you no more."

"I know," she said. "I know."

She kinda calmed herself down a bit then, and in just a little bit I turned a loose of her.

"That was slicker'n owl shit," ole Paw said. "I ain't seed shooting like that in a long time. Maybe never. I wouldn't a believed it."

"I guess I'll have to take this one back into town now," Rice said.

"I guess," I said.

We loaded ole Alf up on his own horse, and Rice mounted up and led it on into town. It was just me and Paw and Sally again.

"Where'd you learn to shoot like that, boy?" Paw asked me.

"Around," I said.

"I bet you could take that Texas lawman," he said. "I bet you could take him quicker'n a blink."

Chapter Sixteen

I spent a while that night a wondering if ole Paw was right about that, but then I tried to give off thinking about it at all. I didn't like it, 'cause I knowed I wouldn't like the way a shoot-out between me and Rice was to come out no matter whichaway it come. Fin'ly I just went ahead and went to bed, but I never went to sleep. I waited till I heared a horse a coming. I let it get close enough, and then I said, "That you, Rice?"

"It's me," he said, and I could tell that it was, so I settled on down to sleep. We never talked till morning. As usual, he was up first and a cooking. After we had all et, me and Rice got off by ourselfs so we could talk free.

"What about that Alf?" I said.

"It's all right," he said. "I told them what happened. Actually, they seemed a bit relieved. Apparently he was some kind of local bully."

"He got friends?" I asked.

"No one special that I could tell," Rice said.

I was thinking about how might near ever'one I had kilt had friends and cousins and brothers and such that come a looking for me. Anyhow, the Alfie business seemed to be more or less settled, and so I fig-

gered I should tell ole Rice what I had found out
about Clell from ole Paw. I told him how that outlaw
he had captured told me that ole Clell had never left
town whenever we chased them others out. I told him
that the outlaw had figgered that Clell had waited till
we was out a town and then lit out, most likely for
his hideout back yonder west in them mountains. I
said that I figgered it was the same one that we had
camped down beneath it that time. He hummed a bit
and rubbed his chin, and then he pushed his hat back
and scratched his head.

"There's something wrong with that story," he
said.

"What's that?" I asked him.

"We followed seven outlaws out here," Rice said.
"We've accounted for seven, and Clell ain't one of
them. Yet this one here tells you that Clell stayed in
town and then rode off."

I hadn't thought a that. "Well," I said, "could be
we counted wrong."

"I don't think so," Rice said.

"They was seven to start with all right," I said.
"Three was kilt in the street. I kilt one out here. You
kilt that first one we follered. One group a citizens
kilt another one out on the trail, and you got this one
here captured."

"That's seven," Rice said.

"It is?" I said.

"It is," he said.

"Well, I'll be," I said. "What're you going to do
now?"

"I guess I'll head back west," he said. "How about
you?"

"Me too," I said. "I ain't give up on ole Clell. You

oughta know that much about me by now."

"I reckon I do," he said. "All right then. What are your intentions regarding those two over there?"

"Oh," I said, "you mean ole Sally there and that there outlaw?"

"That was my meaning," he said.

"Well," I said, "I ain't got intentions about ole Sally. She wanted to get away from Alf. I helped her. That's all. Now that Alf ain't no problem, she can go back down into Lowry if she wants to or if she wants to go on out west with us and find her a place out there, then she can ride along, I guess. I ain't talked to her about that none since I shot that ole Alf."

"All right," Rice said. "We'll talk to her. What about the other one?"

I tried real fast to figger a reason for keeping ole Paw alive and out a jail without telling Rice that he was my paw.

"I kinda figgered," I said, talking kinda slow so I could think more about it while I was a talking, "I kinda figgered that maybe we had ought to take him along with us till we catch up with ole Clell. He might be some kinda help along the way."

"Well," Rice said, a scratching his head again, "you did get more information out of him than I did. Even though some of it doesn't seem to make sense. All right. We'll take him along."

We talked to Sally after that, and she said that she didn't have no desire to go back down into Lowry. It wasn't nothing there for her but just only bad memories. She said that she had much ruther go on west with us, and whenever we found her a good enough town, why, she'd just drop off there and wouldn't be no more worry to us. We agreed to carry her along. Then we packed on up and headed on out.

There was lots a tracks along the way, but a course, we didn't have no way a telling if any of them belonged to the horse ole Clell was a riding. It was long about noon, I guess, when ole Paw rid up alongside me and spoke to me in a kinda low and secret like voice.

"You see them prints there with the crook in the right forefront shoe?" he said.

I squinted down at the tracks in the road, and then I seen a print kinda like what he said.

"I see it," I said.

"That's ole Clell's horse," he said.

"Then we're on his trail all right," I said.

Paw just kinda nodded. He knowed that I wanted to kill Clell and that Clell wanted to kill me. He didn't like talking to no law, but then I weren't no law, and I was his own son. I reckon after all that did mean something to the old son of a bitch. I didn't rush on up to ole Rice to tell him what Paw had said to me, but whenever we stopped a little later to eat, and whenever Paw went out to the bushes to relieve hisself, I set down alongside a Rice.

"We're on ole Clell's trail all right," I said.

"Oh?" he said. "How do you know that?"

"Just trust me, Rice," I said. "We're on his trail."

We didn't talk no more about it after that, but around mid-afternoon, Rice give me a look and looked down at the tracks on the road, and I tuck me a look down at them and just nodded my head. We rid on. We didn't never see no sign a anyone being ahead of us on the road, but then I figgered that 'cause we had gone on back to Lowry, ole Clell had got a real good lead on us. Our best hope a catching him was if Paw was right about where he was a heading.

We made another camp that night, and we had et our evening meal so Paw was untied. I knowed that ole Rice would tie him up again before we all bedded down, but for the time being, Rice had found him a chance to set with ole Sally, and they was a talking real quiet like off a little ways from us. Paw was standing by the fire, and I was just a setting there on my saddle a sipping some coffee.

"You could take that lawman right now," Paw said.

"Never mind about that," I said.

"What's the matter, boy?" he said. "You don't want to save your own ole paw from a hanging?"

"It ain't that," I said.

"Well, what then?" he said. "Tell me. I just don't see no other way, boy."

"There'll be another way," I said. "I'm a thinking on it."

"Come here," said Paw.

I never even thought about it. I just stood up and walked over to him. Doing what your ole paw tells you to do without even thinking on it first is a hard habit to get out of, even if you ain't seed him for a spell. He was still taller'n me and a hell of a lot tougher looking.

"You don't want to do it," he said, "then give me your pistol. I'll do it myself."

"I ain't giving you no gun," I said.

Well, he smacked me a good one right across the chops. He was still my ole paw all right. I flew backwards and landed hard on my ass. I was some surprised by that, I can tell you, and besides that, it smarted some. I wiped at my face with the sleeve a my left arm, and at the same time, I whupped out my

Colt with my right hand. Paw was a coming at me, but whenever I thumbed back that hammer and he found hisself a looking down the barrel and that Colt cocked, he stopped all right.

"You wouldn't shoot your ole paw," he said.

"You ever hit me again," I said, "you ever try to get my gun, you'll damn sure find out. Now set down."

Paw set on his saddle, and he commenced to laughing. 'Bout then Rice come a walking over.

"What's going on here?" he said.

"Ain't nothing wrong here," I said.

He looked at the gun still in my hand. I eased down the hammer and holstered the Colt.

"It's all right," I said.

He give Paw a look, and then he walked back over to where he had left ole Sally. Paw's laughing had toned down to a kind a chuckle.

"What's so damn funny?" I asked him.

"I guess you've growed up, boy," he said. "I reckon I won't be a slapping you down no more. I done it a bunch a times, but I guess I won't be doing it no more. I tell you, son, I ain't never seed a faster gun than what you got. Why, you're a—"

"I know," I said. "I'm a regular Billy the Kid."

"That's it," he said. "That's exactly what I was a thinking. How'd you know?"

"It's been said before," I told him.

I went and poured myself a cup a coffee. Then I looked over at Paw. "You want some?" I asked him.

"Naw," he said.

I tuck me a sip, and it was plenty hot. I like to a blistered my top lip. I didn't let on though. I said, "How's Maw?"

"Aw, she's all right," he said. "She ain't changed none."

"You got any money?" I said.

"Hell, no," he said. "I'm flat-ass broke. That's how come I—Well, I ain't got none."

"I got me a share of that reward money," I said. "I'll give you some to take home for her whenever it's time for you to go."

"You meaning to get me out a this?" he said.

"You heared me," I told him. "Now go on to bed."

He kinda smiled at me, and he said, "Okay."

He went on to bed, and I did too. I don't know what Rice and Sally done.

It was the middle a the next morning. The dry land had got kinda rugged what with cracks in the ground and gullies and dry washes and such. The trail was kinda narrow, and Rice was riding in front. Sally was right behind him, then Paw, and I was taking up the rear. Of a sudden, I heared a shot ring out from somewhere up front.

"Take cover," Rice hollered.

I rid my ole horse down into a ravine off the side a the road, and ever'one else done the same thing. We all jumped off our horses. Paw and Sally hunkered down low, and me and ole Rice pulled our guns out and peeped up over the edge of the ravine.

"What is it?" I yelled out to him.

"Bandits, I guess," he called back. "Come on up here."

I made my way past Paw and Sally and three horses in that narrow gully and come up beside ole Rice.

"Over there," he said.

I looked and seed a few heads peeking out from behind some rises in the rough ground.

"How many?" I said.

"I'd say eight," Rice said.

"What the hell do they want?" I asked him.

"They didn't say," he said, and I felt kinda foolish. He still could do that to me. Just then Paw come a sidling up to me.

"You say eight?" he said. "There's only two a you. Give me a gun, and I'll help fight them off."

"Just keep your head down," Rice told him.

"Give me a gun," Paw said. "We'll have us a fighting chance then."

I looked ole Rice in the eyeball.

"Hell," he said, "give him one."

"There's a Winchester back yonder on my horse," I told Paw. "Go get it."

"But don't shoot unless I shoot first," Rice said.

"I got you," Paw said, and still hunkered way down, he run back toward ole horse to get the gun. Pretty soon I seed him lay up over the edge a that ravine ready and waiting.

"Well," I said to Rice, "what the hell're we going to do now?"

He never answered me. Instead, he give out a yell to them owlhoots.

"Hey," he hollered. "You out there. What do you want with us?"

"We just want to talk is all," come the answer.

"You got a funny way of showing it," Rice yelled.

"That shot was a accident," the voice come back. "Let's talk."

"One of you come out and walk this way," Rice said. "I'll meet you."

"All right," the voice answered. "No shooting now."

"No shooting," said Rice.

Pretty soon we seed this feller come up outa the ground and start walking toward where we was at. He weren't holding no gun in his hands. Rice let him walk pretty close before he started up outa the ravine. I grabbed hold a his arm, and he looked at me.

"They can pick you off if you go up there," I said.

"If they do," he said, "you kill that one."

"I'll do her," I said, and I let him go, and he crawled on outa there. Then he walked on a few steps to meet up with that feller. Whenever they stopped, they was close enough for me to hear what they was a saying. Then I knowed how come ole Rice to wait so long before he clumb out over the edge, and I thought to myself that was some clever a him to do thataway. You see, they was standing a whole lot closer to us than they was to that bushwhacker's pals.

"Howdy," said the stranger.

"What do you want with us?" Rice said.

"We don't mean no harm," the stranger said. "We thought you might want to sell some horses."

"We've just got enough for ourselves," said Rice.

"Any extry grub?" the stranger said.

"Sorry," said Rice. "We travel light."

"Maybe you'd like to sell us that little gal you got with you," the ugly feller said.

"Why don't you and your friends just mount up and ride on out of here before someone gets hurt?" said Rice. "We don't have anything to talk about."

"I'll tell you something, mister smart talker," said the stranger. "We watched you coming. There's four of you and eight of us. And one of you is a gal. You give us the gal and her horse, and we'll let the rest of you go. Otherwise, we'll just kill the three of you men and take her anyway."

"You got one thing wrong, mister," Rice said.

"What's that?" the other guy said.

"We'll only have seven to fight," said Rice.

"How's that?" the man said.

Rice raised an arm, motioning back toward the way the man had come from.

"You see the distance you had to walk to get over here?" he said. "You'll never make it back."

The man's eyes opened up real wide, and his mouth kinda dropped open too. He stammered.

"You mean—You mean—"

He turned and started in to run. At the same time ole Rice turned and run a couple a steps and then tuck a dive back into our hole.

"Kill him," he yelled.

I kinda hesitated. I hadn't never shot no one in the back before. Then I heared the shot, and I knowed that it was my ole Winchester. Paw had did it. The running man kinda jerked, but he kept a running. He run a few more steps, but he looked kinda like a rag doll a running, with his arms a flailing around loose and his head a bobbing, and then he kinda pitched forward and plowed headfirst into the ground. He was dead enough. Paw had got him good.

Then the bullets come a flying hot and heavy, and all of us scrunched ourselfs down till the shooting slowed. After a while, I peeked out, and so did Rice. I seed one a them bastards out there, but it was too long a shot for just my Colt.

"Paw," I said.

"I see him," said Paw, and just then he shot, and

I could see the blood fly off from that feller's head when the bullet hit him. Paw always had been good with a rifle. I knowed that. Why, he just only tuck one bullet out with him whenever he went to hunt, and he always brung something back for supper. That was the way he had taught me. But growing up the way I done, I had never had no pistol in my hand, and that's how come me to have to be taught to gun-fight by ole Tex back then at the Boxwood.

"Six to go," Paw said.

"Kid," Rice said to me, "I think that if you were to make your way down the ravine and sneak out down there, you could cross over and get behind them. You think you could do that?"

"I bet I could," I said. I didn't wait for him to say nothing more. I just hunkered over real good and started running through that gully. Ever' now and then I heared a shot, but I couldn't rightly tell where they was coming from, my side or theirs. I kept on a running and a hoping that none a them owlhoots' shots was a hitting their marks. When I had gone on about as far as I thought I needed to go, I stopped, and I tuck myself a real keerful peek up over the edge. It sure enough looked like as if I had made it far enough, so real slow and easy, I clumb on out over the edge. No one tuck no shots at me, so I run across the way for a distance.

I had me a pretty good idea where them skunks was hid out, even though the lay a the land looked some different from my new view of it, so I moved cautious like along to get myself behind them. I thought I was getting close enough all right, but still whenever I seed that first hat right up ahead of me, it just stopped me real abrupt. I really weren't ready for it. I seed the hat, and it was just a little ways ahead. I sneaked on up a little more till I could see the whole feller, well, most of him anyhow. The trouble was, I didn't have no way a knowing if he was the last of them or the first of them or if he was somewheres in the middle. I decided I couldn't let that worry me none.

Now I just told you, I think, that I never shot no one in the back before, and the thought a doing it kinda bothered me somewhat, but I figgered that this was a different situation. These guys, after all, was a shooting at us and had ever' intention a killing us off, all 'cept poor ole Sally, and I knowed why they didn't mean to kill her. So I didn't figger this to be nothing at all like bushwhacking. This was smack in the middle of a fight, and I had just managed to get myself in a better position than what he was in. That's all. I leveled my Colt, and I cocked it, and I put a bullet smack between his wing bones.

Chapter Seventeen

Well, ole Paw had got two of them, and I had got one, so what started out to be eight was now just only five. The odds was getting to look a whole lot better. But I was in a pickle. Like I done said, I didn't have no idea where the rest of them was at, and I sure didn't want to lay myself open for one a them to shoot at me while I was a hunting them. Then I heared another shot, and I could tell that it come from across the way. It was shot from a six-gun too, so I knowed that ole Rice had shot it. I wondered why he had did that, trying to hit someone at that distance with just only a revolver, but I soon found out, for another shot answered it, and it come from the side I was on, and it come from my right side, so then I knowed where at least one a the road agents was at, more or less.

I slipped on down real easy like to right beside what was left a that feller I had plugged, and it kinda give me the willies. I'd kilt them before, but I'd never snuggled up to one of them like that. I tried to just ignore what it was I was a nesting with and look down the way to see could I spot me one a his pardners. I didn't see no one. I begun to sneak on down to the right. I had only just gone a few feet whenever

I heared someone on down thataway say, "Zack, is that you?"

I give my own voice a kinda harsh whisperlike sound, and I said, "Yeah."

Of a sudden a man come around a curve in that embankment with his gun out and ready for action, and he said, "No, it ain't." He pulled the trigger, and I throwed myself hard into the wall to my right just as his shot went off, and his bullet thudded into the dirt over to my left. Just as I hit that wall, I got off a shot. It tore into that bastard's right shoulder and crippled it. I didn't see no sense in leaving him like that, so I shot again and hit him square in the chest. He dropped dead with that one. There was four to go.

Then I heared some scrambling, and I figgered they was trying to get away, so I commenced to running on down that natural hallway, and I come around another curve, and there they was. They had scrambled outa their hole and was running for their horses. The problem for them was that they had exposed their backsides. I tuck one of them down with my Colt, and Paw got one from off across the way with my Winchester. They yelped and fell back down into the hole. The other two got mounted and tuck off fast. Paw got off another shot but missed, and I tuck out after them.

"Let them go," Rice shouted.

I looked back toward ole Rice and then looked after them outlaws again. Then I kinda shrugged and put my Colt away and started into walking back over where Rice and them was at. It was a long enough walk, but I sure weren't ready for what I seed whenever I got back over there. I looked down into that ravine, and there was Paw with my Winchester, and he had it pointed right at ole Rice.

"Paw," I said. "Put that thing down."

"I ain't going to jail," he said.

"Put it down," I said.

"Hell, boy," he said, "they might hang me."

"You don't put that rifle down," I said, "I'll kill you right here."

Paw kinda humphed, and he said, "You're fast, boy. Fast as I've ever seed, but I'm holding this here Winchester in my hands, and it's done got a shell in the chamber."

"You got it pointing at ole Rice there too," I said. "I can kill you fast as you can pull that trigger. He'll be dead, but so will you. What's the profit in that?"

Paw looked at me. Then he looked at Rice. He looked back at me, and then he said, "Shit," and he throwed that Winchester down. Rice run over and picked it up. Paw stuck his hands out in front of him.

"I reckon you'll be tying me up again," he said.

"No," Rice said. "There's no need. Just go get on your horse."

Paw done what Rice said, and I slid on down into the gully to get my own horse. Rice come over to me.

"Thanks, Kid," he said.

"It's all right," I said.

"Your paw, huh?" he said.

"I slipped up," I said. "I never meant to let you know that."

"I guess I know now why you didn't want me turning him in back there," said Rice.

"I know he ain't no good," I said, "but he's my paw. I never knowed he was with them bank robbers though, not till you come riding into my camp with him that night. I swear I never. I was just trailing ole Clell like I told you."

"I believe you, Kid," he said. "Let's get mounted and go gather up those stray outlaw horses."

We done that, and we burried them ones that we'd kilt. Not me nor Rice nor Paw recognized a one of them neither. The only thing we knowed about them was just only one first name, 'cause I'd heared that one call out to Zack. We went through their pockets and all and kept what little money they had on them. We also packed up their guns and ammunition. They didn't have nothing else on them that was worth keeping, so we burried the rest of it along with them. Then pretty soon we was a riding the trail again. This time we was leading a string a six riderless horses along behind us.

No one was saying much. I was thinking about Paw, and I was considering how I had come close to shooting him back there. I wondered what it would a felt like to have to kill my own paw, and I wondered if I had did the right thing by standing him off. What if he hadn't a backed down the way he done? I reckon I'd a shot him like I said I would. Then I'd a had to live with the certain fact that I had kilt my own paw. I didn't like to think about that, but one thing I was sure was glad of, I was sure glad that ole Paw had dropped that Winchester when he did.

But there was something else a bothering me, and it had to do with Paw too. That was what ole Rice had pointed out, that what Paw had told me about ole Clell just didn't add up. The only way it seemed that Paw could a been telling the truth was if there had been eight outlaws and not just only seven, but we had counted seven whenever we first seed them, and we had follered them, and we had counted the kilt and captured ones too. It sure seemed like as if ole Paw had been lying to me, and if he had lied about Clell, then whose crookedy hoof print was we a follering anyhow? And how come him to be lying to me?

The trail kinda widened up a little 'bout then, and Paw slowed his horse down so that I come up alongside of him. I wished that he had just kept on ahead a me the way he had been. I didn't want to talk to him just then. I didn't even really want to see him, 'cause I weren't for sure just how I was going to deal with him lying to me the way he done. We rid along quiet like that for a ways. Then he said, " 'Kid,' huh? Like Billy the Kid?"

"They just started in to calling me that," I said. "I let it go, 'cause I didn't want no one to be calling me by my right name. You and Maw give me a shitty name."

"How many men you kilt, Kid?" Paw said.

"I don't rightly know," I said. "I ain't kept count."

"You ain't kept count?" said Paw. "Why, hell, boy, you oughta be carving a notch on the handle a that there Colt each time you gun one down."

"I ain't no hired gun hand," I said, "and I don't want to be tuck for one."

"Well, it's a bit late for that, ain't it?" he said. "They say you're a regular Billy the Kid. It's done gone too far for you to be getting soft over that gunfighter label. You're a wearing it, boy. It's on you. You might just as well go on ahead and carve them notches."

"I think there was nine," I said.

"What?" he said.

"I think I kilt nine," I said. "That's counting that

first one. Joe Pigg. The one I hit with the ax handle. I think there was nine all told."

"Nine," he said. "By God." And he sure sounded proud. "Is that counting them just now? I mean back there on the road?"

"It's nine counting them," I said. "I think."

"By God," Paw said. "I reckon I'm sure enough lucky that I never pissed you off too much. There was twice now when you mighta kilt me. Nine men. By God."

When we camped later that evening, Paw come and set with me, and he tuck up that same conversation.

"Tell me who they was," he said. "Count them off."

"Well," I said, and I was a thinking real hard, "there was ole Joe Pigg what I hit in the head."

"Yeah, yeah," Paw said. "Go on."

"Then there was his cousin or something who come to the Boxwood a looking to get me for killing his kin," I said. "I kilt him, but he had friends with him, and they shot me up some. My friends kilt the rest of them."

"That's two," Paw said.

"Then I shot Harley Hook in Ass Grove," I said. "He was nekkid, but he had a gun in his hand."

"That's three," said Paw, "and that's why Clell and them was after you, huh? Well, go on."

"Well, there was this feller called Clinch," I said. "Him and his pal come on me and ole Zeb in the mountains, and I kilt the both of them."

"Who the hell is Zeb?" Paw said. "Never mind.

You can tell me later. Let's see. That's up to five now. Okay. Keep going."

"I kilt Asa Hook after him and Clell beat ole Zeb up," I said.

"Zeb again," said Paw. "All right. That makes six. Go on."

"Then I kilt one a them outlaws out on the trail," I said. "I thought it was Clell at first, but it weren't. I don't know his name."

"That's seven," Paw said. "Okay. Okay."

"I kilt Alfie," I said.

"Eight," said Paw. He was a getting real excited, and I couldn't help it. He had got me thataway too.

"And three a them bushwhackers back down the road," I said.

"Eleven," said Paw, and he like to of jumped up and down for joy. "That's eleven all told. Hell, boy, you said maybe nine, and it's eleven. By God, you are a regular Billy the Kid."

"There's more," I said. "Once I shot off a man's left ear."

Why, hell fire, me and ole Paw set up for the longest just a carrying on like that, and for the first time, I was a getting to where I felt real proud a being a gunfighter and a regular Billy the Kid. Old Paw, he never before in my whole life carried on like that over me, like he thought that I had did real good, you know? I mean, like he was real proud a me. Proud that I was his own kid. It felt good. When I was younger and still a living at home with him and Maw, even whenever I went out with just only one bullet and come home with a squirrel or something, he never bragged on me nor nothing, never told me I done good. So I was really having me a good time with ole

Paw. Hell, likely it was the only good time I ever had with him. I guess that ole Rice got kinda sick a listening to us, 'cause he interrupted us there in a bit.

"We all need to get some sleep," he said, but I believe that I could detect some kinda disgust in his voice. I didn't say nothing though. I just agreed with him, and I laid out blankets for me and Paw.

There ain't a whole lot for me to tell you about after that, not while we was just a riding along, and not till we had made it all the way back out to the mountains and was there where we had hid and watched Clell and them other outlaws ride down from that there cabin they had. We got out there and we set us up a camp right where we had been before. We was trying to decide our next move.

"That there's where I believe he went to," Paw said, a looking up that mountain.

"How do we get to it without him seeing us a coming?" I said. "That there's a awful narrow trail."

"There's another'n north a here," Paw said. "You go up thataway, and then you come back south kinda 'long a ridge there. You ride in right above the cabin."

"You can lead us up there," Rice said. "But we have to find a safe place for Sally first."

"No, Bill," she said. "I'll ride along with you. I'll be all right. After all, there's only one of him."

Rice give Paw a look.

"Is that right, Parmlee?" he said. "Is he going to be alone up there?"

Paw give a shrug.

"Damned if I know," he said. "I ain't for sure he's even up there. I told you I figgered he'd be going there."

"We follered his tracks the whole way," I said.

"Someone else could be up there with him," Paw said.

"Who's left?" said Rice. "Who could it be?"

"No one that I know," Paw said. "Ever'one I knowed rid out east with us. You know what come of all a them."

Ole Paw, he was just a trying to aggravate ole Rice, but he was a aggravating me too. Here he was a saying that there could be more up there, but he didn't know of no more who they could be. Well, we knowed that we wasn't going nowhere that night, and it looked like we wasn't going to have to take ole Sally nowhere special, not just yet, so we figgered on bedding down there at our campsite and going up the mountain in the morning. We all laid out our bedding. I was walking back over to ole horse for some reason or other, and I happened to walk close by ole Rice. He reached out and laid a hand on my shoulder. I stopped and give him a look.

"I thought you resented that gunfighter label," he said.

"What do you mean?" I said.

"You threatened to kill me once if I called you a regular Billy the Kid where anyone could hear me. Remember that?" he said. "You said you didn't want to be known as a gunfighter."

"Well," I said, "if I got that reputation, I guess I'll just have to live with it."

"Or die with it," Rice said.

"Yeah," I said. "That risk comes along with the reputation, I reckon. What the hell are you complaining about anyhow? You're a professional manhunter. You've kilt some, I reckon."

"I've had to kill a few," he said.

"So what's the difference?" I said.

"I'm not bragging on it," he said. "I'm not counting them up and talking about notching my gun handle."

I felt my face a getting hot and tears a building up in my eyes.

"I ain't cut no notches on my gun," I said. "And I ain't a fixing to neither."

I hurried away from him then for fear that my voice would crack and he'd be able to tell that I was about to cry. I sure didn't want that to happen.

In the morning, Paw showed us that other trail up the mountain, and we tuck it. It was slow going, but we made our way over to where we was looking down on that cabin, but we was suspicious right away, 'cause it was kinda cold up there, and there weren't no smoke coming out the chimbley. We slipped on down there kinda keerful anyhow, just in case, and Rice made Paw call out to Clell and then go in first. We went on in then, and sure enough there weren't no one there.

"He's been here though," Paw said.

"How do you know that?" Rice asked him.

Paw stuck his hand inside the stove.

"First off," he said, "there's been a fire in here not too long ago. And I seed them telltale horse prints outside." Then he picked up a dirty shirt and held it out for us to look at. "And this here is what he was a wearing when we all rid outa here."

"Then we'll just have to go back down and look for his trail again," Rice said.

"It's near about noon, ain't it?" Paw said. "Why

don't we eat right here indoors for a change?"

We built a fire in the stove and had us a good hot
meal there in the cabin. When we was all done, we
went on out and mounted up again and headed back
down. It didn't take too much studying down on the
trail to find that one peculiar hoof print, and when we
found it, we seed that ole Clell was a headed back
south again. We follered him. While we was riding
along, I was thinking how that ole Rice and Sally had
been cozying up to each other of late. At first I guess
it got my goat just a little, but I got to thinking about
it, and I come to decide that it was not a bad thing at
all.

I sure didn't have no plans that included her, and
if ole Rice didn't get sweet on her, why, we was just
going to have to dump her somewhere in Colorady in
some mining town or other. That didn't seem like
such a good idea. So I thought, maybe ole Rice will
get so sweet on her that he'll take her along on back
to Texas, and she'll be all right then. I never worried
too much about the life of whores, but then I never
met one before ole Sally what wanted to get away
from where she was at and what she was a doing for
a living.

Then too, we was headed back toward where ole
Red was at. I sure didn't want no women getting in
no fights over me. That got me to thinking about ole
Red again, and then about ole Zeb. I wondered how
he was a doing. I hoped that I had left him enough
money to take keer a all a his needs for all that time
I had been gone away from him. And then I had me
another thought. It just come on me sudden like, and
I didn't like it worth a damn. It was Clell what with
the help a his brother had beat up ole Zeb in the first

place. Why, hell, ole Zeb could put Clell in the jail-house. If Clell knowed that, then Clell might go after Zeb again.

"Hey, Rice," I said. "Can we hurry it up a little here?"

We rid on a little faster, but we couldn't really go much faster, 'cause it wouldn't a been good for the horses. A course I knowed that my own self, but I was sure a worrying over ole Zeb all of a sudden, and I wanted to get back to that town. Then whenever the day was done we had to stop and camp for the night. I couldn't hardly stand that, but there just weren't no way around it. I et what ole Rice cooked up, and I drunk a bunch a coffee. Then I rolled me a cigareet and smoked it. Ole Paw wondered what was eating at me.

"You started to ask me about ole Zeb a while back," I said.

"Yeah," he said. "You brung up that name a couple a times."

"Well," I said, "ole Zeb was my pardner for a spell. He tuck keer a me in the mountains, and he taught me a lot a things that I never knowed before. He was—"

I stopped short, 'cause I caught myself about to say that ole Zeb was like a paw to me, and I guess that he really was kinda like that, but it didn't seem like the right thing to say to ole Paw's face.

"He was a real pardner," I said. "Then Clell and that other Hook beat him up real bad and stole all his money, just 'cause he had beat them in a poker game."

"Ole Clell never could stand to lose," Paw said.

"Well, Zeb is laid up in that town yonder where

we're a headed, and Clell is headed there too," I said. "If Zeb was to spot Clell, why, he could tell the law and have ole Clell arrested."

"And if Clell was to spot Zeb first—" Paw said.

"Yeah," I said, "you got it."

Chapter Eighteen

We got on into that town just before dark, and for the first time I noticed as we was riding in that its name was Fosterville. I seed it on the sign just outside a town. Ole Rice said that he'd get us some rooms in the hotel, and I let him take keer of it, 'cause I was mighty all-fired anxious to check up on ole Zeb. I hurried right on over to the room I'd left him in, and damned if he weren't gone. That worried me some, but the lady what run the boarding house said that he was just fine.

"He got to feeling better," she said, "and I couldn't keep him down without I hit him over the head with a rolling pin or something. Likely you'll find him around town somewheres."

I asked her if I owed her any money, but she said that ole Zeb had paid for ever'thing, so I guess I left him with enough money. I thanked her kindly for all her help, and then I went out a hunting him. I couldn't help but think about how the last time I went a hunting ole Zeb in this here town, he was a laying out in a alley all beat up, and then I was thinking too that one a them bastards what done it was back in town. I tell you I was rushing around from place to place.

I found ole Red back in the same place where I

met her, and I run right up to her. She was a talking to a mining feller, and he kind a resented my intruding on the conversation like that. Red just leaned over close to his ear and whispered something, and he kind a lost the color in his face and excused hisself and faded away.

"Where's Zeb?" I asked her.

"Can't you even say howdy?" she said.

"Howdy, Red," I said. "Where's Zeb?"

"He's all right," she said. "He's upstairs with one of the gals just now, likely having himself a grand ole time."

"You sure?" I said.

"You want to go look in on him?" she said.

"Well, I just been worried about him is all," I said.

"You didn't flatter me none too much the way you come up to me, Kid," she said. "I guess you sure didn't miss me none. I bet you never even give me a second thought while you was away."

"I did too," I said. "Why, hell, I thought about you most ever'day."

"I'll bet," she said.

"Say," I said, "what was it you said to that mining feller while ago?"

"What?" she said.

"You know," I said, "that feller you was with what didn't want me messing in. What was it you said to him to make him go off like that?"

"Oh, that," she said. "I just told him that you was the one what killed Asa Hook in here not long ago, the one they call the regular Billy the Kid."

"Oh," I said, "that ole line again." But I had to admit to myself that it did come in handy sometimes. When I come into that there room, I meant to talk to ole Red and find out what I could about Zeb no matter what, but I was just as glad that I never had to kill that mining feller. "You real sure that ole Zeb is okay?" I said.

"I'm sure, Kid," she said. "I seen him just before he went upstairs."

"You ain't seed Clell Hook, have you?" I asked her.

"Clell? No," she said. "You didn't get him?"

I shuck my head. "Nope," I said. "He's got clean away, and we follered him right back here too. That's how come me to be so worried about Zeb."

"I ain't seen him in here," she said, "but I'll sure keep my eyes peeled."

"Well, maybe I had ought to look around town," I said. "See if maybe I can spot him."

"You said 'we'," she said.

"Huh?" I said.

"You said, 'we followed him back here.' Who's 'we'?" she asked me.

"Oh," I said. "Well, along the trail I kind a got myself hooked up with a feller from Texas what's after ole Clell too. Name a Bill Rice. A gal come along with us from out in Kansas, but that's a long story. Her name's Sally, and Sally and ole Rice are off somewheres getting us rooms." I never mentioned ole Paw.

"Is she with him or with you?" Red asked me.

I knowed right away what she was a getting at, and I told her, "She's with ole Rice." It weren't no lie neither. 'Course, I never bothered telling Red how it was me what had been in the sack with Sally and what stole her out a town and kilt a man for her. But then, she never asked me about none a them things neither. All she asked about was just who was ole Sally with at that time, and what I told her was the whole truth a the matter.

"Why go looking around for Clell?" she said. "If you stick close to Zeb, then if Clell comes around, you'll be there to look out for Zeb. What if you was to leave here to go looking and then he come right on in here, and Zeb just upstairs and not suspecting any trouble?"

"Say," I said, "you're right about that. Why don't I just get me a bottle and a glass and set right down here? Better yet, why don't I get me a bottle and two glasses, and you set with me?"

"I can go you one better than that, Kid," she said. "Why don't you get the bottle and the two glasses, and then why don't you and me go upstairs where we can be alone?"

"What if Clell comes in, and I don't know about it?" I said. "What if we got ourselfs occupied in one a them rooms, and then ole Zeb gets done and goes downstairs and there's Clell just a waiting for him?"

"I can take care of that," she said. "Come on."

She led me down to the far end a the bar where the barkeep was hanging out, and she motioned for him to lean over close to her.

"I'm going upstairs with the Kid," she said. "If ole Zeb Pike comes down, or if Clell Hook comes in, you get yourself upstairs fast and tell me. Don't worry about what you might be interrupting. Just do it."

He looked a little bit uncertain, and he give me a look, but I give him a real hard one back, and I said, "Do what she says."

"Okay," he said, and so then me and ole Red went on over to the stairs and started up. I noticed that mining feller giving me a kinda mean look, but he didn't worry me none. I never knowed a miner what was a gunfighter, and ole Red had done scared him off once just only by mentioning my name. We got up to the landing, and I couldn't help myself. I turned around to look down over all the crowd, but I didn't see no sign a Clell. I went on down the hall and into a room with Red.

I was sure glad that I had tuck a share a that reward money or else I wouldn't a been able to afford a tumble with ole Red, and by the time she had got me settled down about ole Zeb and Clell, I was ready for her. I had only just barely touched her, and I was already telling myself that a the three gals I had got me some experience with, she was the best one of all. 'Course, like I think I done told you, I most usual felt thataway about the one I was with at the time.

She closed the door, but she never locked it, so I made sure that my Colt was real handy on the back of a chair right there beside the bed. While I was a setting that up, Red was pouring us a couple a drinks. I was thinking about pulling off my boots, when I heared some footsteps out in the hallway. I grabbed my Colt and bolted for the door. Easy like I pulled it open just a tad and peeked out, and damned if it weren't ole Zeb and his gal a headed for the stairs. I jerked that door on open wide.

"Zeb," I said.

"Hey, Kid," he said. "It's you! I didn't think you was ever coming back."

"Come on in here," I said, "and let's have us a party."

Red come over to stand beside me then. "Howdy, Zeb," she said.

"Howdy, Red. Well, Kid," he said, "we was all done—you know—and we was going back down to get us a drink or two."

"We got a bottle right in here," I said. "Come on in."

The gal stood out in the hall. "I don't know if I should," she said.

"I'll tell you what you should," Red told her. "You run down and get two more glasses and then bring them back up here. Hurry it up."

The gal hustled off, and the other three of us went back into the room.

"Zeb," I said, "I'm sure tickled to see you up and around."

"Ah, hell," he said, "they can't keep me down. You oughta know that."

"Well, I guess, maybe I did," I said, "but I still didn't like seeing you laid up like that."

Red had done poured two glasses a whiskey, but we hadn't neither one touched them yet, so she handed one to ole Zeb, and he tuck to it like he hadn't had none for at least six weeks, but I sure knowed better than that. She give me the other glass, and just about then that other gal come back with two more glasses. In another minute, we was all setting there drinking and telling tales and having a good time. The other gal's name was Dolly. Me and Red was setting side by side on the bed, and ole Zeb, he was setting in a chair with Dolly on his knee. After a while, there come a lull in the conversation. I tuck advantage of it.

"Zeb," I said, "I got to tell you. I never caught up with ole Clell."

"Ah, that's all right," he said. "You tried. That's what counts."

"No," I said. "I mean, that ain't all. He's here."

"Here?" Zeb said. "Here where?"

"Somewhere in this here town," I said. "We follered him here."

Well, I had to go all through just who that "we" was again, and I done it again, still without making no mention a my ole paw.

"Hell," Zeb said, "leave him to that Texan. I don't give a shit. Unless he comes messing with us, then you can kill him. Otherwise, just leave the Texan have him."

I didn't say nothing to that, but I didn't much like Zeb's idea. I had swore that I was going to get Clell, and I meant to. Besides, I thought, ole Zeb seems to a forgot that Clell was out to kill me. Well, we partied in the room till we run out a whiskey, and then we decided to all of us go on downstairs and have some more drinks. We done that, and we was all a setting around a big round table when ole Rice come in and found me. I interduced him to ever'one and invited him to set with us and have a drink. He set down.

"I'll have one," he said, "but don't you think you're being a bit careless, what with Clell Hook likely being in town?"

"I can take keer a Clell anytime," I said.

"Have you ever tried shooting as drunk as you are right now?" he asked me.

"Why, he kin shoot the whiskers off a cat," Zeb said. "Don't you worry none about my pardner, Kid Parmlee here. He's a regular—"

"Billy the Kid," said Rice. "I know."

"Well," I said, and I could tell that I was talking

kinda blurry, "have you seed ole Clell around any-wheres?"

"No," said Rice, "I ain't seen him, but he's here somewhere. That's almost certain."

"Say," I said, "where's—"

"Sally's sleeping in her room," said Rice, "and . . . my prisoner is handcuffed to the bed in my room. They're okay."

"Prisoner?" said Red. She give me a look. "Is he a lawman?"

"Yeah," I said. "I guess I forgot to mention that. It's okay though. He's from Texas."

I was afraid that either me or ole Rice was going to have to give a long explanation a what he was a doing in Colorady, but just then ole Jim Chastain, the local sheriff, come a walking up. He stopped right across the table from me and give me a stare.

"Why, howdy, Sheriff," I said.

"Kid," he said, "I was hoping that I wouldn't see you here again."

"That ain't a nice thing to say to me," I told him. "I ain't done nothing wrong in this here town."

"Trouble follows you," he said.

"If it's trouble a follering him," Zeb said, "then by rights you oughta be locking up the trouble. Like that Clell Hook what beat me up and robbed me, him and his worthless and now dead brother."

"Clell Hook is the trouble," said Chastain. "He's in town, and he's got three more with him."

"Three more?" I said. "Ain't there no end to them?"

"Do you know who they are, Sheriff?" Rice asked.

"I know them," Chastain said. "But who the hell are you?"

"Bill Rice," Rice said, standing up to offer his hand to Chastain. Then he told the sheriff what it was he was a doing in Colorady, and how he couldn't do nothing official, but they sure as hell did want ole Clell back in Texas so they could hang him up to a tall tree. After he listened to all that talk, ole Chastain shuck Rice by the hand.

"I'll help you all I can," said Chastain, "but I have to be careful. Clell's not wanted here."

"I know that," said Rice. "Can you tell me who's with him?"

"Jody and Eddie Hook," Chastain said, "and Stanley Pigg."

"Another Pigg?" I said.

"I told you about those three," Rice said.

"I thought maybe they was some a the ones we done kilt," I said.

"No such luck," said Rice.

"What's all this?" Chastain said. "You killed some of them?"

He kinda looked around to see if there was anyone close enough to us to be a listening in on our conversation, and when he seed that there weren't, he turned back to face Rice again.

"Sit down," Rice said, "and I'll tell you all about it." So they set, and Rice told him the whole tale a how we follered them outlaws back east and helped stop them from robbing that bank but only ole Clell slipped by us somehow. When he was all did, I guess he figgered he'd earned hisself a second drink, 'cause he went and poured him one.

"So where the hell are they?" I asked.

"The condition you're in," Chastain said, "I wouldn't tell you if I knew."

"What the hell—"

"Shut up, Kid," Rice said.

"You got no business talking to me like that," I said.

"Neither one a you," said Zeb. "Why, Kid Parmlee'll take on the both a you."

Just then ole Red snuggled up to me and shoved a hand right down in my crotch. "Calm down, Kid," she said. "You're trying to fight the wrong people here."

Dolly tuck up the cue and begun to rubbing on ole Zeb, and the both of us stopped fussing right off, but I don't think that we was none too calmed down. It's just that we was getting wrought up over something entire different.

"I think I'd better take you all over to my hotel," said ole Rice.

"We don't need to go over there," I said. "We can just go upstairs."

"I got a prisoner over there," Rice said. "I might need your help."

I kinda puzzled over that, but even in my drunkenness, I figgered that maybe ole Rice was right somehow.

"All right," I said. "Let's go."

The gals was holding me and Zeb up and making us walk sorta straight, and Chastain and Rice was walking along behind us. We was about to go out the front swinging doors when the barkeep called out something.

"Hey, you," he said. "Red and Dolly. You can't leave here like that."

Chastain walked over to the bar and give the barkeep a look and said, "I can close this place down if I want to, can't I?"

The barkeep kinda gulped, and he said, "Yeah. I guess so."

"Then I reckon I can take those two gals out of here if I have a reason to," Chastain said.

"Yes sir," said the barkeep, and we all went on outside. Well, I couldn't rightly say just where we went to after that, but we wound up somewheres in a sure enough hotel and not just no whorehouse. Rice went and arranged for extry rooms, and he had them all right there together too. Me and ole Zeb and our two gals went into one room together. I guess ole Rice figgered that me and Zeb was too drunk to do anything anyhow, and besides that, even if we was to try, well, we had already did it earlier in the evening. What he didn't know was that maybe ole Zeb had did it, but I sure never. Anyhow, I couldn't by then, I was so drunked up.

I guess I slept all right, but my head sure did hurt like hell whenever I woke up the next morning, and the first thing I knowed, the gals was insisting that we all get baths before we do anything else. Me and Zeb was a wanting some grub real bad, and Paw, he was too. I heard him once from down the hall, but the gals insisted, and ole Rice and ole Chastain, they agreed with them. So we had to wait while baths was drawed and while ever'one what was in line before us got his or her bath, and they never even let us stay in the room and watch the gals a doing theirs neither. I was in a pretty foul mood by the time I was all shined up and smart.

Anyhow, we fin'ly got us all set down together in a restrunt downstairs in that there hotel, and we got

us some breakfasts ordered up. I think they had to
raid the henhouse for us too, and we all drunk up
enough coffee for a army. It made me feel some better, but my head was still a throbbing. I hoped that I
wouldn't run into no Hookses nor Piggses till after-
noon at least. When we was done eating and was just
a setting and making small talk and drinking more
coffee, I got out my makings and rolled me a cigareet.
Then I went to hunting a match, but I couldn't find
none in my pockets. Red said she'd get me one, and
she got up and left the table. By and by, she come
back and give me a match. I lit up that smoke, and
then Red said, "I seen four men across the street, and
one of them is Clell Hook."

I started in to jump up, but ole Rice stopped me.
"Take it easy," he said. "Just take a casual stroll over
there to the window and look out. Don't let them see
you."

So I done what he said. I just kinda strolled a puffing my cigareet, and I walked over close to the front
winder and sidled up to it, keeping myself kinda hid,
and I looked out and across the street. There was that
damn Clell all right, and he was with three other men.
I figgered it had to be that Stanley Pigg, and them
two other Hookses, Jody and Eddie. They was a
rough-looking bunch, all right, and I figgered if I was
to have to face any one of them in a fistfight, why,
I'd a been scared to death. He could a broke me like
a matchstick.

But I never had no intention a facing any of them
thataway. That woulda been just plain downright stupid, and I ain't that. I ain't too bright, I guess, but
I'm that smart I don't fight no one what can whup
my ass. I know that I can face anyone with my Colt

though, so if I got to fight, that's the way I mean to do it.

I went back over to the table and set back down. "I seed them all right," I said.

"All four?" Chastain asked.

"There's four of them," I said.

Rice got up and tuck his turn and sauntered over by the winder. He stayed for a spell and then come back.

"They're a rough-looking bunch, all right," he said, "and they're well armed."

"It'll just take one bullet to stop each one of them," I said. "What're we waiting for?"

"Just sit tight, Kid," Chastain said. "I can't have you starting a fight in my town. Especially if I get drawn into it."

"Then just stay out," I said. "Me and Rice can handle them four."

"What about me?" said ole Zeb. "God damn it, just give me a shotgun, and I'll take them out two at a time."

"I don't want you getting into no fight," I said to Zeb, and the only reason I can think of that I went and said that is that I had come to think that I just had to take keer a the old fart. That made me think about ole Paw in there locked up to the bed. Oh, he weren't in there starving. Rice had got someone to take him in a breakfast all right. But I was thinking about how I was so all-fired pertective a ole Zeb, and I weren't that way atall about Paw. Well, maybe a little.

"I don't want anyone getting into a fight," Chastain said. "Not just now anyway."

"I don't know what time would be a better time," I said.

"Take it easy, Kid," said Rice. "So far here, we have the sheriff on our side. Let's try to keep it that way."

"What I need to do," Chastain said, "is find out if I can legally arrest those men for crimes committed in Kansas and Texas."

"If you know they're wanted," Rice said, "then—"

"There's paperwork that has to be done," Chastain said, interrupting ole Rice. "I can't do it just on your say-so."

"What's the matter?" I said. "Don't you believe him? Hell, he's the most honestest man I ever knowed."

"It's not that, Kid," Chastain said. "It's just that there's a legal way to go about it. Give me some time to send a few telegrams. I'll get back to you a little later."

Well, having done said that, he got up and walked right on outa there. I sipped some more coffee, but what was left in my cup had done got cold. I made a face at it, and Red went to get me some fresh.

"Be patient, Kid," Rice said. "Give him a little time."

"I got another question for you," I said.

"What's that?" he said.

"Are me and you going to fight it out over ole Clell before we all go fight them four?" I said. "'Cause if we get in a big fight with them guys, it ain't going to be easy for you to keep ole Clell alive, now is it?"

"You're right about that," Rice said. "We'll just have to wait and see what happens. I don't think we'll have to fight over him."

He stood up then like as if he was a going some-wheres. I asked him where he was a headed, and he said to check on his prisoner.

"Let me do that for you," I said.

"Go on," he said, and he set back down. I tuck a fresh cup a coffee and went on back upstairs to where our rooms was at, and I found Paw a hooked to that there bed. He had done et his breakfast, so I give him that coffee. He tuck it and slurped at it and give me the eye.

"This the way you allow your own paw to be treated?" he said. "Like a dog?"

"I wouldn't treat no dog like that," I said.

"But it's all right for your paw?" he said.

"I never said that, Paw," I told him. "It ain't me a doing this to you."

"But you ain't doing nothing to stop it, are you?" he said. "And you're pardnering with that lawman. You might as well be doing it."

He throwed that cup and spilt all the rest a the coffee all over the floor. It made me jump back outa the way.

"What the hell'd you do that for?" I asked him.

"I don't need no coffee from no one that would chain up his own old man like this," he said. "I don't need no pity. And when they fin'ly stretch my ole neck, I don't want to see you a crying in the crowd neither."

"You old bastard," I said, "I never asked you to go out and rob no banks with no outlaws, and Maw never either. Whatever mess you got in, you got in it your own self, so don't go looking for me to get you out of it."

I turned around and started outa the room, but he stopped me.

"Wait a minute, Melvin," he said. I whirled on him with my Colt out and cocked, and his eyes opened wide as saucers, and he put his arms up in front a his face as best he could, being handcuffed like he was.

"Don't never say that again," I told him. "I'll kill you. I'll make you number thirteen."

Chapter Nineteen

Well, I never kilt ole Paw, of course, but what I done instead is I looked that bed frame over real good, and I found out that if I was to pull the pieces apart there where ole Paw was handcuffed, why we could slip them cuffs right offa the bed frame, and he'd be a loose. He'd be free as a skunk. So I done that, and ole Paw, he helt his hands out toward me. They was still cuffed together a course.

"I can't do nothing about that," I said, "and even if I could, I wouldn't. I done too much already. You're on your own now. Just get the hell outa my life." I dug in my pocket and give him all my money, and I felt stupid for doing it, but I couldn't help myself none. "Take this and get home to Maw," I said. "I hope I don't never see you again. Now get on outa here, and go out the back way too."

I left that room and never even waited to see what Paw was going to do. I guessed that he done what I told him and went on out the back way. I went back on down into the eating part a the hotel, and there was ole Rice a talking with Chastain again. I guess Chastain had come back around while I was in the room with Paw. The gals had gone on back to work, I guess, all but ole Sally Goodin, who didn't have no work to go to. I got myself another cup a coffee and set down at the table with ole Zeb. He had done gone and got him a bottle a good whiskey. That was one thing about ole Zeb, no matter what was his circumstance nor how drunk he was nor what, he always managed to get real good whiskey to drink.

"Have a drink, Kid," he said, and he shoved the bottle over at me. I shoved it right back towards him.

"I might have to do some killing here in a while," I said. "I better not."

"Yeah," he said. "Likely you're right about that."

I was a looking at ole Rice and wondering what him and Chastain was talking about, but I was also feeling guilty about Paw and wondering if Rice would suspect me whenever he found out that Paw was gone. A course, if he was to say anything about it to me, it was my full intention to deny ever' bit of it and claim to be innocent as a nekkid, newborn babe. I was a wondering too just how come me to go and do what it was I had did. It's true enough that I didn't really want ole Paw to hang up by his scrawny ole neck till he was dead, but I ain't sure yet that's the real and main reason I turned him a loose. I think I went and turned him a loose 'cause I just didn't want to have to see no more of him. I was sick in tired a looking at him and a listening to him yap. Anyhow, I think so, but I ain't for sure.

Something or other was making me feel right ornery for some reason. I guess it was 'cause I was a feeling guilty, and I was trying to cover it up or something, and I drank down my coffee, and then I stood up and hitched my britches. I set a mean look on my face, checked my Colt for its slickeriness in the holster, and then I walked right on over to where ole

Rice and ole Chastain was a talking in them low tones like as if they was a trying to keep something or another to theirselfs.

"I ain't waiting forever for you two to figger out the right and proper way to do this job," I said. "I got me one killing to do for sure, and likely now it's got to be four. Y'all can go on and talk all day if you're a mind to. I mean to be getting to it."

"Hold on there a minute," Rice said. "Just listen to what Jim's got to say."

"I figured out that I can arrest those men and hold them for a good while just on suspicion alone," Chastain said. "That should give us plenty of time to get all the right paperwork from Texas and Kansas."

"So you think them four will just walk right over to your jailhouse with you real calm like, do you?" I said.

"No, I don't think that," Chastain said. "I propose to deputize both you and Bill Rice. If they submit to arrest, then everything will be okay. If they want to fight instead, well, three to four's not such bad odds. Especially when one of the three is a regular Billy the Kid."

"I'd ruther you not to use that saying," I said. "And what's that depitize you said? Does that mean make me a depitty?"

"That's what it means," said Chastain. "It'd be temporary. You'd be my deputy just till we get this mess taken care of."

"I don't like the sound a that," I said. "I got a bad enough reputation as it is."

"That's the only way for it," Rice said. "Otherwise you'll have the law after you."

"Not if they draw on me first," I said.

"How could I ever believe that?" Chastain said. "You've already stated within my hearing that you mean to kill those four men."

"They'd draw first," I said. "They always has. Most always."

"Just do it our way this time," Rice said. "Hell, chances are it will all turn out the way you want it to anyhow. It's like you said. Do you really expect those four to just hand over their guns and go peacefully along to jail?"

"Well, all right," I said. Then I looked ole Chastain in the eye. "If you make me a depitty, do you have go telling it all around?"

"I'll keep it as quiet as I can, Kid," he said.

"I'll do her then," I said.

I walked over to the winder and looked out to that place across the street where them four had been hanging, but they was gone. I stood there a minute a thinking about the strange ways a the world. Ole Chastain had kicked me outa town the last time I was there. Here he was fixing to depitize me. I went back over to Chastain and Rice.

"If you'd a come to this here conclusion about what we're going to do some little while ago," I said, "we coulda walked right over there across the street and tuck keer of it, but the bastards is gone now."

"We'll find them," Chastain said. "Are you two ready for this?"

"Ready as I'll ever be," Rice said.

"I been ready," I said. "Let's go get them."

The three of us headed for the door then, and ole Zeb hopped up from his chair.

"Where you going?" he said.

"We're going after them Hookses and Pigg," I

said. "You just set there and drink your whiskey. I'll come back and see you when the job's been did."

"Get me a shotgun, and I'll go along," Zeb said.

"Set down, Zeb," I said. "I don't want you a getting in the way."

He set back down then and went to sipping his whiskey. He didn't look too disappointed.

"Bill," said Sally. She'd been quiet all this time. "Be careful. You too, Kid."

"Don't worry none," I said. "I won't let him get hurt."

"We'll be careful," Rice said, and he give her a quick hug. I liked the look a that. I figgered that was for real off a my hands now. Rice had done tuck her on. I decided that I'd have to be real keerful that nothing happened to him out there in the streets.

We walked on outside then and crossed the street. The place over there where I had seen them four lounging in front of was a saloon, so we went inside. We stopped just inside the door and looked over the crowd. None of us seed none a them, but there was several in there giving us the hard eye. If you're a drinking and having a good time in a saloon, the last person you want to see come a walking in is the local law. I guess they was wondering too who the two characters with him was. Anyhow, in a minute or so, ole Chastain said, "Let's go." We turned around and left that place.

We walked on down the street, and ever' place we passed, we looked in the winders or the door. When we come to the next saloon, we went inside the way we had did at the last one. We never seed none of them in there neither. Well, our stroll down the street went on like that for quite a spell, and I was getting some frustrated. We had just come out of a place and was back on the sidewalk, and I turned to face ole Chastain.

"Well, goddamn it," I said, "where the hell are they hiding out at?"

"I don't know any more than you do, Kid," he said. "We've checked all the saloons and most of the eating places. We've got a couple of hotels and a whore-house or two left. We'll just keep looking."

"I'm 'bout to get fed up with your way a doing things already," I said.

Long about noon, we still hadn't seed hide nor hair of them bastards, and we all of us started in to getting hungry, so we decided to go get us some grub. We went into a hash house that was right close to where we was at, and we put on the feed bag for a while. I stuffed myself pretty good with that greasy hash and taters and such. We washed it all down with several cups a coffee, and then ole Rice, he waved at the gal what brought the food out. She come over and asked what was it he was a wanting.

"Can you fix me up a plate to take out of here with me?" he asked her.

She said that she could do that and then went off to take keer of it.

"Ain't you et enough?" I said.

"I'm thinking about your paw," he said. "I can't let him go hungry over there."

I don't know if my face showed out what come over me with that or not, but I just said, "Hell, he'll be all right. You don't need to do that."

He didn't agree none with me on that issue, so we waited for the plate to get brung out to us, and then we walked back over to our hotel, and Rice, he tuck

that plate into his room. He come back out looking
pretty damn disgusted.

"He's broke loose," he said. And he give me a
look. "At least that's what it looks like. He's gone."

"Well," I kinda stammered, "how'd he do it?"

"The bed frame's been pulled apart," Rice said.
"Wherever he is, he's still wearing my handcuffs."

"He shouldn't be hard to find like that," Chastain
said. "We'll spread the word around town to watch
out for him."

"What're we going to do now?" I asked. I was sure
feeling guilty like. You know how you feel whenever
you sneak something to eat before suppertime and
your maw starts in to wondering what happened to it,
and you're trying to play innocent? That's kinda like
how I was a feeling just then. Ole Rice, he never
accused me direct, but he give me some looks. I made
out like I never noticed.

"We'll just keep on doing what we were doing,"
Chastain said. "Let's go."

We went on back out again and started back on
our rounds, and Chastain told someone out there
about ole Paw and told him to pass the word around
town to be on the lookout. I was sure hoping that Paw
got hisself out a town and off safe somewheres. I
didn't want to see no more a him, and then too, I was
kinda skeered that if they caught him, he might tell
on me that I was the one what turned him a loose.

We was a walking along the sidewalk headed for
one a the places we hadn't yet looked in, when back
behind us someone yelled and a shot was fired, and
we all jerked out our six-guns and ducked for cover
and turned around a looking for wherever the shot
come from. I kinda looked to see if any of us was

hit, but we wasn't. I had ducked into a doorway and
was a peeking out to see what I could see, and there
back down the street was a feller a standing on the
sidewalk with a gun in his hand and his legs real
wobbly like. As we watched him there, he fell over
on his face. We all run down there.

Chastain bent over the fresh corpus to check it out.
Me and Rice was kinda crouched and ready for a fight
and a looking around, but we couldn't see no one who
looked like he might be a shooter. Chastain grabbed
a handful a shirt shoulder and rolled the poor unfortunate over.

"Eddie Hook," he said. Then he just kinda looked
around and yelled out at anyone and ever'one out on
the street. "Where'd the shot come from?"

An old-timer standing out in the middle a the street
pointed and said, "I seen him. He run around the corner a the gen'ral store there."

The three of us tuck off all together, but I was the
first one around the corner, being little and skinny and
all. Rice and Chastain come right up behind me. We
didn't see no one, so we all run on to the back a the
building and looked up and down the alley.

"Shit," said Chastain.

"What now?" I said.

"There's no telling where he went," said Rice.
"Whoever he is."

"We'll just keep doing what we been doing," said
Chastain.

"Yeah?" I said. "Well, I vote we do it on our own.
At least me. You two can stick together if you want."

"Look," Chastain said. "I already told you—"

But ole Rice, he stopped him clear. "I think you
ought to let him go, Jim," he said. "He might be right.

If we split up, we can cover three times the territory in the same amount of time. If any of us sees any one of them, why, we can send a runner to find the others."

"You hear that, Kid?" Chastain said. "You spot any of them, don't start shooting. Send for Bill and me. Just keep your eyes on them till we get there."

"Sure," I said, but to my own self I thought, Like hell. 'Specially if I spot that damn Clell. I'll just blow his ass away, and then I'll call for help. Anyhow, we all went our separate ways. I decided to amble on down that alley, which was the last place we knowed of the shooter being. We hadn't tuck time to talk about it, but I figgered the other two was wondering about the same thing what I was wondering about. Who the hell shot that there Hook? And why?

Whoever done it had almost for sure saved the life of either me or Rice or Chastain, 'cause that Hook had a gun in his hand, and from the looks of it, he was leveling down on one of us from the back. I wondered just then where ole Zeb was at, but then I kinda pushed that thought aside, 'cause even when Zeb had said he wanted to come along with us, he had called for a shotgun. It weren't no shotgun what killed that Eddie Hook. It was a six-gun.

I slipped on down that alley a keeping my Colt ready in my hand, ready for damn near anything. I come to a door what I didn't know what it was, but I opened it anyhow and stuck my head in. It was just only the back door a the gen'ral store. I shoulda knowed. The man in there kinda jumped and looked around.

"Anyone come a running into here?" I asked him.

"No," he said.

I closed the door and moved on down the alley, and ever' door I come to, I done that same thing. No one nowhere along the line admitted to seeing no one come in through his back door. I stood there in the alley asking myself where in the hell that shooter coulda gone to. Then I said to hell with him. What'd I want with him anyhow? Hell, he done us a favor, whoever the hell he was. I wanted Clell Hook, and them other two. I wanted them other two 'cause I was for sure that they'd eventual come after me if they was able. But I wanted Clell the most.

What I hoped would happen was I hoped that ole Rice would come on that Stanley Pigg and kill him, and ole Chastain would come on Jody Hook and kill him, and me, I'd come on Clell and finish up my job what I had promised ole Zeb I would take keer of. That was how I was wanting things to come out, but you know, things never does work out just exactly to my satisfaction. Then I heared some shots.

I tuck off in the way I was thinking they come from, and I run back around to the main street and down toward the end. I seed ole Rice a ducked down behind a water trough, and I figgered if he was hiding from flying lead, why, I hadn't oughta just leave my ass out in the open, so I ducked into a doorway.

"Rice," I said.

"In the stable," he said.

"Where's Chastain?" I said.

"Across the street," he answered me.

'Bout then I seed a head pop up from the opening to the barn loft, and I sent a shot at it. It was a long shot with a six-gun, so all I done was I kicked some splinters at him, and he ducked back down. Whoever it was, I couldn't recognize him, but I did see that he was a holding a six-gun in his hand.

Ole Jim Chastain, he started working his way down the street toward the stable. He kept his back pressed against the walls a the buildings as he moved, but pretty soon, he was halfway on down there. Me and Rice was still away back. I seed the big front barn door creak open just a crack, and I seed a hand with a gun come a poking out. Before I could yell or do anything, it fired a shot, and I seed Chastain drop to one knee. Me and Rice both fired shots at that door, but all we done was just make whoever that was duck back inside.

I seed that someone run over to Chastain and helped him inside a building. I guessed that he'd be all right. I hoped so. But seeing him get shot like that made me mad, and I come outa my doorway and run down the sidewalk toward that barn. I passed by a couple a doorways and then ducked into another one. I was some closer than I had been before. Then I heared Rice yell out at me.

"Kid," he said, "be careful. You damn fool."

"You be keerful, you son of a bitch," I hollered. "I aim to get them bastards."

I run right out in the middle a the street then, and I fired a shot up into the loft. Then I called out in my biggest voice, "Show yourselfs, you coward peckerwoods. Piggs and Hogs."

I tell you what, bullets started flying from up in the loft and from down at the front door, and they kicked up dirt all around me. It must a been some kinda miracle what kept any of them from hitting me, 'cept I don't know who would make such a miracle happen for me. But I musta looked a sight, 'cause when the bullets started hitting close to my feet, I hopped up and down and danced a while before I come to my senses and run for cover. There was a store across the street what had a front porch on it with space underneath that porch, and I tuck me a flying dive, and hit the dirt and rolled right under the porch. Just as I rolled under there, I heared a bullet thunk into the wood right over me.

I asked myself, What did that Rice call me? A damn fool? Hell, I guessed that he was most nearly right about that. I heared some more shots, and I wondered where they was coming from. I guessed that ole Rice was trading shots with them in the barn. I scooted on my belly till I got myself in a position close underneath the edge a the porch where I could peek out and see the barn. The first thing I noticed was that from my new position, whenever that barn door opened, the way it done whenever that bastard shot Chastain, I could see in there. I had me a whole new angle. I got myself set to try one a my best shots ever, and sure enough, pretty soon that door creaked open a crack again.

I leveled my Colt and held her steady, and I tuck a fine bead on the bastard just inside the barn door. I don't know exactly what he thought he was a doing. I guess he was looking for me. He oughta had knowed that he had already put Chastain outa commission, and he was looking and aiming in the wrong direction for ole Rice. But he didn't know where I was at. He musta wanted a little better look, 'cause he pushed that door a little bit wider open, and then I squeezed my trigger. Damn, but that shot was loud down under that porch.

The ole boy standing in the doorway a the barn

give a twitch. I knowed I'd hit him. I didn't know how serious though till I seed him let go a his gun and let it fall to the ground. He still just stood there for a bit, and then he wobbled, and then he fell back. I didn't know if he was dead or not, but I knowed he was out a commission. I could tell that much.

Well, I knowed there was still one up in the loft, and then there was one more somewheres. There weren't no way a knowing if he was in there in the barn with them or not. Only them two had showed theirselfs. I tried to get me a look at ole Rice to see what he might be up to, but I couldn't really get no good look at him. Then I realized what I had did to myself. I had gone and got myself pinned down underneath that there porch. It was one thing to go a rolling underneath it for cover, but it would be a whole different story to try to come a crawling back out without getting a bullet in my back or my head or somewheres. I guessed I'd be down there till the fight was over with and done. I just hoped that ole Rice would win it.

I heared another couple a shots, and then I got myself a idea. I felt kinda stupid it had tuck me so long to come up with it, but the damn porch had three sides—well, anyhow, it had a front and two sides—so I fin'ly realized that I could make my way to the side that was the furtherest away from the barn. It would be the blind side as far as them in the barn was concerned. So I scrunched and scooted myself around till I was headed thataway, and then I bellied all the way across the length a that porch till I reached the far side.

I come out from under that porch sideways still a laying flat on the ground. Then I wormed my way back to the back end a the porch where I could come upright a leaning on the front wall a the building. I done that real slow, and as I done it, I seed that fella up in the loft take a shot at Rice and make water splash in the trough. It was his last mistake though, 'cause Rice come back at him real quick. He hit him, I think in the chest, and the feller wobbled and fell forward outa the loft. He landed *kerplunk* down on the ground in front a the front door. He never moved no more.

I stood on up then, but I was still a holding my Colt ready. I knowed there was one more of them yet, but like I said, I didn't have no way a knowing where he might be. I looked over at ole Rice, and I seed that he was a standing up from behind that watering trough.

"Be keerful, you damn fool," I hollered out to him. "There's one more yet."

"Let's move on in," he said.

So Rice headed for the barn door from his side a the street, and I come at it from my side. We was a moving in on it from two different directions and from different distances, so if the last one in there was to try to shoot one of us, the other'n would get a good chance at him. I was hoping he had figgered that out as good as me. Rice got to the barn before me, and he stood there a hesitating a bit. He looked back at me and seed that I had him covered good. He leaned over and tuck hold a the shirt a that dead one there what had fell from the loft and drug him off to one side. Then he waited for me to come on up.

When I got there, the two of us was a standing there in front a the barn door a looking stupid. We knowed there was another dead'un just inside the

door, and we knowed there was another live one, the
last a the bunch, somewheres. I nodded toward the
body what he had pulled off to one side.

"Who was he?" I whispered.

"Not Clell," he said.

I was just a dying to see the one inside the door.
I reached over to get a hold a the door, and Rice put
a hand on my arm.

"Stay back out of the way," he said.

I nodded, and then I swung that door real hard to
get it wide open. I stepped to the side as I done that,
and so did ole Rice. We waited, and no one tuck no
shots at us. We kinda stepped into the doorway, but
it was just only half the doorway, 'cause, you know,
them old barns has two big front doors, and I had just
only swung one of them open. We could see the dead
fella there. I just couldn't wait no more. I moved right
on over there and rolled him over onto his back, and
it weren't Clell. I sure as hell was disappointed. I
straightened my ass up and walked over beside ole
Rice again.

"It ain't him," I said. "And he ain't inside there
neither."

I weren't standing in the wide-open doorway no
more. I was standing just in front a the other half a
the door or the other door or however you keer to
look at. And just then I heared someone give a loud
"Hyaw," and something hit that loose barn door and
sent it a flying open and a knocking me flat on my
ass, and ole Rice too, and a big stallion come a rushing out just as I was trying to get back up on my feet.
He run into me and sent me a whirling. I only got a
glimpse a the rider on his back, and I was so dizzy

that I never even got my Colt out much less had a chance to use it.

I heared ole Rice get off a shot. I knowed it was Rice 'cause it was so close by me.

"Did you get him?" I shouted.

"Hell, no," he said. "Let's get some horses and get after him."

"Who was it?" I yelled. "Did you see him?"

"It's Clell, Kid," Rice said. "God damn it, let's go."

Chapter Twenty

Well, me and ole Rice, we grabbed up the closest two saddled horses without worrying about who they belonged to, and we skeedaddled out a town on ole Clell's trail. He was already outa sight, but we seed which way he was headed all right. We rid them horses like hell meaning to catch up with the bastard, and they was pretty good horses all right. If I'd a had a chance, I'd ruther of been on ole horse though, but sometimes you just ain't got no choice. We was outa town some ways, and we still hadn't caught sight a Clell, when of a sudden something come a flying right at my head, and I just barely ducked it in time. As it was a flying by me, I realized what the hell it was. It was a horseshoe.

'Bout that time too, the horse ole Rice was on started slowing hisself mighty fast, and ole Rice like to of lost his seat, but he hung on all right. I jerked back on the reins a mine and pulled him around.

"He lost a shoe," I yelled.

"Keep after Clell," Rice hollered back at me, and I turned my horse again and commenced on the trail. I rid that animal as hard as I dared to for as long as I dared, and then I slowed him to a walk. I looked ever' whichaway, and I couldn't pick up no sign a

Clell. I couldn't find no place where he coulda got off the trail neither. I can't tell you how bad I wanted to find that skunk. I wanted to find him for all the reasons I done told you about, but I wanted to find him, too, 'cause ole Rice had been forced to quit the trail, and he was a counting on me to take keer a the situation.

Well, I stayed out all damn day, and I was hungry as hell and tired. I weren't thirsty for I had come across a pool a good water, so me and the horse was both satisfied in that way. When the sun got low in the west, I decided that I had failed my duty that day. I rid back into town with my head a hanging. I found ole Rice at the hotel. He told me that ole Zeb was done passed out, and he said that Chastain had only just tuck a bullet in the thigh. He would be okay. I was glad to hear that. But I weren't very happy to have to tell him about how my day had gone.

"I never seed nothing of him," I said. "Never."

"Well," Rice said, "he gave us the slip all right."

It was awful good of ole Rice to include hisself in that remark, but he didn't really deserve to be stuck in there with me. He'd had to a dropped outa the race early on account a the horse he was on. It weren't his fault. It was me. I'm the one what was out all day on a good horse and never seed the man I was a chasing.

I got myself something to eat, and then I tuck a bottle up to my room and drunk myself to sleep. The next morning I went down to get some breakfast, and there was Zeb and Rice and even ole Chastain. Sally was there a setting with Rice. I went on over and set with them. A course, the talk was all about the shooting that tuck place the day before. The two men what we kilt was Stanley Pigg and Jody Hook. After that the talk turned to me and Rice a chasing ole Clell outa town and coming back empty-handed.

"Kid," ole Zeb said, "let's forget about that Clell. I'm a itching to get back to the mountains and sniff out some color. Pack up and ride along with me. What do you say?"

"I don't know, Zeb," I said. "If I don't go on ahead and get that Clell now, why, he's liable to come a sneaking up on either me or you one a these days."

"Well, then," he said, "you can take him when he comes a sneaking. You can do it. I seed you do it before. Might be easier to let him come after us than for you to keep on a trying to chase him down."

I thought about that, and I figgered that ole Zeb could be right there. I sure hadn't had no luck tracking nor chasing Clell. I didn't want to give up so easy though, 'special not with ole Rice a setting there.

"Rice," I said, "you going to keep after ole Clell?"

"That's what I was sent here for," he said.

"What about my paw?" I said.

"He was a part of that gang," said Rice, "and he was my prisoner, and he escaped. I don't take kindly to that. I do have some kind of professional reputation to maintain."

"Well, how about this?" I said. "Suppose you go on after Clell and forget you ever seed my paw. Forget that you even know anything about him. What I'll do for you in exchange for that is I won't ride along with you no more. Thataway you and me won't have to fight over ole Clell. I'll promise to quit trying to kill him, and I'll just leave him for you and the Texas hangman. What do you say?"

He set there and thunk a minute. I knowed he was thinking hard, 'cause he shoved his hat back and scratched his head. "Are you really willing to give up your claim on Clell Hook?" he said.

"I promise you, Rice," I said.

He stuck his hand out for me to take, and I tuck it and shuck it.

"It's a deal," he said.

"Thanks," I said.

Well, I was outa the manhunting business. By and by, ever'one got up and went somewheres. Ever'one 'cept me and ole Zeb. We had each just got our cups filled back up with coffee, and I had put a bunch a cream and sugar in mine.

"When we taking out a here?" I asked him.

"The sooner the better," he said.

"Let's pack up and go right now," I said.

"Right now?" he said.

"Yeah," I said. "I got no reason to hang around this ole town."

"All right," he said. "We'll do her. Just let me fin-ish this here coffee."

"Yeah," I said. "I'll finish mine too. Zeb?"

"What?" he said.

"Can we go find your peak and climb it?" I asked him.

"You wanta climb up ole Pike's Peak?" he said.

"That's just what I want to do," I said.

We packed up ever'thing we owned, and we loaded it all on Bernice Burro and on one a the extry horses we had. Then we went on over to the gen'ral store where Zeb bought up a whole bunch a supplies for us, including a canvas tent and a good heavy coat for each of us. He bought a lamp and a stove what burned kerosene, and he bought a can of kerosene to burn in them. We had food in tins, and jerky and hardtack. We got plenty a bullets and flour and gravy and coffee and a few bottles a whiskey. Fin'ly we packed all that on the extry horse, and we rid outa town. We never even told no one what we was a doing nor where we was a going.

It was a long and slow trail, but it was relaxing riding along like that, back on ole horse and with just only ole Zeb and Bernice and the horses for company. I was needing to relax too. I had got myself pretty high strung out a chasing all them outlaws and killing and such. We rid along just east a the big Rocky Mountains, and all the way along, I could see the snow on top and the low clouds a hovering there. It was sure pretty, but I was anxious to see that Pike's Peak. A course, I knowed by then that it weren't really ole Zeb's mountain like what he had told me, but I never let on to Zeb that I had found that out about him.

Well, the farther north we rid, the higher up we was a going and the colder it got. I was sure glad that ole Zeb had picked up them two winter coats, 'cause pretty soon we had to stop and break them out. About noon we stopped and het up some beans and made some coffee over a campfire. Then we cleaned up the camp and headed out again. We rid all day, and toward the evening dark, we found us a campsite for the night. We built another fire and laid out our blankets. Then we had us another meal. We was just a setting and drinking coffee. The sun had done gone down, and ole Zeb come up with a hell of a surprise for me.

"Kid," he said, "I seed who it was that shot that Eddie Hook in the back and kept him from shooting ole Rice in his back."

"You did?" I said. "How come you never told?"

"I didn't think it was no one else's business," he said.

"Well, who was it?" I asked him.

"It were your own ole paw," he said. "He done it."

"Paw?" I said. "You sure? You really seed him do it?"

"I seed him," he said. "Clear as a trout in a mountain stream. There ain't no mistake about it."

Well, that really set me to thinking. Here I had been a saying that ole Paw had never give me nothing but ten dollars and old Swayback. A course that had never been quite true. He used to give me a dime now and then, and I guess he did give me the food I et, at least some of it. I done my share a hunting too though. But anyhow, now it was different. Now he had maybe kilt a man to keep that man from killing me. 'Course, there weren't no way a knowing just who Eddie Hook was a taking a bead on, but it coulda been me. And Paw had kilt him, and him one a the same gang too.

Now that thought just almost made me teary-eyed, and I went to bed that night a thinking thoughts a my old home back in West Texas with Maw and Paw and Farty. I couldn't help it. I tried to think about screwing ole Red or Sally or even Sherry Chute, but it never worked. Them thoughts a my childhood home just kept intruding, and whenever I fin'ly went off to sleep, why, damned if I didn't dream a me being out a hunting squirrel with just one bullet for my rifle gun and ole Farty a running alongside a me with his tongue a hanging out and his tail a wagging.

In the morning after breakfast, we broke camp and headed north again. The air was a getting cleaner and crisper all the time. It was even getting a little harder to breathe, but the farther we traveled I started in to kinda get used to it. I shot a antelope the second day on the trail, and so we had us some fresh meat, and it sure was good the way ole Zeb fixed it up, and he fixed biscuit and gravy to go with it too. After a couple a days, we come to a small mining town, and we spent a night inside a hotel and et a couple a meals what someone else had cooked. Ole Zeb, he appreciated that, but I thought that his cooking was better than what we got in town.

We passed on the chance a getting drunk in a saloon, and ole Zeb, he never even got hisself into no poker games. We moved on out, and in another three days we come to Cripple Creek. To get there, though, we had to turn west and go up into the mountains. Cripple Creek was a ways up there too, and it musta had a hundred thousand people crowded into it. Ever'one was a scraping and scratching to get rich. If they wasn't digging their own claims, they was working for big miners, or else they was trying ever' whichaway to steal from the ones what was working. We went on through it as fast as we could.

We rid on out into them mountains on narrer windy roads that sometimes was just trails, and then fin'ly, with the mountains arising up all around us, ole Zeb stopped.

"There she be," he said.

"What?" I said.

"Right there, Kid," he said. "Right in front a you a rising up to a fine point. Pike's Peak."

I looked at that mountain or peak or whatever is the proper name for it, and I seed that pointy top on it, and I just set there a staring in wonderment. Pike's

Peak. I forgot all about ole Zeb's lies. I was setting
there a looking at his mountain. The mountain what
was named after my pardner. It was the greatest sight
I had ever saw in my whole entire life. I felt like as
if ole Zeb had tuck me to a real secret place and
pulled something outa a corner and unwrapped it and
showed it to me, and it was something that he never
showed no one else. 'Course, there weren't no way
he could a kept Pike's Peak a secret like that, but that
was the way I felt about it just at that time.

I couldn't recollect that Maw nor Paw had ever
tuck me into no church, but if they had a I prob'ly
woulda felt something like what I felt like a looking
at ole Zeb's mountain. Why, I was so damn struck
dumb that I couldn't think a nothing to say. I know
my mouth was a hanging open and my eyes was wide.

"Well," Zeb said, a disturbing my trance, "you still
a thinking you want to climb up there?"

"Can it be did?" I said.

"Why, hell, boy," he said, "I told you that I done
it. I was the first white man to do it. That's how come
it to have my name on it."

"Would you take me up there?" I asked him.

"We'll make us a camp over yonder way," he said.
"We'll start up it first thing in the morning."

"It's a dangerous thing, climbing a mountain," Zeb
was saying. We was sipping coffee setting in front of
our canvas tent with a campfire a going. The air was
cold, and the hot coffee tasted good and warmed our
guts. "You get up yonder where it's snowy and icy,
you got to make damn sure of ever' toehold and fin-
gerhold. One slip and you'll fall clean down to hell.
You got to know just the right way to go up there

too. Hell, you could climb for days, and then find out
that all you'd did was climb up to a dead end."

"You know the right way up there though," I said.

"I sure do," he said. "I'll get you up there safe and
sound all right. You just foller me and do ever'thing
I say. You'll be all right, and you'll be right up there
on top a looking down at the whole damn world."

"I can't hardly wait, Zeb," I said. "I tell you. I ain't
never wanted to do something so bad in my whole
entire life. I wish it was morning already. Hell, I'm a
raring to go."

"You'd best get a good night's sleep, Kid," he said.
"You'll need all your strength and energy when we
get started up that peak."

I give a kinda nervous laugh. "I ain't sleepy," I
said. "I couldn't sleep if I had to."

"Break out a bottle a that whiskey," he said. "We'll
just drink you to sleep."

Well, I done like he said. I dug out a bottle and a
couple a tin cups, and I poured us each a drink, and
we commenced to getting drunk. For a while I kept
my awestruck mood, but pretty soon after a few good
drinks, I commenced to getting silly, and ole Zeb, he
did too. We sung a few silly songs we knowed, and
ole Zeb actual got up and danced around the fire once
or twice. We talked about ever'thing we had did together and about ever'one the both of us knowed.

Then we went to talking about a hunting gold and
a getting rich and all like that, and Zeb got to going
on again about opry houses and such truck. I didn't
know what that was all about, so I told him that whenever we got rich, I was a going to buy us a whole
herd a whores, and that got him to laughing so that
he was a rolling on the ground.

"Look out, Zeb," I said. "You like to of rolled into the fire."

He set up then and caught his breath. "That woulda made a hell of an explosion," he said, "all the alcohol that's in me."

The both of us laughed pretty hard at that, and then I caught my head a nodding, and ole Zeb, he seed it too.

"Let's go to sleep," he said, and we did, and I dreamed a being on top a that mountain.

It was two weeks later whenever me and Zeb rid back into Fosterville. We stopped right in front a the sheriff's office and went in to find ole Jim Chastain. He was sure surprised to see us. He come out from behind his desk a holding out his hand to be shuck. He was limping somewhat and toting a walking stick, but other than that, he seemed just fine. I was glad a that.

"I didn't know if I'd ever see you two again," he said. "Sit down."

We all tuck chairs and set, and ole Zeb, he reached under his big coat and come out with a bottle. Chastain got us each a glass, and Zeb poured a round a drinks. Chastain held his glass up and said, "To old friends," and we all clunk our glasses together.

"Is ole Rice still around?" I asked.

"No," Chastain said. "He gave up on ever finding Clell Hook. He headed back for Texas a couple of days after you two rode out. He took that Sally Goodin along with him, too."

"Well, I'm glad to hear that," I said, and I really was too. I had been a wondering off and on what would become a her. I kinda ducked my head then, and I said, "You, uh, you ain't seed my paw around, have you?"

"I never saw him after the day he got loose from Bill Rice," Chastain said. "I did have a man who came up from Ash Grove tell me an interesting tale though."

"Oh?" I said. "What was that?"

"Seems a feller rode into Ash Grove and stopped by the blacksmith shop," Chastain said. "He was wearing a pair of handcuffs and asked the smithy to cut him loose. Said it was a practical joke some friends had played on him."

"The smithy cut him loose?" I asked.

"Yeah," he said. "The man rode out of town and hasn't been seen since."

"Well," said ole Zeb, "I wonder who that mighta been."

"What have you two been doing all this time?" Chastain asked us.

"We went up to Zeb's mountain," I said. "We clumb up to the top. All the way."

"Zeb's mountain?" Chastain said.

"Pike's Peak," said Zeb.

"Oh," Chastain said. "I get it. Well, what did you do that for?"

"It was just something I wanted to do," I told him, "and ole Zeb, he showed me the way up there. It was the most wonderfullest thing I've ever saw, I can tell you that. It was covered with snow, and it was cold. And something happened while we was up there that you might like to hear about."

Chastain turned his glass up and emptied it. He held it out toward Zeb, and Zeb filled it back up. Then he poured his own and mine full again.

"I'm listening," Chastain said.

"Well," I went on, "we clumb clean up to the top a that peak. It was a hard climb too. At first it was just like walking up a real steep hill, but then it got steeper and steeper, and pretty soon we was on all fours, a grabbing with our hands and pulling ourselfs up, and then we got to snow and ice, and we had to really be keerful then. Ole Zeb, he tied a rope around his own waist and then he tied the other end around me, and he clumb first. That was in case I was to fall, but it worried me lest I fall and pull him after me, but I never.

"I slipped once and slid a ways, but Zeb stopped me with the rope. I looked back behind me and seed where I woulda slud to if I had a kept going. If ole Zeb hadn't a caught me like he done, I'd a gone clean down to China. Anyhow, we made it up there, and I stood right up there on top. It ain't really quite pointy up there. It just looks thataway from down below.

"Well, we started back down, and it was even tougher than going up, but we made it most nearly back to the bottom. We was on a kinda ledge, and it was all covered up with snow, and then all of a sudden, I seed him down there a looking up at us, and he had a rifle gun in his hands."

"Who'd you see?" said Chastain.

I tuck a drink a whiskey.

"It was ole Clell," I said.

"Clell Hook?" Chastain said.

"The same ole snake shit," said ole Zeb. "It were him all right. He musta follered us up there. And he were a waiting for us to come back down."

"Well," I said, "I went for my gun. I knowed what I had promised ole Rice, but Rice weren't there, and

I was, and Clell, he was a raising that rifle to his shoulder to kill either me or Zeb or both of us, so I figgered that my promise didn't hardly count under them circumstances."

"I wouldn't think so," Chastain said.

"But ole Zeb, he stopped me," I said. "He told me not to shoot, and then he made me back way up outa Clell's line a sight, back against a kinda wall there at the far back side a that ledge we was on. Well just as I started back; Clell tuck a shot at me. Me and Zeb, we just barely got back in time, 'cause it seemed like as if that whole damn ledge just went and collapsed. It was all just snow, and it just dropped off the side a the mountain. God a'mighty, it roared when it went down, and underneath that roar, I thought I heard ole Clell a screaming real hideous like too.

"Anyhow, we waited it all out, and whenever it fin'ly stopped falling and roaring and such, ole Zeb said we could move on. It was tougher going though, and Zeb, he led me on down real slow and keerful, and we made it back to our camp all right. I asked him where was Clell at, and he said that he was buried under so much snow that no one would see nothing a him again till maybe next spring, if then. And that's the all of it. We headed back down here to tell about it—what happened to Clell."

"I'll be damned," Chastain said.

My throat was all dry from so much talking, and I tuck me another drink.

"I'll write up a report and send it around to all the law-enforcement agencies that have dodgers on Clell Hook," Chastain said, "including Bill Rice."

"Tell ole Rice," I said, "that I kept my word. I never shot Clell. Will you tell him that for me?"

"I'll tell him," Chastain said.

Well, we set around and visited some more with ole Chastain, and then we tuck out. We went over to that saloon where ole Red was a working, and she was sure glad to see us. She grabbed a friend for ole Zeb, and the four of us went upstairs for a party, and we sure damn had us a good one. We didn't get us much sleep that night, I can tell you that. The next morning, me and Zeb packed to head on out again. I had it in mind to go out and find us some more a that "pocket money," and ole Zeb was dead set on locating his bonanza. We said our so-longs to ole Red and the other gal and stopped by to tell Chastain we'd be a seeing him someday. Then we headed out back toward them mountains a gold.

We was out a couple a days whenever we heared some gunshots up ahead of us, and we decided to go investigate. We come on a scene up there where there was a couple a guys a shooting at one guy. The two was up high in the rocks, and the one was kinda down in a low spot across the road from them. It looked to me like as if them two had tried to ambush the one feller, but he had managed to duck behind some fell logs and was a shooting back.

Now I never did like no ambushers and I never did like no two against one. I told ole Zeb, "I'm a going to help that feller out."

"Go to it," he said.

Well, none a the shooters on either side had saw me yet, so I clumb down offa ole horse, and I started making my way through them rocks. I managed to get myself close enough, and I had a clear shot at one a the ambushers.

"Hey," I called out. "Throw out your guns."

The feller turned and tuck a wild shot at me, and I dropped him dead with one shot from my Colt. I run on down there and ducked behind another boulder, and the other shooter come a running out then to see who had shot his pard. I seed him and tuck a shot, but I shot too quick. He ducked back behind a rock.

"Throw out your gun and come on out," I said. "I won't kill you."

"Who the hell are you?" he said.

"They call me Kid Parmlee," I said.

"They say you're a regular Billy the Kid," the man said, "but you don't scare me. Come and get me if you want me."

I scooted backwards and went up around another clump a rocks and worked my way back down towards him, but I come up on his back side. He was a peeking around the corner a that rock he was hiding behind a looking over where he thought I was at. There wasn't nothing between the two of us. I stood there with my Colt a hanging down to my side in my right hand.

"Here I am," I said.

He spun around real fast and snapped off a shot at me, but it went wide. I raised my Colt up and give him a slug right in his chest, dead center. He coughed and fell back against the rock. Then he just kinda slid down till he was a setting up on the ground and leaning back against the rock. He was dead. I moved over to one a the rocks what they had been shooting over, and I kinda peeked up over the edge. The feller down there tuck a shot at me, and it chipped rock not far from me. I felt some of it sting my cheek.

"Hey, you down there," I yelled. "Don't shoot."

I waited a minute, and then he called back.

"Who're you?" he said.

"I ain't one a them what was a shooting at you," I said. "I done kilt them."

"Come on out," he said.

I did, but I kept my Colt in my hand just in case. I started walking toward that feller. I had got about halfway to him when he stood up. I didn't recognize him at first, but then all of a sudden he yelled out like it was time for a big celebration.

"By God," he said, "that makes fifteen."

"Paw?" I said.

Zeb come a riding on down then, and he brung ole horse and all our other animals along with him. Paw got out his horse. He looked at me, and he looked at Zeb.

"Do you keer if I was to ride along a spell with you?" he said.

I looked up at ole Zeb a setting there on his horse. He give a kinda shrug.

"It don't make me no nevermind," he said.

I looked back at Paw. I thought about all the times he'd whupped me when I was a kid. I recalled all the times he'd left me and Maw to do for ourselfs when he was off doing whatever it was he done, robbing banks maybe. I thought about the dimes he give me now and then for candy, and I thought 'special about the ten dollars and ole Swayback and then how he had shot that Eddie Hook.

"Ah, hell," I said, "mount up and come on along."